Hanging by a Hair

A BAD HAIR DAY MYSTERY

Hanging by a Hair

Nancy J. Cohen

FIVE STAR
A part of Gale, Cengage Learning

Farmington Hills, Mich • San Francisco • New York • Waterville, Maine
Meriden, Conn • Mason, Ohio • Chicago

Publisher's Note: The recipes contained at the back of this book are supplied by the author. The Publisher is not responsible for your specific health or allergy needs that may require medical supervision. The Publisher is not responsible for any adverse reactions to the recipes contained in this book.

This novel is a work of fiction. Names, characters, places and incidents are either the product of the author's imagination, or, if real, used fictitiously.

The publisher bears no responsibility for the quality of information provided through author or third-party Web sites and does not have any control over, nor assume any responsibility for, information contained in these sites. Providing these sites should not be construed as an endorsement or approval by the publisher of these organizations or of the positions they may take on various issues.

LIBRARY OF CONGRESS CATALOGING-IN-PUBLICATION DATA

Cohen, Nancy J., 1948–
Hanging by a hair : A Bad Hair Day Mystery / Nancy J. Cohen.
— First Edition.
pages cm. — (Bad hair day mystery)
ISBN-13: 978-1-4328-2814-1 (hardcover)
ISBN-10: 1-4328-2814-2 (hardcover)
1. Shore, Marla (Fictitious character)—Fiction. 2. Women detectives—Florida—Fiction. 3. Beauty operators—Fiction. 4. Florida—Fiction. I. Title.
PS3553.O4258H37 2014
813'.54—dc23 2013041350

First Edition. First Printing: April 2014
Find us on Facebook– https://www.facebook.com/FiveStarCengage
Visit our website– http://www.gale.cengage.com/fivestar/
Contact Five Star™ Publishing at FiveStar@cengage.com

Printed in the United States of America
1 2 3 4 5 6 7 18 17 16 15 14

ACKNOWLEDGMENTS

Thanks to Robin Burcell, author of *The Black List* and former police officer, detective, and forensic artist, for answering my questions on police procedure and forensics.

As always, with gratitude to Detective R.C. White from Fort Lauderdale Police (retired). Thank you for your detailed responses to my crime-related questions.

CAST OF CHARACTERS

(In Alphabetical Order)

ALAN KRABBER —President of Royal Oaks Homeowners Association, retired insurance company owner. Marla and Dalton's next-door neighbor.

ANGELA GOODHART —Blond graphic designer and Marla's neighbor on the next street over. She works from home and is single.

BEAMIS WOODHOUSE —Building supplier who is Krabber's cousin. He claims the window leaks aren't his fault.

CHERRY HUNTER —A divorcee with two children, Cherry is treasurer for Royal Oaks HOA. She's a history professor who specializes in Native American cultures.

DEBBIE MORRIS —A real estate agent, Debbie is secretary for the HOA. She has strawberry blond hair and is a wife and mother. Her sister Hannah has been ill.

ERIK MANSFIELD —Construction company owner bidding for a lucrative contract from HOA to build a playground in the Royal Oaks community.

ETHAN LINDBERG —Gayle's son and owner of Steers Industries, a manufacturer of polyvinyl extrusions. He sold his product to Beamis Woodhouse's company.

GAYLE LINDBERG —Alan Krabber's former flame. Married to Donald, she has three children, lives on Marco Island and runs a clothing shop.

GENE URIS —Vice President of Royal Oaks HOA who takes over as acting president in the wake of a vacancy. He supports the playground bid from Erik Mansfield. Gene is a furniture store manager at Lemmings and Sons.

HERB POLTICE —The shaman for the Immowakee tribe is Cherry's distant cousin. His office is located in a nearby casino. He's concerned with respecting the ancestral spirits.

KATHERINE MINNETTI —A detective newly transferred to the Palm Haven police force, Kat is Dalton's new partner.

PHILIP BYRD —Krabber's nephew and heir, Philip is a travel writer for the Global Rainforest Foundation.

RON CLOAKMAN —Developer of the master community including Royal Oaks, Ron stands to lose millions if Krabber's secret is exposed.

SUSAN FEINBERG —Marla's neighbor on the other side of Krabber's house. Married with two children, Susan is a consulting editor for a women's magazine and a blogger.

**Author's Note: This cast is limited to the principals in *Hanging by a Hair* and does not include recurring characters like Marla's friends, relatives, and salon personnel.

Chapter One

Marla Vail sat wedged between her husband Dalton in the aisle seat and a young couple on the other side. Her temples throbbed from the stark overhead lighting and the musty odor of old carpet in their community clubhouse. Or maybe her headache was induced by Alan Krabber, president of the Royal Oaks Homeowners Association. He ran their annual meeting with the subtlety of a drill sergeant.

Krabber sat at a long table facing the members. Flanking him to his left were the other Board officers. He addressed one of the residents in an exasperated tone.

"I don't care how long your sister is visiting, lady. City code says recreational vehicles have to be parked in a side yard, and that includes trailers like hers. They're supposed to be blocked from view by a solid fence or dense shrubbery."

"But my sister is only staying for two weeks. It's not like her trailer will be there forever." The elderly woman's voice quaked.

"Doesn't matter." Krabber glared at her. "The rules stand. We can't make exceptions. If you don't want the vehicle on your property, tell her to leave it at the community center."

Marla gritted her teeth. She and Dalton had the misfortune to live next door to the president. Alan Krabber had already aggravated them by digging a big hole in his backyard. The open pit, waiting for a propane tank to fuel a standby generator, was hazardous to pets and small children. But that wasn't the only reason why Marla's blood pressure elevated. Now Alan had the chutzpah to quote city code when he'd violated it.

Dalton raised his hand after the older lady resumed her seat.

"Pardon me," he said after Krabber gestured for him to speak, "but wouldn't those rules also apply to the boat parked in your driveway?"

"Nah." Krabber's mouth curved in a disdainful smirk. He was a heavy-set guy with receding brown hair above a wide forehead and wire-rimmed glasses. "My boat is a modest size, and it's not as unsightly as a trailer."

"You just said no exceptions can be made. Aren't you being hypocritical?"

The president jabbed his pudgy finger in the air. "You know, you've already complained to me about the construction crew in my backyard and the paved walkway on the side of my house. Why don't you let this one go, buddy?"

Dalton stiffened. "You can't condemn a resident's trailer in one breath and excuse your own transgression in the next. The code applies to everyone. Just because you're president doesn't mean you can skirt the rules."

Marla noticed the tense look on his face and swallowed. A homicide detective in the local police force, Dalton had a tendency to play by the book.

She tugged on his shirt. "Dalton, we're new here," she said in a hushed tone. "Maybe we should discuss this with Alan in private."

He glared at her, a lock of peppery hair falling across his forehead. "No way. Mr. Krabber has clearly stated the code and insisted that woman follow it to the letter. He can't be allowed to mow everyone over and then do what he wants. If he intends to keep his boat on his property, he has to hide it from view as the code states."

His face as red as a sunburned tourist, Krabber leaned forward. "You've been in this neighborhood for how long now, buddy?" He counted on his fingers. "This is March, and you moved in around the end of January. Things have been just fine without your input. But to make you happy, I'll consider your objections."

"You'll have to do more than that, or I'll report you to code enforcement."

A thin guy raised his hand. "You know, he's right, Alan. Maybe we should take a vote."

Murmurs of consent wafted through the room. A show of hands reinforced the rule.

Marla breathed a sigh of relief when Dalton resumed his seat with a satisfied grunt. This wasn't how she'd imagined their first homeowners' meeting.

He shot her a reproving glance. "What? Someone has to uphold the law, and it might as well be me. Our neighbors agreed that Alan should follow the code, so I'm not alone. The vote went in my favor."

Oh, joy. Maybe you should run for office. You can ticket people for speeding down the side streets or putting their trash out the night before pickup day.

Dalton couldn't hold still when they got to the budget. His hand shot up when Gene Uris, the vice president, called for questions. Gene pointed to him with a pained glance, as though he knew a troublemaker when he saw one.

"What's this line item for security listed at one hundred and forty thousand dollars? Can you please tell us exactly what that covers?" Dalton asked in a polite voice.

Marla, aware of stares directed their way, wished he'd sit through their first meeting without being so vocal. Maybe she should have come alone if she wanted to meet their neighbors in a friendly fashion. Then again, did any homeowners' meeting exist without contention?

"We have video surveillance around the clubhouse and at the

main entrance. And we pay for a private guard from 10 p.m. to 6 a.m." Gene glowered at Dalton. A bearded fellow who looked to be in his forties, the Board member had carefully styled hair and large front teeth.

"Oh, yeah? I've never met this guy." Dalton wagged his finger in the air. "What does he do, sit in the office all night?"

"He patrols the neighborhood and watches for anything irregular."

"Why, have there been incidents?"

Krabber snorted, as though Dalton's attitude was to be expected. "We've had a few break-ins, but it was determined some neighborhood kids were involved. And we've had thefts from unlocked cars in driveways. Otherwise, our record is pretty good for a community this size."

"I'm not implying otherwise." Dalton's placating tone would have suited a hostage situation. "But this amount of money budgeted to security seems awfully high. Have you gotten bids from different companies?"

"Of course, we did." Debbie Morris, the secretary, spoke in a defensive tone. She tucked a strand of strawberry blond hair behind her ear. Wedged between the taller men, she looked diminutive with her petite frame.

The fourth Board member, treasurer Cherry Hunter, was an attractive woman with raven hair and high cheekbones. She sat on the far end from Alan Krabber and kept relatively quiet. Shouldn't she be the one answering questions about the budget?

"Maybe it's time to reevaluate the need for a night guard," Dalton persisted. "Some local communities have set up neighborhood watches, for example. I'd be happy to head up a security committee."

Marla rolled her eyes. Was her husband turning into a political animal? Hopefully people would understand that Dalton meant well.

She tried to smooth things over after the meeting adjourned and members segued into the kitchen for coffee and dessert. March being the month of Purim, Marla had brought store-made hamantaschen. She munched on an apricot-filled pastry while chatting with her new neighbors.

During a break in conversation, she aimed toward Alan Krabber. He stood across the room from where Dalton was engaged with an elderly gent.

The association president wore a dress shirt tucked into a pair of belted trousers. A hint of stubble shadowed his jaw as he stuffed a chocolate chip cookie into his mouth. His flabby neck quivered as he chewed. Her glance rose to the retreating hairline crowning his square face. He kept his walnut hair combed neatly back.

She tapped his arm. "Hi, there. I'm sorry for the fuss about your boat, but I happen to believe my husband is right to support the city code. We have two dogs and are interested in putting up a fence ourselves. Maybe we should get together and exchange ideas since we share a common boundary."

Normally Marla would approach the woman of the household to make a conciliatory gesture, but her neighbor lived alone. His closest family in the area was a nephew.

Krabber's gaze turned crafty behind his wire-rimmed spectacles. "Sure, we could discuss it together. Why don't you come over next time your hot-headed spouse is at work? We'll have an intimate chat, just the two of us."

"Who are you calling hot-headed? And did you just hit on my wife?" Dalton loomed over them, his mouth thinned and his eyes narrowed.

"Hey, buddy, loosen up. I didn't mean to offend anyone."

Dalton leaned forward, his jugular veins prominent. "If I recall, the first time we met, you made inappropriate remarks to Marla, too. I won't tolerate that behavior."

"Hey, you tolerated a lot more by marrying her kind."

"What does that mean?"

"You should know. You're not one of them." Krabber winked. "If I were you, I'd think about saving her soul while there's still time."

Dalton's fists curled, while Marla's stomach sank to her toes. She couldn't believe she'd just heard a racist remark in earshot of everyone. In this era of diversity, and especially in South Florida, it was a rare occurrence.

A sudden hush fell over the room, and shocked glances turned in their direction. Marla sucked in a breath to calm herself. She didn't want to give anyone more fodder for gossip.

"Come on, honey, it's time we left." Her body trembling, she took Dalton's arm. "If Mr. Krabber can't appreciate the benefit of different cultures living in harmony, it's his loss."

Krabber didn't deign to respond. With a snort of disgust, he turned on his heel and strode to the coffeemaker.

"Alan, what's gotten into you?" another guy said, trailing after him. "I've never heard you speak like that before. You should apologize."

While people filed around Krabber with murmurs of agreement, a blond woman approached Marla and Dalton.

"Hi, I'm Angela Goodhart. Please don't mind Alan. I'm sure he didn't mean to be so rude. He was just trying to get a rise out of you, Mr. Vail, for leading a vote against him."

Dalton's mouth turned down. "I should report his remarks. We have witnesses."

Marla tightened her fingers on his sleeve. "I don't think so. We've caused enough waves. By the way, Angela, I like how you do your hair," she said to change the subject. "I'm a hairdresser, and I own the Cut 'N Dye salon in town. If you come in, I'll give you a discount on your first appointment." She handed over a business card.

"Thanks." Angela tucked the card into her purse. "What days are you there?"

"We're open Tuesdays through Saturdays. I have a full client list, but I'd fit you in." She gave a broad smile. Talking about the work she loved always energized her.

"So you're married to a detective, huh? It must be difficult to settle into a routine when he works irregular hours. I've seen cop shows on TV and sometimes the guys are barely home."

Marla nodded absently, her attention drawn to Krabber, who'd gotten into a close discussion with some other men. They shot occasional glances her way.

"Marla, I think we should leave." Dalton took her arm and tugged her toward the door.

"Nice meeting you, Angela," Marla called.

Before they reached the exit, the treasurer planted herself in front of them.

"You're onto something," Cherry said in a slurred tone, making Marla wonder if she'd been drinking before the meeting. Her stick-straight black hair hung down to her shoulders. "That man has secrets to hide. Better not push him. You don't know what he'll do."

Marla got an inkling of what Cherry meant when a plastic bag of dog poop showed up on their circular driveway the next day. She'd just stepped outside at seven o'clock on Friday morning with Lucky and Spooks—their golden retriever and cream-colored poodle—when she noticed the item lying on the asphalt. Hauling on the dogs' leashes, she veered over to verify her observation. Then she rushed back inside to inform her husband.

"I'll bet it's him," Dalton said, rising from the breakfast table where he sat drinking coffee and watching the news. "Let me get my fingerprint kit. I can prove it."

"Dalton, that's absurd. What are you going to do, arrest our next-door neighbor for defiling our property? It's a prank, that's all. The best response is to show no reaction."

He winced. "You're right, as usual. Man, how did we luck out? He's such a jerk."

"We don't know for sure that he's responsible. It could have been anyone. Let's just dispose of the bag and pretend like it never happened. That'll deflate his balloon."

Brianna shuffled into the kitchen in her pajamas. Dalton's fourteen-year-old daughter cringed at the bright light. "Why are you so loud in the morning?"

"Sorry." Dalton pointed to the tea kettle–shaped clock mounted on the wall. "You're running late. I'll have to drive you to school again. Go and get dressed."

"I'm taking the dogs out." Marla gave her a warm smile. "Do you want scrambled eggs? I can make them as soon as I get back." She'd inherited the teen along with her husband. It still amazed her that she had taken on the role of stepmother.

"Okay, and I'll have whole wheat toast, please." Brianna headed toward her bedroom.

Dalton opened the garage door, donned a pair of gardening gloves, and threw the offensive bag in the trash. Marla took the dogs out through the garage and strode down the street with them until they did their business. She didn't go near Krabber's house, heading in the opposite direction. The street was quiet except for an older couple. She guessed they were dedicated walkers from their running shoes and brisk pace.

She sighed, regarding the pristine neighborhood. They'd been delighted to find new housing since Palm Haven was mostly built out. While construction had started here two years ago, empty lots had still been available when she and Dalton had come looking. Evidently, Alan Krabber had been one of the earlier residents. He must have made out well before he retired, because he owned the only two-story house on the block.

The morning's incident fled from her mind when she went

into work at ten o'clock. Time raced by as it always did on weekends. Friday and Saturday were hectic at the salon. On Sunday, she and her new family went shopping. While she and Dalton had supplied many of the furnishings for their new home from their previously separate households, they still lacked necessities like a lamp table for the living room and a file cabinet for the home office. They enjoyed searching for accessories together.

Finally, she could relax alone on Monday after Dalton had gone to work and Brianna to school. She hoped to catch up on bookkeeping from the salon and to figure out what they needed to do next on the house.

Her peace shattered mid-morning when a banging noise sounded outside. Oh, great. Construction must have resumed on their neighbor's standby generator. Krabber had been waiting for the propane tank to be delivered. Having a backup power source was desirable in South Florida, where hurricanes could knock out power for days at a time. Marla had considered installing a unit herself until she'd learned about the twenty-thousand-dollar price tag.

She rushed to the window in Brianna's room and peeked through the blinds. Dirt was still piled in mounds around the hole in Krabber's backyard, so the noise didn't originate there. Her stomach knotted as she viewed a couple of brawny men erecting a wood fence between their houses. Her eyes narrowed as she assessed the distance.

Considering how their sprinklers were so far over, toward Krabber's property, she and Dalton had done a survey. It revealed that their neighbor had erected his path of round stones partially on their land. Dalton had requested Krabber move the pavers to his side of the boundary, but so far, he'd done nothing. And now this!

Back in the kitchen, Marla grabbed her house keys and cell

phone. She darted outside to confront the two workmen. Perspiration ran down their swarthy faces. Their truck, parked at the curb, showed no visible license plate.

"Hello, I live next door." She pointed to her house. "Isn't that fence going to put our sprinkler pipes on Mr. Krabber's side of the property? Look, you can see where the heads are located." The grass cutters had cut a clear strip around them.

The taller guy paused, a hammer in his hand. "You'll have to talk to the boss about it. We're just doing what he hired us to do."

"Do you have a permit?"

The guys glanced at each other, then the first one spoke. "You don't need no permit for a fence this size. See? It'll extend from that one already fixed along the rear boundary. If you need to get to your sprinklers, you can come through the gate."

"I can't do that! I'd be trespassing on Mr. Krabber's property. This makes no sense whatsoever." She propped her hands on her hips. "Are you sure about the permit? I thought the city required one for any kind of construction."

"Only for fences of a certain length, miss. This here is under the regulation footage."

Was that true? Could she be mistaken?

She glared at them, but they'd resumed their banging. "I want to see his survey. It should clearly show our property line." She'd raised her voice to be heard.

The foreman—if that's what he was—pulled a soiled piece of paper from his pocket and shoved it in her face. "See, we got one."

Marla squinted in the sunlight. "This looks like a drawing of the fence. If I'm not mistaken, it will intrude on our property. You have to stop construction immediately."

The laundry room door burst open and Krabber sauntered outside. "What's causing the ruckus? Lady, I can hear you hol-

lering all the way inside my house."

"Did you get an official survey before hiring these men? Because I have one, and this fence looks to be on our land."

"Is that so?" Krabber's double chin rippled as he spoke, his squirrel-like eyes scrunched under his wide brow. Crumbs dotted his sport shirt.

"See where my sprinkler heads are located? The piping will clearly end up behind your fence. You're violating the property line, same as with that path there."

He shrugged. "I just assumed the boundary ran halfway between our houses."

"Well, you assumed wrong. Your piece of land is smaller than ours."

"I'll check into it. Meanwhile, boys, get that fence up as planned. We can always move it later. Then be sure to plant my hedge before you go."

Marla glanced into his yard and blinked twice. She hadn't noticed that lineup of potted plants from Brie's bedroom window.

"You're not planting ficus, are you? That's the worst kind of tree to edge your lawn. They're a nuisance to maintain. The roots will extend toward our house and may end up cracking our sprinkler pipes. I thought those trees were on the city's disapproved list?"

Krabber jabbed a finger in the air. "Look, nobody can tell me what I can plant in my yard. They're allowable if I keep them trimmed."

Oh, right. And you're going to pay your grass cutters to trim the branches on my side of the fence?

She compressed her lips. These workmen could be lying about the permit. Considering how their truck had no visible tag, she'd guess they were fly-by-night laborers willing to do any job that paid cash.

"I'm calling Dalton." She whipped out her cell phone. "Your stone path also infringes on our property. This is getting out of hand."

If Krabber didn't make amends, she and Dalton would be forced to file a code violation. Marla would rather avoid that unpleasantness. Normally, she wouldn't bother Dalton at work, but this construction had to be stopped before the fence became a permanent fixture.

The UPS truck chose that moment to squeal to a halt in front of Krabber's house. He stomped toward the front to retrieve a package while she dialed Dalton's office number.

Fortunately, her husband was available and made it home within twenty minutes.

Krabber had disappeared inside his house with his parcel. She quickly filled Dalton in on the details and then turned to the workmen, who regarded the newcomer with wary expressions.

"Guys, this is my husband, Detective Dalton Vail with the Palm Haven police force."

The workmen exchanged startled glances. Her words had the galvanizing effect of making them pack up their tools. Wood planks littered the ground.

The foreman rapped on the laundry room door. "Yo, Mr. Krabber. You're needed out here."

Krabber waddled outside, his forehead creased. "Are you still here?" he said to Marla.

"Yes, I am. You remember my husband, Dalton."

"How could I forget? Whaddya want, buddy?"

Across the street, the garage door rumbled open. Jeanie, a stay-at-home mom, emerged outside. She waved at Marla from the driveway, where she appeared with her two children in tow. Marla waved back, offering a stiff grin. Jeanie set out a lawn chair while her kids—a boy and a girl—stooped over the asphalt to draw something with chalk. Watching them, a wave of nostalgia hit Marla. She'd played hopscotch on the sidewalk in her youth.

Her attention swung back to Dalton, who addressed Krabber in a reasonable tone. "The city requires a permit for any type of fencing. Do you have one?"

"These guys say I don't require a permit for a fence this size."

"That's right." The foreman shot a dark glance at his partner. "And since the last hurricane, you don't need approval for any work under twenty-five hundred dollars."

"That's hogwash." Dalton shook his head. "No matter the size or the cost, a permit is required. You're operating illegally if you don't have one."

The foreman turned to Krabber. "We want our money, dude. You can settle this after we leave."

Krabber scowled at him. "I don't owe you anything. You didn't finish the job, and our agreement said payment upon completion."

The foreman's shoulders hunched. "You're not thinking of stiffing us, are you? Because if so, I know what you've been—"

"Hey, you'll get paid. I'd planned to go to the bank later this afternoon. Come back tomorrow. We should have this sorted out by then."

"Are you guys licensed and insured?" Dalton focused on the two men with laser intensity. "If so, I'd like to see that license. You should know better than to put up a fence without a survey or a permit."

"Sure, we'll go get it." Without a backward glance, they high-tailed it to their truck, hopped in, and sped away before Marla thought to point out to Dalton the missing tag.

Dalton snorted, as though he'd known their type. Returning his attention to their neighbor, he raised his eyebrows. "How about showing us your so-called 'survey'?" While waiting for a reply, he folded his arms across his chest and stood with his feet spread apart.

Krabber slipped inside his house through the side door and reappeared within minutes. He waved a document in the air, flicking it at Dalton rather fast. Marla caught a glimpse of an official looking paper.

"Here, I have one. So back off, buddy."

Dalton remained firm, his face as stony as those round pavers on Krabber's path. "This fence and that trail extend onto our property. Remove them both, or we'll sue for compliance."

Marla tapped his arm. "Dalton, he's planning to put ficus trees near our boundary. See?"

Dalton's voice rose. "You're doing everything you can to decrease the value of our property. And when is that hole going to be filled in, huh? It's an accident waiting to happen."

Krabber's face purpled and his veins protruded. "Lots of folks have standby generators in South Florida. We're following standard procedure."

"He's right, Dalton." Marla spoke in a mollifying tone as her husband looked about ready to pop out of his skin. "If he agrees to move his fence, get a proper survey and permit, and change the location of those stones, we'll be satisfied."

"Don't think because you're our association president that you can break the rules," Dalton said. "I know guys like you. You'll stomp on anyone who gets in your path. Well, I won't stand idly by while you make an exception of yourself. No matter what it takes, I'll see that you comply with the law."

Chapter Two

"Dalton, what's wrong with you? Normally you're the one who calms people in a situation." Surely her husband had reason to be upset with their neighbor, but usually he kept his cool. Hoping he wasn't short-tempered because he regretted the changes in his life, Marla strode beside him on the way back to their house.

He must have heard the quiver in her tone because inside their foyer, he spun to face her. "You're right. I've been on a short fuse lately, and I should have told you why sooner."

Uh, oh. She swallowed her doubts, waiting to hear him out.

His jaw tightened. "I have a new partner at work."

"So? That's good news, isn't it?" Relief washed through her. Was that all? His tense mood had nothing to do with her or their marriage?

He grimaced. "Not in this case. I'd hoped it might be temporary, and you wouldn't need to know."

"Dalton, I want to know everything that affects you. It hurts me when you bottle things up, and then I worry that I'm the cause."

He shook his head. "Never. You're my solace and my strength. I didn't want to add to your burdens."

Her mouth pursed. "Then don't keep your problems from me. We're here for each other, remember? Anyway, I thought you had taken on more administrative duties. Why would you even need a partner?"

"The captain felt we were too short-staffed after Sergeant Weber's retirement."

Marla had attended the officer's farewell party with Dalton, but she still didn't understand why he'd be disturbed by the assignment. "Is this person anyone I know?"

"Lieutenant Minnetti transferred from another precinct. Katherine Minnetti."

"Oh." Her brow folded. "You've worked with female officers before, so what's different this time?" Did the woman's equal rank bother him? That shouldn't matter.

"You'll understand when you meet her." He glanced at his watch. "I have to get back. It's her first week, and I'm supposed to be showing her the ropes."

"Give it time, Dalton. You're good at what you do. You always notice those little details other people miss. She can learn a lot from you."

His face softened. "And you always make me feel better about things." He drew her into his arms for a lingering kiss.

Held so securely, Marla wished he didn't have to leave. She inhaled his male scent, spice cologne mixed with Irish Spring soap, and a warm glow filled her. How gratifying to be involved in his life and to be able to offer comfort. She wanted nothing more than to retreat to the bedroom and show the man how much she cared.

"I'll stop by code enforcement on my way to the station," Dalton said, his tone husky as he broke their embrace.

"Will you be home for dinner?"

"I should be. We don't have any cases right now, so it's a good opportunity to train Kat and to get caught up on paperwork."

"All right. I'm sorry to have called you away from your desk."

Giving her a lazy grin, he stroked her cheek. "Don't ever be sorry. We're a team now."

Her heart sang as she observed his tall figure retreating down the driveway toward his sedan. She shut the front door, her mind turning to the myriad tasks ahead.

With quiet descending over the neighborhood once more, she got a lot accomplished. In fact, it wasn't until the next day that Alan Krabber again entered her thoughts. She went to take the dogs out in the morning and noticed a rescue truck next door.

Oh, dear. Had the man experienced a heart attack? An accident? Maybe he'd fallen into that dangerous pit in his backyard. As she stood gaping, a police car pulled up to the curb, parked, and disgorged two officers.

Yanking on the dogs' leashes, she rushed back inside the house to summon her husband. Brianna was in the kitchen, where the heady aroma of brewed coffee scented the air. The teen, spooning cereal into her mouth, glanced up at Marla's hasty entrance. Brie took one look at Marla's face and put her utensil down.

"Marla, what's wrong?"

"Where's your father? Is he dressed yet?"

"I'm right here." His tall frame filled the doorway. He wore a sky blue dress shirt tucked into black trousers. He'd brushed his peppery hair off his forehead.

"Something's happened at Alan's house. There's a police car and a rescue truck."

"Damn." He patted his pockets. "Where's my cell phone? I might have gotten a call."

"It's probably still on the night stand. Funny, I didn't hear any sirens, did you?"

"Nope." He disappeared and returned several minutes later, his face somber.

"What is it?" She put down the dish towel in her hand.

"I'm afraid it's bad news. Alan Krabber is dead."

Marla clapped a hand to her mouth. "Oh, no. That's impossible. Why, we just spoke to him the other day."

"That's horrible, Dad." Brianna stared at her father.

"I know." Dalton gave the two of them a cautionary glare. "I'm meeting my partner next door. We'll conduct a preliminary investigation. It's routine for cases like this."

Despite the chills running up and down her spine, Marla's curiosity overwhelmed her. She wanted to meet the woman but knew Dalton wouldn't allow her into a crime scene. Wait a minute. Did that mean their neighbor had been killed?

"Was Alan murdered?" she asked in a hoarse tone.

"It appears to be a possible suicide. I'll know more once I check out the scene." Dalton compressed his mouth, going into work mode. She could see it in his stony eyes.

Marla's gut churned. She couldn't believe Alan was gone. But a suicide victim? He'd given no indication of depression yesterday. He wouldn't have been doing all that construction without planning to stick around, would he? Then again, how well had they truly known him?

"Guys, I'll be late for school." Brie took her empty bowl to the sink.

Marla gestured. "Get your backpack. I'll give you a ride to the bus stop." The dogs nudged her, their leashes trailing on the floor. "Poor babies. We really need to fence in our yard to let them out."

"They can wait a few more minutes." Dalton's gaze warmed. "I'm glad you're here to share these things. It sure makes my life easier. I want you to know that."

She grinned, pleased by his words of appreciation. "Women are used to multitasking. Look, can you call me as soon as you know something solid? Otherwise, I'll worry all day." Good Lord, she hoped they hadn't pushed their grumpy neighbor over the edge with their argument. She'd already purged enough guilt from her system to fuel a lifetime of regrets.

"It would have to be him." Dalton rubbed his brow.

Shadows ringed his eyes. He hadn't slept well. Marla had heard him get up in the night. Used to receiving phone calls at any hour, he often had restless cycles. She'd fallen back to sleep, and this morning she'd awakened to his tall form stretched beside her.

"Good luck, Dad!" Her ponytail swinging, Brie breezed back into the kitchen, her backpack slung over her shoulders. She grabbed her purse from the counter. "Come on, Marla, or Spooks and Lucky will do their business in here."

Marla drove Brie to the bus stop and then returned home to take the dogs out. Next door, the melee had been joined by a crime scene van. Was that routine too, or did Dalton suspect all wasn't as it seemed?

Various neighbors emerged, gawking at the scene. Marla caught the narrowed glance of the young mother from across the street. She waved and got no answering response. Jeanie must have gotten an eyeful yesterday, Marla thought with growing concern. How much of their dispute had she overheard?

One of the uniformed officers began canvassing the neighborhood, starting with the woman on the other side of Alan's house. She, too, was a mom with kids.

At thirty-seven, Marla had no children of her own. She was grateful to have acquired a stepdaughter in Brie, who was turning fifteen this month. More kids weren't in the cards. Marla had too many things she wanted to do. Instead, Brianna would benefit from their full attention, and Marla could focus on her business, new family, and wish list of travel plans.

Like that will ever happen, she thought with a mounting sense of gloom.

Unable to resist the compulsion, she wandered next door before leaving for work. So she'd be a few minutes late at the salon. Luis, her handsome Latino receptionist, could open the shop.

She approached one of the uniforms assigned to crowd control. Maybe she could coax him to talk or at least tell her who owned the silver Prius in Alan's driveway.

"Hi, I'm Detective Vail's wife. We live next door. I can't believe our neighbor killed himself. Is it true?"

His keen gaze assessed her. "Sorry, ma'am, but I don't know the details." His cool tone told her he wouldn't relate them even if he had been informed. "Would you like me to relay a message to the lieutenant for you?" He put a hand on his radio.

"No, thanks, I won't bother him." With a shrug, Marla turned toward the sidewalk.

She hadn't gotten far when one of the neighbors stopped her.

"I hear Alan hanged himself." The woman pressed a hand to her chest. "His death will affect the entire community. This is such a shock."

Marla nodded, too choked to speak. Why would Alan have been erecting a fence around his property if he didn't mean to hang around?

Oops, bad word choice.

How had he done it? Strung himself over the shower rod? Thrown himself over the second-floor balcony, if he had one? Bile rose in her throat. The guy was a big man. He might have choked slowly, his body twitching. Had he regretted his actions in those last minutes?

Shoving those troubling thoughts aside, she nodded at the neighbors who stood around in clusters, chatting amongst themselves. She'd have liked to linger and get the scoop on what was going down, but Dalton could fill her in later. Time to leave for work. Besides, guilt tore at her. Even though she knew they weren't responsible, she and Dalton had been rather adamant in their disagreement over the property line.

She swallowed hard as she strode toward her open garage. How much would that affect his investigation? Would bias cloud his judgment?

It's not your problem. Focus on your own job.

Nonetheless, Marla kept her cell phone close during her morning appointments, hoping Dalton would call and reassure her. Familiar noises made her jumpy. The background music seemed too loud. The whirr of blow dryers and the splash of water seemed to echo in her ears. And the chatter of customers seemed to rise in a crescendo.

When noon came and her phone remained silent, she turned to Nicole at the next station. The cinnamon-skinned stylist had been her confidant through other cases, and Marla had to talk about this now, or she'd *plotz*. You're not going to burst out of your skin, an inner voice said. Instead, the words spilled from her mouth.

"Nicole, you'll never believe what's happened," Marla said after Nicole switched off her hand-held dryer. "Our next door neighbor was found dead this morning."

While waiting for her twelve-thirty appointment, the other stylist had cleaned her chair of stray hairs. The shampoo girl's broom picked up the debris.

Nicole's brown eyes popped. "You're kidding, girl." She plunked the dryer down on the counter.

Marla paused midway to arranging a stack of foils for her next client. "Do I ever joke about such matters? The man is . . . *was* president of our homeowners' association. Dalton complained about him in front of everyone at our annual meeting."

"Oh, great. Nice way to meet your neighbors."

"Tell me about it. Then yesterday, I caught Alan—that's his name—trying to put up a fence on our side of the property line." Marla furtively glanced around to make sure no one else could overhear. "He wouldn't listen to reason, so I called Dalton."

"This just keeps getting better." Nicole's expression alternated between morbid fascination and sympathy. "Go on."

"Dalton asked if Alan had a permit for the fence and if the workers had a license. They didn't have a survey, either. Dalton threatened to sue if Alan didn't comply with regulations."

"Your neighbor must have been angry. He'd have had to pay those laborers."

"Not according to what he told them when they asked for payment. He said their agreement was based on a completed job. They weren't too happy when they took off."

"And now the fellow is dead?"

"Rumor has it he hanged himself, but I haven't heard confirmation from Dalton. Bless my bones, I wish he'd call."

"Why would he be involved if it's a suicide?" Nicole glanced up as Luis signaled from the front. Her next customer had arrived.

"His team investigates any unattended deaths."

"Who called this in, then?"

Marla stared at her. "You know, I hadn't even thought about that. I have no idea."

Clients distracted her all afternoon but still she worried. Why didn't Dalton call? He'd know she would be waiting for news.

Who would plan Alan's funeral? His nephew?

Marla berated herself for knowing so little about him. Here they'd confronted a man who might have had suicidal tendencies. Their dispute may have contributed to his problems, but she doubted Alan had killed himself over a property line. She and Dalton couldn't stand by and do nothing about the land issue. Regret mixed with anger. If Alan had followed the laws, she wouldn't have his demise weighing on her conscience.

Impatient to learn more, she finished work early. Would

Dalton be home for dinner as promised, or would he be engaged in this new case? Had he left her any messages?

Dalton's car wasn't in the driveway when Marla got home at five-thirty, but her mother's white Chevrolet was there. She groaned inwardly, hoping Ma's boyfriend Roger hadn't come along. His boisterous manner would aggravate her sour mood.

"Hello?" she called upon entering. Voices emanated from the kitchen so she headed in that direction. She had to heat up the casserole she'd made the other day, anyway.

Ma sat across from Brie at the kitchen table. The teen's history book was open and she scribbled notes into a notebook. Good, Brie was getting her homework done before her evening dance class. But what were they discussing?

Anita glanced up and grinned at Marla's entrance. She waved an idle greeting, her red-painted fingernails flashing in the air. Her white layered hair was a contrast to the navy blouse she wore over a pair of white cropped pants. A pair of gold chains hung from her neck.

"Hi, Ma. How are things?" Marla tossed her purse on the counter and stooped to pet the dogs who danced around her ankles. After they'd calmed down, she refilled their water dishes.

"Brie's birthday is in less than two weeks. I offered to take her shopping for her present, but she wants money toward an iPhone."

Marla frowned. "I know, and Dalton disapproves. He's afraid she'll spend all her time playing with apps." The teen had one of their hand-me-down phones. It was ancient with a miniscule screen. She really did need an upgrade but Marla could understand Dalton's concern.

"All my friends have one," Brie said with a moue of discontent. Her puppy dog eyes swung toward Marla. "You'll talk to Dad, right?"

"We'll see." Marla hesitated to act as a buffer between

Brianna and her father. Brie often asked her to intervene when Dalton was being intransigent, feeling a woman would be more sympathetic to her needs. "Ma, how come Roger didn't come with you?"

Anita averted her gaze. "I haven't heard from him in two days. That concerns me. It's unlike him not to call."

"Two days is nothing. Maybe he went out of town or is busy with his golfing buddies."

Her mother gave Marla a pained glance. "It's more than that. Whenever I've talked to him lately, he's seemed more distant. I can't put my finger on it, but things aren't the same."

While Marla held no fondness for the portly fellow who liked to eat, he did make her widowed mother happy. She'd thought they were on the verge of moving in together.

She turned the oven on and retrieved the casserole from the refrigerator. Busy getting out the dishes and utensils, she sought an appropriate reply.

"I'm sorry you're upset. Maybe Roger's lack of communication has nothing to do with you and will blow over."

Anita gave a desolate shrug. "I hope you're right. So Brie, are you all set for your birthday luncheon?"

The teen glanced up from her book. "What's there to do? We're just going to Jasmine's on the Intracoastal. It'll be nice."

Marla wagged her eyebrows at Anita in warning. Brie hadn't wanted a party, saying she'd prefer to have the money instead, but Marla knew that wasn't the real reason. Ever since her mother died, Brie had invited friends over for a barbecue on her birthday. Dalton's parents, Kate and John, had flown down for the occasion. But this would be the first time Marla's family would be involved. She suspected the teen would be embarrassed by having her friends around so many relatives.

Nonetheless, Marla had planned a surprise. She'd suggested they go to a restaurant this year since Anita and Roger were coming, along with Marla's brother Michael and his family. Brie had agreed, not knowing Marla had invited ten of her girlfriends to join them.

Anita pushed herself up from her chair. "I suppose I should go. Dalton will be home any minute and you have dinner preparations under way. We'll talk again soon."

"You can stay for dinner. I've made my chicken spaghetti casserole. We'll have more than enough for company."

Anita knew she had a standing invitation whenever she stopped in, although Marla wished she'd give advance notice of her visits.

"That's okay. I'm playing mah jongg later, and I need to get ready, but thanks anyway." Anita grasped her purse. "Have a good dance class tonight, bubula." She bent to give the teen a quick kiss on the forehead.

"Thanks." Brianna's eyebrows lifted. "I hear the garage door. Dad is home."

Brie scooted to her feet to unlock the inner door while Marla escorted Anita to the foyer.

"Ma, I'm sure everything will turn out all right with Roger."

Anita gave her a troubled glance. "Do you think he's sick? Maybe I should stop by his place. He might need me."

"His son, Barry, is around to help. If you've left messages, it's up to him to respond."

She did agree that it was unusual for Roger not to call back promptly. That had always been his habit, almost to the point of annoyance when he phoned Anita several times a day. Perhaps a temporary issue had come up that kept him occupied.

Her mother's problems fled her mind as Marla bustled into the kitchen to greet Dalton, but he wasn't there. Brie sat alone at the table, biting her lip in concentration as she resumed her homework.

"Where's your father?" Marla stuck the baking dish into the

oven and set the timer.

"He went to get washed. Gosh, a girl can't get anything done with all the commotion around here."

"You could go into the study. It would be quieter."

"No, thanks. How much time until the food is ready?"

"A half hour or so."

Questions burning on her tongue about the day's case, Marla hustled to the bedroom. Dalton was locking his gun into the safe they'd installed for that purpose. His heavy-duty belt lay across the bed, along with his tie. His face looked haggard, and sympathy seeped into her pores.

"How'd it go today?" She leaned against the door frame.

"Okay."

"That's it? There's crime scene tape across Alan's front door. Does that mean something you can share?"

Dalton's mouth tightened. "Yes, it means the case is under investigation."

"But what about the evidence indicating a suicide? And who called in the death to the police? Where was Alan found? Did he really hang himself?"

"You know I can't discuss the details." After adding his extra pack of ammo, Dalton punched in the code to lock the safe. Then he laid out his radio, cell phone, badge and cuffs in a neat row on top of their dresser.

"For heaven's sake, we'd just spoken to the man. Do you think our conversation pushed him over the edge?"

"It's not our fault. Don't think that for a minute." Dalton shot her a dark glare before striding into the bathroom to scrub his face with water. Patting his skin dry with a towel, he glanced at her in the mirror to where she'd followed behind. "Marla, give me some space, will you? I just got home. I'll tell you more when I've relaxed."

"I've been worried all day. I thought you would call me at

work, knowing I'd be anxious to hear from you. Can't you at least tell me what's being made public?"

He unbuttoned the top few buttons of his shirt. "Soon, all right? Let's eat first."

She studied his stern features and tense shoulders. Craving an affectionate response and not this chilly reception, she decided to cease her probing questions for now.

Maybe he was hungry. Didn't Ma always say to talk about important issues after a man had his meal? Nonetheless, he could offer her a crumb of information.

He headed to the study and picked up the mail she'd stacked on their desk.

Marla trailed after him, wondering how to improve his mood. Normally she wouldn't pester him about a case, but this one involved someone they had both known. She watched him set each envelope down without reading it, his gaze turned inward. Something was definitely off kilter, and it might have nothing to do with her.

"Dalton, I know you're upset." She hoped her soft tone would soothe him. "So am I. We couldn't have known Alan was so depressed. He didn't show it, although his anger could have been a manifestation."

Dalton had been quite vocal also, she remembered. The men had shouted at each other. Had her husband gone to code enforcement as planned and filed a complaint? Did guilt afflict him like it did her?

His lips thinned as he stalked into the kitchen. Clearly he wasn't in the mood to talk, but it wasn't healthy for him to keep his feelings restrained. Was this what it meant to live with a cop? Officers preferred to leave the ugliness of their world behind when they stepped inside the haven of their home. Maybe it was wrong of her to pry.

Focusing on her wifely duties, she grabbed a potholder and

cracked the oven door to check on the casserole. It was bubbly around the edges. Almost done.

Dalton gave his daughter a perfunctory greeting and turned on the news. They kept a small TV in the kitchen. He liked to hear what local newscasters were saying about police matters. With an irritated glance, Brie slammed her book closed.

"I'll finish this later. Marla, I'm going to pack my bag for dance class. Don't forget the monthly check is due today."

"It's already in my purse. I'm giving this dish ten more minutes and then dinner will be ready."

"Okay." Brie halted halfway toward the door and whirled around. Maybe she'd noticed her father's long face. Or maybe she'd picked up on Marla's subdued tone.

"Dad, what's the matter? I know you didn't like our neighbor, but you're usually able to be objective about a case. What's so different about this one?"

Dalton's morose gaze fell upon them. For a long moment, he didn't speak.

"If you must know," he said finally in a funereal tone, "I've been removed from the case."

"What?" Marla and Brie said in unison.

"It's a potential homicide, and I'm a person of interest."

Chapter Three

"You're a what?" Marla gaped at Dalton, but she couldn't wait for a response. Words bubbled from her mouth. "And since when is it a homicide? You've been removed from the case? That's impossible. It's your district."

"Whoa, slow down." Dalton sank into his favorite chair at the kitchen table. "I'll tell you what I know if you promise not to speak a word about this to anyone."

"Sure, Dad." Brie, her eyes sparkling with curiosity, retraced her steps and resumed her seat. The teen enjoyed the challenge of a puzzle, same as her father. Unlike him, she watched crime shows on television. He was more into the nature and history channels.

Marla leaned against the counter. "Why don't you start from the beginning? What did you find when you went next door?"

"Krabber was hanging from his second-story balcony. He had a computer cable wrapped around his neck, and he'd left a signed suicide note on his desk."

"So what tipped you off about that scenario?"

"A number of things. The knot looked wrong, and the angle of his body didn't seem right. The chair next to the rail didn't have any footprint impression, which it would have had if he'd stood on it before jumping over. And there's more."

"Your observations are important. How can you be excluded from the case?"

"The neighbor across the street reported that she'd seen me

arguing with the man. And other people mentioned my complaints at the meeting."

She lifted her chin. "You had every right to protest. Alan meant to violate the rules."

"Our late president has his supporters. The chief removed me for conflict of interest. My new partner will take over, and I'm temporarily reassigned to another division."

Ouch. No wonder you're grumpy. "Conflict of interest, not person of interest?"

He leveled his gaze on her. "I used the wrong term before. Conflict of interest is the excuse the chief used, although I could be considered a suspect. No one at the station really believes that. Still, it's protocol. I'm involved, so someone else has to take over."

"Do you really think our neighbor was murdered, Dad?" Brianna tilted her head as she regarded her father.

"We'll know for sure after the M.E. completes his examination and the toxicology results come in. Marla, be prepared to be questioned. Kat may come around and ask you about my whereabouts last night."

"You were home all night with me." But how about when she'd awakened and his side of the bed was empty? She had fallen back to sleep and didn't know when he'd returned. His partner might ask if he could have slipped outside in that interval and gone next door.

"Just tell the truth, and it'll be fine."

Shortly thereafter, Marla turned off the oven and donned a pair of insulated gloves to remove the casserole to the ceramic stove top. They muddled through dinner, the teen's dance class, and bedtime preparations.

When Marla lay in her nightgown later by Dalton's side, she traced a finger up his muscled arm. "I have faith in you, and so will your colleagues. This storm will blow over."

"I lost my temper, Marla." Lying on his back and folding his arms behind his head, he contemplated the ceiling. "I let that man get to me and I blew my stack. It's not a great beginning to my partnership with Kat for her to hear about it from the citizens of our community."

"Once she gets to know you, you'll earn her respect. What's she like?"

"Tough as steel and just as hard-edged. I can't read her well enough to know more. She won't discuss the reasons for her transfer."

Marla trailed her hand downward, meaning to distract him from his worries and reinforce her claim to his attentions.

"Forget about everything else for now. I love you. That's all that matters." She rolled sideways and pressed her lips to his. Their world narrowed until it was just the two of them, and any other reality ceased to exist.

"How can I help him, Nicole?" Marla asked the next morning at work. "Dalton has never been pulled from a case in all the time I've known him. This could smear his reputation, both at work and in our new community. It's even worse with his new partner taking over."

The stylist's eyebrows shot up. "Oh? What's this?"

"He's got a lady detective working with him now. I haven't met her yet."

"And now she's working his case." Nicole blinked. "You want to know what to do? If it turns out to be a homicide, find the killer. You're experienced at sleuthing. Who else would have reason to want that man dead?"

They both stood by their stations drinking freshly made coffee and waiting for their first customers to arrive. Nicole's brown eyes sparked as they always did when Marla got embroiled in a murder investigation. Her friend devoured mystery novels as though they were brain candy.

"How can I go about it?" Marla propped a hand on her hip. "I can't just knock on doors and ask nosy questions. I'm not a cop."

"No, but use the skills you have."

She considered Nicole's advice. "You may be onto something. Our new neighbors are all potential customers. I could offer them an incentive to come into the salon."

Nicole grinned, showing a flash of white teeth. "There you go, girlfriend. Bring the informants to you."

Marla gave the other stylist a quick embrace. "I knew I could count on your insight. Listen, don't repeat a word of this to anyone. I promised Dalton I'd keep my mouth shut."

"My lips are sealed as tight as a perm wave."

Their clients arrived, and Marla kept busy until ten-fifteen when Luis approached her. The receptionist stroked his mustache. "Dara is late again, and her customer is complaining. What should I do? She isn't answering her cell phone."

Marla glanced at her watch. "Did she know she had a ten o'clock?"

"I reminded her yesterday."

"See if Jennifer will cover for her. I don't think she has anyone until eleven."

"Jen covered for Dara the last time, and she got stiffed for ninety dollars. She had to honor Dara's discount to the woman."

Her comb in hand and in the middle of a cut, Marla frowned. "Just see if she'll do it, okay? I have to talk to Dara. She has no respect for her customers or for the rest of us. Speaking of discounts, Luis, can you make up a couple of hundred coupons for me? I want to stick them in people's doors in my new neighborhood."

"I'll get on it." His eyes gleamed as he gave her a onceover. "Nice dress, by the way."

Marla glanced down at her ankle-length maxi. "Thanks. I need to exercise more. My clothes are starting to get tight."

"In all the right places, I'd say."

She swatted him on the shoulder. "You're incorrigible. Go back to work."

Time flew past until six o'clock when Marla finished with her last client. She called Brie to make sure the teen had gotten home okay.

"Have you heard from Dad?" Brie asked in a plaintive tone.

"No, he hasn't contacted me." She wondered what occupied him. Had he been assigned a dull desk job? "I'll be home soon. I just have one more issue to settle here."

Marla intercepted Dara on her way to the door. Tote bag swinging from her arm, Dara chewed a piece of gum, her face sullen. Her nose ring quivered with each motion of her jaw. She wore her spiked black hair in a short, boyish style.

"Can I have a few words with you, please? Let's step outside." The late-afternoon air was warm but delightfully dry. It would have been a great day for the local park. Folding her arms across her chest, Marla got to the point. "Jennifer doesn't appreciate having to take your clients when you're late. This has been happening on a regular basis lately. Not only do you fail to respect anyone else's time, but your steep discounts put the rest of us at a disadvantage."

"What are ya saying, Marla?" Dara stuck out her lower lip. "You want me to leave and take my customers with me? 'Cause your place sucks. You have too many rules."

"They're simply rules of common courtesy and professional behavior. You're a good stylist, and you have a loyal clientele. But if you can't make an effort to get along with your colleagues and show up for appointments, maybe this isn't the salon for you."

Dara kicked at a discarded cigarette butt on the ground.

"Jennifer doesn't like me. She's a spoiled brat, expecting everyone to kowtow to her because she's your favorite."

Marla drew in a deep breath to calm herself. "That is so untrue. And this is about you, not Jennifer. It's your actions that are unacceptable."

Dara's lips tightened and her eyes scrunched. "All right, I'll try to get here earlier. But I don't like being picked on because I'm not a straight arrow like you."

What's that supposed to mean? At the moment, Marla didn't know and didn't care. She just wanted to go home.

"Consider yourself on probation." She didn't like treating a fellow stylist like a schoolgirl, but Dara needed to improve her social behavior if she wanted to fit in. Why did the young woman's customers keep returning when her rudeness extended to them, too? "One more infraction, and we'll have to discuss your continuation at the salon."

Fortunately, her stylists worked on commission rather than renting their chairs. It had been her experience that independent operators felt little sense of obligation to the staff as a whole. Marla could have settled for a steady income each month that way, but preferred to have more control. For one thing, she'd rather keep the shelves stocked herself. And by offering continuing education classes and special events, she tried to foster team spirit. An environment where they all benefited from sharing resources encouraged cooperation. Exceptions like Dara disrupted the harmony in what was already a competitive business.

Luis didn't get around to producing her coupons until the next day. Since Thursdays were her late day at work, it wasn't until the weekend that Marla got to pass them around. Brianna offered to help. Sunday found them zigzagging through the neighborhood, leaving coupons in doorways, while Dalton stayed home to read the newspaper.

"Isn't the annual picnic coming up soon?" Marla asked him when they returned, weary but triumphant. The police department held an event every year so officers and their families could bond. Marla looked forward to meeting Dalton's colleagues as his wife. While many of them had attended the wedding, she hadn't been involved in their personal lives before.

"It's July 4th weekend, like always." Seated at the kitchen table, Dalton buried his face in the sports section. "I don't know that we'll go this year, though."

"Why not?" She busied herself putting away the breakfast dishes. Brianna had gone to her room to call her friends and make plans for later.

Dalton shrugged. "We've gone for a couple of years in a row. Maybe we should do something different for the holiday."

"I was just your girlfriend when we went before. Now I'm your wife." She wanted to feel included, not be greeted with polite smiles and surface chatter. Maybe the women would talk about things that truly concerned them in front of her since her status had changed.

"It's not for a while yet. We don't have to decide right this minute."

Glancing at his bent head, she swallowed her retort. His reassignment was taking a heavy toll on his ego, and in his job, he couldn't afford to lose focus. She hoped he'd rejoin his team before his morale dipped any lower.

She dropped the subject, suggesting they go to the park while the humidity remained low. A brisk walk might lift his spirits, plus they both needed the exercise.

After dropping Brianna off at a friend's house, they headed over to Central Park. Dalton didn't say much, responding to her chatty conversation with curt responses. The brooding look on his face deepened her concern, but she didn't know how to ease his troubles when he wouldn't talk about them.

Heaving a deep sigh, she switched her gaze to the lake where a duck family waddled along the bank. Ducks didn't have to deal with work problems or awkward relationships. She studied the ripples on the water, palm fronds swaying in a light breeze, and a yellow butterfly alighting on a flowering plant. If only her life was so peaceful. Was she up to par to deal with Dalton's affairs? How had things gotten so complicated so fast?

Life got even more complicated on Monday morning when a loud knock on the front door took her away from household bookkeeping. Wearing jeans and a short-sleeved top, she strode toward the foyer, wondering who would stop by so early. Lucky and Spooks accompanied her, barking madly and thrusting themselves at the door. She shooed them aside to peer through the peephole. A woman stood on the front porch, her skirt suit indicating she meant business.

"Yes?" Marla asked. "Who is it?" She wasn't in the mood for solicitations.

"Detectives Minnetti and Langley. We'd like to ask you a few questions."

Marla felt the blood drain from her face. *Great, just what I need this morning.*

"Let me get the dogs locked up, and then I'll let you in."

A few minutes later, Marla swung the door wide. "Dalton has told me about you. I'm so glad we're finally able to meet." *Although I wish the circumstances were different.*

"Likewise, Mrs. Vail." Detective Minnetti strode inside, along with a somber-faced man in a jacket and tie whom Marla had met before. Detective Langley flashed her a sheepish grin and mumbled that he was Minnetti's current partner on the case.

"Please come in and have a seat." She ushered her guests into the living room.

The detectives sat on the camel-colored sofa, while Marla sank onto the matching loveseat. A cherry wood cocktail table separated them. A faux suede armchair completed the conversational area. One wall held a shelving unit with knickknacks, which she and Dalton had decided would reflect their new life and not their separate pasts.

Marla folded her hands in her lap. Realizing she was swinging her crossed leg back and forth, she stilled. The dogs continued their barking from the kitchen where she'd confined them behind a doggie gate. After an awkward interval where Marla waited on edge for the detectives to begin, the animals quieted and silence reigned for a few blessed seconds.

"Marla . . . may I call you by your first name?" Minnetti began.

"Please do." She moistened her lips.

"As you might have guessed, we're here to talk about your neighbor, Alan Krabber. What can you tell me about him? And do you mind if I take notes?"

"Go ahead." As the detective withdrew a notebook and pen from her handbag, Marla studied her. The woman could have been a model with her height, slim figure, and refined features, but her eyes were stone cold.

Minnetti couldn't be all that bad. She'd taken particular care with her jet black hair. The short layered cut had not a hair out of place. It highlighted her bone structure and firm chin. Marla couldn't have done better herself if the woman had sat in her salon chair.

"We didn't know Alan all that well." Marla stumbled over the words, regret assailing her. "Dalton and I introduced ourselves when we first moved in, but the man mostly kept to himself."

"Was he friendly during your first meet?"

"I'd say he was polite. He's not . . . wasn't an overly garrulous man. However, he did like telling others what to do."

"How so?" Minnetti leaned forward, an interested expression on her face.

"He made sure to point out to us the days of trash delivery and certain rules. You know, keeping the roof clean and our yard free of debris. Not that he was one to follow regulations."

"What do you mean?"

"Well, he tried to park his boat in his driveway. That's explicitly against city code, which Dalton pointed out to him at the homeowners' meeting."

Minnetti's lips compressed. "Tell me about that night."

The dogs whined. Marla desperately wished she could put them out in a fenced-in yard.

She shifted her position. "Alan wanted to keep his boat in plain sight. Dalton protested, and another member called for a vote. The result was that Alan had to comply with the rules. He wasn't exempt because of his role as president."

"You said your husband protested. In what manner?" Detective Langley hunched forward, his dark eyes fixed on her.

"Dalton reiterated that the rules were intended to be followed by everyone, especially after Alan had just reinforced the same regulations for another resident."

Minnetti consulted her notes. "So it was determined that Mr. Krabber had to build a fence to be in compliance with city code."

"That is correct."

"Did your husband raise any other issues at the meeting?"

"During the budget discussion, he mentioned the line item for security. Dalton wondered why the cost was so high and offered to head up a committee to look into our options."

"How was his mood at the time?"

"Excuse me?" She raised her eyebrows, needing clarification.

"Did he seem hostile?"

Marla straightened her shoulders. "He was annoyed by Alan's attitude, and rightfully so."

"Did Lieutenant Vail discuss these issues with the association president at the reception following the meeting?"

"Not really." Marla surmised this is why it took so long for the detectives to interview her. They must have been interrogating other witnesses, as well as waiting for test results on Krabber's body.

Minnetti tapped her chin. "Yet I have one witness here who says your husband addressed Mr. Krabber in an angry tone and leaned forward in a threatening manner."

Marla's blood flashed hot. "Alan hit on me. It wasn't the first time. When we moved into the community and made an effort to introduce ourselves to the neighbors, Alan implied he could entertain me if I got bored. He said he liked to lie out by the pool in his birthday suit. Ugh." She shuddered at the image that came to mind.

"So Lieutenant Vail took offense at Mr. Krabber's words?"

"Yes, he did, especially when Alan's remarks turned nasty." Even now, the memory made her stomach clench.

"What happened after this confrontation?"

"Alan walked away and the situation defused itself."

"When was the next time either one of you encountered him?" The detective's pen scratched on her notepad. A lock of hair fell across her face, and she absently tucked it behind her ear.

Marla cleared her throat, which had suddenly gone dry. "I'm sorry, can I get you guys a drink? I should have offered you something sooner."

Minnetti exchanged a glance with Langley, who'd been scanning the living room with an eagle eye while the two of them talked. "No, thank you. Please continue."

"The next morning, we found a plastic bag of dog poop on our driveway."

"Is that right?" Minnetti arched a penciled eyebrow.

"We thought Alan might be the culprit, but we just disposed

of the bag and let it go."

"Which day was this?"

"Friday. I didn't see our neighbor again until Monday morning, when I heard a banging noise next door. At first, I thought construction must have resumed on the underground propane tank he's putting in to run a standby generator. But when I looked out the window, I saw a couple of workmen putting up a fence next door between our properties."

Langley's brow creased. "Wasn't that per the rule to hide his boat from view?"

"Yes, except that he hadn't done a survey or gotten a permit. Those men were constructing the fence on our land."

"How did you know that?" He brushed a piece of imaginary lint off his trousers.

Marla sat forward as their neighbor's affront riled her again. "We'd done a survey. I went outside to talk to the handymen. They didn't have a visible tag on their truck. That should have raised my suspicions."

"About what?" Minnetti took over the conversation again.

"Illegal work being done."

"So you went out alone to confront them?"

"That's right." She jumped up, her nerves crawling. "I need a cup of coffee. Are you sure I can't get you something? A glass of water, perhaps?"

"No, we're good." Minnetti replied for both.

In the kitchen, Marla drew in a shaky breath. She was so afraid she might say something that would cast blame on Dalton. But he'd advised her to tell the truth, and that's what she would do. He could deal with the fallout.

The dogs roused from their slumber at her arrival and nudged her for attention. Stroking the fur on the golden retriever, she willed herself to remain calm. The detectives were probably hoping she'd get rattled.

Spooks didn't like being left out. The poodle poked her leg with his wet nose. After giving Lucky a final pat, she grabbed Spooks up in her arms and gave him a quick, comforting squeeze before putting him down. No way would she let anyone harm their "daddy." She'd make these people see that Dalton had nothing to hide.

After giving each dog a biscuit for good behavior, she poured herself a mug of coffee, added sugar and cream, and returned to the living room. Both detectives had risen and were roaming around, peering at the objects on display. At Marla's appearance, they resumed their seats.

"Where was Lieutenant Vail when you went outside on Monday morning?" Minnetti said, eyeing Marla's coffee mug with an impassive expression.

The woman likely would have enjoyed a beverage but wouldn't indulge while on duty. Marla's gaze narrowed as she pondered the reason for her rigid self-control and cool demeanor. Dalton had said he couldn't read her, and Marla agreed. The woman would be a tough nut to crack, but Marla liked challenges when it came to psyching people out.

"Dalton had already left for work, and Brianna was in school."

"Oh yes, that's his daughter? How old is she?"

Lord save me, you're not going to question the girl, are you?

"She'll be fifteen later this month. Look, leave her out of this, okay? It's bad enough that her father was removed from the case. His colleagues should know better. Dalton is the most honest, diligent, and devoted cop I know. He wants to get to the bottom of this more than anyone, especially because he knew the victim. It's frustrating him that he can't be involved."

Silence greeted her tirade. Marla plunked her mug down on the coffee table, dismayed by her outburst. But then the lady detective's face softened and a smile played about her mouth. It transformed her features and made her look more approachable.

"Listen, Marla, we're just doing our job. Your husband may have a sterling reputation, but there have been complaints about him. It's our duty to investigate. No one is making judgments here. If it were me involved, the protocol would be the same."

Marla clasped her hands together. "I'm sorry. I hate to see him troubled."

"You're newlyweds, aren't you?"

"Yes, we got married in December, a second marriage for both of us."

"Tell me, did you realize he had a temper before you wed him?"

"Excuse me?" Marla did a double take. *Is she trying to throw me off guard? If so, that won't work with me. A little sugar won't change my tune.* "Normally, Dalton is very calm in stressful situations. I don't know where you're going with this." She spoke stiffly, insulted by the woman's suggestive tone.

"So you confronted the workmen by yourself, and then what?"

"Mr. Krabber heard us arguing, and he came outside. I asked if he had done a survey or applied for a permit. The fence wasn't the only issue. He'd put a stone path around the side of the house, and it crossed our boundary. And he was planning to plant ficus trees by the property line. You know how far those roots grow. They could crack open our sprinkler pipes."

Marla's voice rose in pitch. How could the detectives not sympathize with her plight? Those were blatant code violations. Nonetheless, the neighbor was dead, and she and Dalton might have been the last ones to see him alive.

Detective Langley, who'd been content to let his partner ask the questions, said, "How did Mr. Krabber respond to your comments?"

"He didn't take me seriously, so I called Dalton. Sometimes a man can be more forceful."

Oops. Those words had slipped from her mouth. She hoped the detective didn't take them the wrong way.

Detective Minnetti riffled through her notes. "I understand a heated discussion ensued between your husband and Mr. Krabber. And that's when your husband said, 'I won't stand idly by while you make an exception of yourself. No matter what it takes, I'll see that you comply.' He didn't mean that he would make the problem disappear, did he? And Alan Krabber along with it?"

Marla, midway to picking up her mug, sloshed coffee on her jeans.

Chapter Four

Marla snapped the leashes onto the dogs' collars as soon as she was free. Her fingers trembling, it took several tries before she got the job done. She grabbed her keys from the kitchen counter and stumbled after the pets in their race to the front door.

No wonder Dalton had been so touchy of late. After meeting his new partner, Marla could sympathize with him. Minnetti appeared competent at her job, but where was her compassion? What had happened to make her so stern? Intuition told Marla it went beyond the horrors she witnessed in her daily job or her attempts to be objective on this case.

Her curiosity aroused, she resolved to get to know the woman.

The balmy air and warm sunshine worked their magic as she strolled along the sidewalk. Her limbs relaxed, her movements becoming more fluid as she let the dogs take the lead. Her gaze darted to the neighboring homes. Were the housewives watching her now through parted curtains, wondering if her husband had been implicated in Krabber's death?

Unfortunately, she hadn't learned any more details about the case. Had Krabber hanged himself or not? Did the evidence indicate otherwise, as Dalton suspected?

Minnetti had asked if Dalton had been home that entire evening. Marla said that as far as she knew, he'd been beside her in bed all night. Had the police woman known she'd been fudging the truth? Should she have said that when she'd awakened in the middle of the night, his side of the bed was empty?

Marla assumed Dalton couldn't sleep and had gone into the family room to watch TV. He did that often in the midst of a case, when pieces of the puzzle jumbled in his head. He'd go back to sleep after an hour or so, and sometimes she'd have to rouse him in the morning. She knew her husband was no murderer, but that would have given him time to go next door.

Wait a minute. They'd turned the alarm on. That would exonerate him. The alarm company could prove he hadn't cracked their perimeter.

Her breath huffed with excitement as she waited by a bougainvillea bush for the pets to complete their business. Lost in thought, she loosened her grip and Spooks dashed forward. The leash ripped from her hand as the cream-colored poodle charged down the street. Lucky surged after him, but Marla yanked on the restraint to hold the bigger dog back.

Meanwhile, Spooks raced in circles in the middle of the road and then plunged toward Krabber's yard.

"Spooks, come here! I'll give you a treat!"

She spared a moment to unlock her front door and nudge Lucky inside.

With one dog secured, she turned and sprinted toward the side of the house where she'd seen Spooks vanish. His furious barking shattered the still air. That excited woof could only mean he'd found a squirrel or something more interesting. As she headed around the corner, she prayed for an easy capture. All she needed was for the neighbors to see her trespassing onto Krabber's property.

The dog's sudden silence raised goose bumps on her flesh.

"Spooks, where are you?" Arriving at Krabber's backyard, she halted. Spooks was nowhere in sight. Where could he have gone?

At the far edge of the lawn was a chain link fence marking the border between Krabber's land and the rear neighbor's plot, whose house faced another road. Pots of ficus trees were still lined up by the side border, ready for planting. And a big hole, surrounded by mounds of dirt, gaped in the center of the yard.

Her pet couldn't have squeezed beneath the fence, could he? Watching from the kitchen window, she'd seen a stray cat pass through it, into her own yard. Spooks could even now be prowling around on the next street over.

Or not. A faint whimper drew her attention. It sounded close by.

Small holes dotted the yard. Maybe the construction had disturbed a creature's underground habitat. A large snake might live there.

Dread weighted her stomach. Did snakes eat small pets? They weren't near a canal where she had to worry about gators. The only place she hadn't looked was in that huge pit. Obviously, Krabber no longer had need of a standby generator. Someone would have to petition his heir to fill in the hole.

She advanced cautiously. Wary of getting too close to an edge that might crumple, she peered down and swallowed convulsively.

Oh, God.

Spooks lay immobile on the bottom.

"Spooks, get up! Do you hear me?"

Moisture blinded her, and her heart pounded in her chest. Now what? She had to get him out and rush him to the vet.

The hole was too deep for her to climb down. She needed a ladder, but no way could she bring the huge one from her garage. It was too heavy for her to lift, let alone transport. Who should she call for help?

She didn't want to bother Dalton, not with the problems he had at work. Fire rescue? She bit back a sob. If she still lived in her townhouse, her neighbor Goat would be there in an instant. She missed the dog groomer now more than anything.

Her fingers fumbled for the cell phone she'd stuck in her pocket. She'd have to call the rescue squad. Her ignominy in Royal Oaks would increase, but what else could she do?

She went out front to await them in case anyone had been observing her flight into Krabber's backyard. Heaven forbid the lady across the street should accuse her of snooping on his property . . . or of attempting to cover up her husband's potential crime.

How would they ever earn anyone's trust in this community?

She paced back and forth, her sandals beating upon the rust-stained cement. The minutes ticked by until a red truck turned the corner. They hadn't put the siren on, for which she was grateful. Marla waved to the occupants, and the vehicle screeched to a halt at the curb. Several guys emerged, hunky fellows in jumpsuits.

"I'm sorry to bring you out for this, but my dog fell down a hole in our neighbor's backyard." She hoped they wouldn't notice the crime scene tape stretched across his front door, and that they weren't the same responders who'd come the day Krabber died.

"What kind of hole, ma'am?"

"It's meant for a propane tank to fuel a standby generator. Follow me."

Hastening toward the rear, she heard the thuds of their booted footsteps. She reached her goal and stared down at Spooks, her heart in her throat. He could be bleeding internally from his injuries. Would she be too late in taking him to the vet?

The rescue team retrieved a ladder. With several men, they made the job look easy as they carried their equipment into the backyard and set it into place. A muscular guy climbed down and scooped the still animal into his arms.

Marla accepted the limp dog with a murmur of appreciation. Her throat choked with tears. She blinked rapidly, refusing to break down.

Spooks twitched as though asleep, and his chest moved. Marla's spirits lifted. He was alive! The only injury she noted was a splotch of blood on his head.

"Is the homeowner in, ma'am? It would be wise for him to put up a temporary barrier until this hole is covered over," the same man asked. His name tag read Kevin Jones.

"I know, but he, uh, isn't available. He died a few days ago."

"Oh, I'm sorry to hear that. Is there a relative to contact, maybe?"

"His nephew is likely responsible." Marla walked alongside the EMT toward the front, eager to get to her car and dash off to the animal hospital. While she'd been waiting for the rescue team, she'd notified the vet's office that she'd be coming in with Spooks.

"We'll see if we can contact him and get something done so this doesn't happen again."

"Thanks, that would be wonderful. My dog got loose and ran back here. If he . . . if he survives, I'll be careful to keep him tightly on the leash hereafter."

After providing her phone number and pointing out her house in case the fellow had further questions, she charged to her garage. Tenderly, she placed Spooks inside her car. Then she took a few precious minutes to unleash Lucky and grab her purse. Fifteen minutes later found her inside the waiting room at the veterinarian. She texted Dalton, not wishing to disrupt his workday but wanting to update him.

She gulped past a lump in her throat. After their recent troubles, she couldn't bear to lose Spooks. He was her constant in this crazy universe. Wishing she'd never moved from her townhouse, she reminded herself of her loving family. They were the reason she'd taken this leap in life. She'd have to make the best of it.

"Mrs. Vail?" A tech signaled to her from the entrance to the inner sanctum.

Marla scurried over and followed the girl into a private treatment room that smelled like disinfectant. She stared at the linoleum floor, her pulse racing, until the inner door opened.

Dr. Nelson strode inside, a pleasant woman with a sympathetic smile and hair a shade darker than Marla's chestnut brown. She wore a white lab coat with a couple of pens sticking from her chest pocket.

"Good news. Spooks has a concussion, but he is awake and moving all limbs. He has some bruising from the fall but no evidence of internal bleeding. I'd like to keep him overnight for observation, and then you can come by tomorrow to take him home."

"Oh, thank you." Marla's eyes filled with tears. "Thank you so much. I was afraid—"

"I know." The doctor smiled. "He's a lucky pooch. We'll take good care of him, Mrs. Vail. Don't you worry."

Her brow aching, Marla retreated to her car. She'd pay the bill tomorrow when she picked Spooks up.

The rest of her day loomed lonely and bleak. Should she go into the salon? No, today was her day off. Surely she could find something else to do to lift her mood. Call her mother? Nope, that would irritate her more than anything. Dial a friend?

She opted for that choice. "Tally? Do you want to meet for coffee? I need some company, and we haven't caught up with each other in a while."

"Sure, Marla. It's quiet in the store, so Angela should be able to handle things for an hour or so. It would be nice to see you." Tally owned the Dress to Kill boutique. Pregnant for several months now, she hadn't cut back on her hours despite her husband's insistence.

Sitting in the coffee shop on a cushioned chair, Marla related everything that had happened since the homeowners' meeting. Upon her conclusion, Marla glanced at her cell phone in case she'd missed a call from the vet.

"Holy smokes, Marla." Tally, a lithe blond, brushed her hair back from her forehead. "I hope Spooks will be okay."

"Me, too."

"You don't think someone else was in the backyard, do you?"

Gripping her ceramic mug, Marla leaned forward. "What do you mean?"

"Well, you heard him barking, right? Maybe he was barking at someone rather than another animal."

Marla stared wide-eyed at her friend. "You're a genius. I would never have thought of that! If you're right, this person might not have wanted to be seen, and so he tossed poor Spooks in the pit to shut him up."

"He would have heard you calling for the dog. You said no one was there when you arrived. The intruder could have run around the other side of the house to get away."

"But why would anyone loiter in Krabber's backyard?"

"Why would anyone want him dead, if he didn't hang himself?"

"Good point." Too many questions plagued her. Damn, she wished Dalton would provide details. She said so aloud.

Tally's eyes glistened with sympathy. "He's not supposed to be involved, remember?"

"He is involved by virtue of Alan being our neighbor. And Tally—" her gaze darted around the room, making sure no one was within hearing range—"Dalton did get up in the middle of the night. I mean, the night before Alan's body was discovered."

"Come on, he's not guilty. No matter how annoyed he was by the guy, Dalton isn't a murderer. What's gotten into you?"

Marla absorbed the chatter around them, the aroma of strong coffee, and the scent of sugary pastries. "I suppose his new partner rattled me. And I'd forgotten about our alarm system being on. That would clear Dalton of any lingering suspicions."

"It might, depending on the time of death. What's this about a new partner?"

"Lieutenant Katherine Minnetti. She's cold as ice and holds the same rank as Dalton."

"A lady?" At Marla's nod, Tally narrowed her eyes. "And now this detective is in charge of a case that would normally have been his to solve. But it's better this way. Dalton couldn't possibly be objective when he knew the victim."

"Maybe." Her mouth compressed. "Why couldn't we have moved into a friendlier neighborhood? I miss Moss and Goat and the other people from my development."

Tally reached over and patted her hand. "You'll make friends eventually. And I wouldn't assume everyone loved your neighbor just because he got elected president."

"I don't know people well enough to evaluate their relationship with him."

Tally gave her a level glance. "You've used your sleuthing abilities before. Dig deeper and see what you can learn."

Marla picked up her spoon and twirled it. "After the fiasco at Jill's wedding when I found her sister dead under the cake table, I vowed to myself that I'd focus on family hereafter. I swore off solving any more cases. That's Dalton's job."

"Coaxing information out of people is what you do best. Cast off your slump and start snooping. Just don't put yourself in the path of danger. Brianna needs you, and so does your husband."

"You're right." Marla paused. "Cherry Hunter, the treasurer, said something at the homeowners' meeting about Alan Krabber having secrets to hide. I wonder what she meant."

"There you go. Find an excuse to chat her up and see what she knows. It's a good place to start."

Marla sneaked a glance at her cell phone again. Nothing. Her heart skipped a beat. Was Spooks all right?

She sought to change the subject. "How are you feeling? Have you been to the doctor lately?"

Tally's expression brightened, and she put a hand to her belly. "I'm having an ultrasound next week. The morning sickness seems to have passed, thank goodness. We've cleared out our spare room so we can make it into a nursery."

The conversation proceeded to baby things, which Marla half paid attention to while worrying about her pet and how she could ease Dalton's burden. He liked her brisket. Maybe she should make that for dinner tonight instead of meatballs.

She waved a fond farewell to Tally after a while and went about her business with a sad heart. Although Marla loved her dearly, Tally would soon be caught up in child care and mommy and me classes and such. She'd have to find friends with kids closer to Brianna's age, but how? Most young mothers developed social networks when their children attended preschool.

Her cell phone trilled on the way to the grocery store. Afraid it might be the vet's office with bad news, Marla pushed the button on her ear piece. "Hello?"

"Hi, it's Dalton. I hear you had a visitor this morning."

She calmed to his low, rumbling tone. "Yes, I met your new partner. She's a peach, isn't she?" Is that why he'd called? Not to ask about Spooks?

"What did you tell her?"

Marla detected a note of strain in his voice. "I related what happened at the homeowners' meeting and how Alan persisted in violating city code."

"Minnetti isn't being too forthcoming about the case. Did

you learn anything new from your conversation with her?"

Just that some of the neighbors have been talking about you.

"Not really. Dalton, you need to let this one go. We may share the same personal feelings toward Alan, but that's the very reason why you shouldn't be involved."

"I know, but it's damn frustrating."

She could almost hear him gnashing his teeth. "Yes, I expect it is, but you have to play this one down. Listen, the alarm was on that night. It'll prove you didn't leave the house."

"Good point. I'm hoping the M.E. will let me take a look at his report. If time of death was within those parameters, I'll advise Minnetti to verify the hours with our security company. It won't put me back on the case, but it'll help alleviate any doubts she might have about me."

"All right. I'm making your favorite brisket for dinner. Will you be home?"

"I suppose so. How is Spooks? I presume he's okay, or you would have called."

"He has a concussion and is staying overnight at the vet, but he'll survive."

As soon as Marla returned home from her errands, she made a quick call to the animal hospital to check on Spooks's status. Satisfied that he was stable, she took Lucky out before putting the brisket in the Dutch oven to simmer and settling down at her computer. She wanted to look up Cherry Hunter's phone number. She accessed the homeowners' association website and found the page listing their officers.

Marla would rather not email Cherry and risk leaving evidence of a message, so she dialed the woman's house phone instead. No one answered. She'd have to try again later.

Later never came. She got caught up on chores, confirming plans with Dalton's parents for dinner later that week, and answering her own email. A call to Luis told her to come in tomorrow morning at nine o'clock for her first appointment. Before she realized how many hours had passed, Brianna breezed in the door, home from school.

It wasn't until the next day that Marla was able to pursue Krabber's case. She wanted more than anything to help Dalton. He'd been morose the entire evening. All through her early appointments she kept wondering what else she could do. During a break at lunch, she phoned the vet. Spooks was fine and she could pick him up after work. The bill would make her checking account considerably lighter.

Luis summoned her for a two o'clock—someone new from the unfamiliar name.

"Marla, this is Susan Feinberg," the receptionist said with his sexy grin. "She has one of your discount coupons and wants a cut and blow."

"Hi, I live in Royal Oaks and thought I'd give your salon a try." The brunette took a seat in Marla's chair. She looked to be in her thirties and had a smattering of freckles across her nose.

"I see you have highlights." Marla ruffled the lady's hair. "Are you happy with this shade?" In her opinion, the strands were too light. They should have been more subtle.

Susan made a face in the mirror. "They're too streaky, the main reason why I've wanted to change stylists. I think they left the bleach on too long."

"I can fix that for you if you wish."

"Could you tone it down? I thought I'd have to wait until my roots started to show."

"No, we can take care of it." Marla signaled to Luis and had him check the schedule to see if she'd have time. It would be a squeeze, but she could manage. "Did you say you live in Royal Oaks?" Marla said after mixing up bowls of solution and returning to her station.

"Yes, I'm in the house two doors down from yours, on the

other side of Alan Krabber."

"Is that right?" She selected a comb. "His death was a horrible tragedy."

"I'll say." Susan's glance met hers in the mirror. "Who'd have thought the man would take his own life? I mean, he wasn't easy to get along with, as you well know, but still—"

"It's hard to believe," Marla finished. She picked up a foil, separated a strand of hair onto it, and painted on one of the solutions with her favorite brush. Her fingers folded the foil automatically. "Did you attend the annual meeting?"

"No, I couldn't. My husband David had to work late, so I was home watching the kids."

"How many children do you have?"

"We have a boy who's eight and a girl who's five. We moved in last June."

"I gather Alan was one of the original residents in the neighborhood."

"That's true. We didn't see much of him. He mostly kept to himself."

"Do you work outside the home?" Marla lifted another strand.

"I'm a consulting editor for a women's magazine, and I write a blog in my spare time, but I do them from my home office. It keeps my mind active." She winked at Marla in the mirror.

"I'll say. So tell me, did you have any problems with Alan?"

"Huh, who didn't? He used to complain about our kids all the time. They were too noisy, or they ran into his yard. I didn't like it when that tractor came to dig up his ground."

Susan seemed eager to talk, so Marla probed deeper. "Why do you think he wanted a big generator like that? I can understand families with young children needing power or old people who can't tolerate the heat without air conditioning, but the man seemed fairly healthy."

"Alan was more concerned with his computers than his a/c.

On bulk trash day, he'd throw out lots of boxes from electronics purchases."

"I gather he was retired. Maybe that was his hobby."

"Computers? It's possible. He didn't strike me as the gamer type, though. He could have been active on the social nets." Susan gave a wicked grin. "Or maybe he played online poker."

"Now, that's a thought. One of my elderly customers loves to play online sweeps. She's actually won some prizes, too." Marla finished applying the solution. Her job done, she put down her brush and set the woman's timer.

Susan twirled in the chair to face Marla. "I heard about your debacle with the fence. It didn't surprise me. Alan was strict to enforce the rules for others but not for himself."

Marla stacked the remaining foils in a roundabout drawer. "Can you think of anyone who might have had a grudge against him?"

"Besides you and me, you mean?" Susan chortled, but then her expression turned serious. "Are you suggesting it wasn't suicide?"

"Not at all, but you never know. He didn't seem despondent to me. Who's his next of kin?" Marla asked as though she didn't possess that knowledge.

"His nephew inherits the estate, I imagine. Alan didn't have anybody else. I felt sorry for him, until I came home from grocery shopping one day and found all our patio furniture in the pool. He'd complained about our kids screaming outside his window the day before, so I'm sure it must have been him. He didn't like children or pets."

Marla wouldn't put it past Krabber, not if he was the one who'd left the bag of dog poop on their driveway. He had a mean streak that he'd kept hidden. How many other people had he offended?

"Did you confront him about it?" She glanced at her watch.

Her next appointment should be arriving any minute. Familiar sounds reached her ears: water splashing, blow dryers whirring, people chatting. Every now and then, she'd hear the cash register drawer open and close.

Susan's eyebrows rose. "Heck, no. The man would only give me his self-righteous crap."

"Tell me about it." Marla tapped the timer. "You have forty minutes. Can I get you a cup of coffee? There's Danish out front, too, if you're hungry."

"No thanks, I'm good." Susan's brows drew together. "Is it true your husband is a police detective?"

"That's right."

"I thought I saw somebody in Alan's backyard yesterday. A dog started barking around that time. Then I saw a rescue truck by the house. Do you know what happened?"

Marla winced at the memory. "My poodle got loose and ran into Alan's yard. I found Spooks lying in that dreadful pit and called 9-1-1. That hole is a hazard."

"Maybe I imagined it, but I thought I'd heard pounding noises from back there before the dog barked. Soon after, a shadow passed our bathroom window on that side. I couldn't see much, but it looked like a figure darting by."

"This could be important. I'll tell Dalton."

"Is he investigating? I mean, the cops aren't just writing off Alan's death, are they?"

"Of course not. It's routine to investigate in cases like this," she said in a noncommittal tone. "Can you think of anything else that might be useful?"

"I don't think so." A pause. "I'm still creeped out about Alan dying next door. I mean, I know it's a terrible thing and all. But Marla, considering the circumstances, maybe we should watch each other's backs until we learn more."

Chapter Five

Marla told Dalton what their neighbor had related Tuesday evening at dinner. "Someone might have thrown Spooks in that pit to shut him up," she concluded, cutting a slice of leftover brisket and forking it into her mouth. "He didn't just fall into the hole chasing a squirrel."

"Possibly." Dalton hunched over his meal while the dogs sniffed at their feet, hoping for handouts or crumbs.

Spooks seemed his usual lively self, to everyone's relief. Brianna lavished extra attention on him, handing him a piece of meat under the table. To be fair, Marla gave a morsel to Lucky.

She ate in silence for a few minutes but then more questions surfaced. "If Spooks did disturb someone back there, what were they doing?"

Dalton's eyebrows lifted. "Looking for something, maybe? At any rate, you should be telling Detective Minnetti about this, not me."

"Oh yeah, how's that going?"

"About as well as you can expect."

She examined his face. "That bad, huh? She isn't keeping you in the loop?"

His glance skittered away. "My other buddies keep me informed."

"You'd think she would have the courtesy to confer with you."

"Why should she?" His gaze swung back. "Kat doesn't know

me well. During her first week on the job, her new partner is removed from a murder case. She's smart to be cautious."

Marla put her fork down. "She has issues, if you ask me. How much were you told about her background?"

"Nothing personal, just that her credentials were impeccable."

"Did she request a transfer or was she given one? You should find out more about her. Once this case clears, you'll be partners again. You need to be with someone you can trust."

He grimaced. "I know. The chief seems to think highly of her, though."

Brianna drank a sip of water. "Dad, did you hear anything else about Mr. Krabber?"

"Preliminary tox screens suggest he may have had meds in his system."

Marla sat up straight. "Really? When were you going to share this news?"

"When we have something more definitive."

"What about the autopsy results?"

"Not in yet, but it shouldn't be long. We don't have a huge backload right now."

"That means the body will be released. I wonder if the nephew will hold a memorial service."

Dalton gave her an oblique glance. "We'll probably remove the crime scene tape tomorrow. Keep a lookout for his car in the driveway. You might want to pay the guy a condolence call."

Marla stared at him. "Are you suggesting I pump the man for information?"

"You never know what might come to light during a friendly conversation."

Brianna shoved her chair back. "Marla, if someone was in Mr. Krabber's backyard yesterday, it's possible that person wasn't searching for something but was looking for a way inside the house."

Marla's attention veered to the teen, who'd fixed her hair in a bun in preparation for dance class. "For what reason?"

"To erase evidence. Or to retrieve an item left behind the night of the murder."

She'd make a great teen detective, Marla thought with a swell of pride. "Those are valid theories, but we have no proof that anyone was actually in the yard."

Dalton rose from the table and took their empty plates to the sink. "Even if this person got inside, our team had already scoured the place."

"They could have missed a minor detail," Brie insisted.

"So is it definitely a homicide now?" Marla asked. "Because if Alan ingested drugs, how could he hang himself? Didn't you say a desk chair was by the rail? How would he climb up on it, let alone fasten a noose around his neck, if he was groggy?"

"I didn't say what kind of meds might be in his blood. And what does it matter? Suicide victims find a way to accomplish the task. Unfortunately, they often give no indication about their intent."

"True, but aren't there warning signs?"

"Sure. They may put their affairs in order, make provisions for their pets, give away articles of value, and even mention death. Hints can be there if you're looking for them, but not always."

"You believe Alan Krabber killed himself like you believe I have two heads." Wishing they had more solid information, she shoved away from the table and stood. "Come on, Brie. I'll do the dishes while you get your dance bag."

After the teen left the kitchen, Marla made fast work of cleaning up. She'd just wiped her hands on a dish towel when Dalton approached from behind. His spice cologne wafted into her nostrils as his hands clamped onto her shoulders and spun her around.

He kissed her soundly then stood back. "Sorry if I've been abrupt lately. I'm itching to be involved on this case. It irks me to have to stand aside while my substitute takes over."

"Lieutenant Minnetti isn't replacing you, Dalton. You're just temporarily reassigned."

"Yeah, to do boring paperwork."

"Such is the responsibility of a higher rank like yours." She gave him a sunny smile, grateful he was confiding in her. Standing on her tiptoes, she kissed him back. "Minnetti will soften once she gets to know you. Now I've got to run, or Brie will be late."

Marla dropped the teen off at the dance studio, parked her Camry, and exited the vehicle. She'd run into a nearby shop to browse. She didn't feel like driving home and back again. Immersed in thought, she didn't at first notice the woman coming out of the jewelry store until they nearly bumped into each other.

"Cherry Hunter, how nice to see you." Marla recognized the Royal Oaks treasurer.

Cherry, who'd been admiring a diamond tennis bracelet on her arm, jerked her head up to regard Marla with a perplexed frown. Obviously she had no idea who Marla was, when seen out of context.

"Oh, hello. Do I know you?"

"I'm Marla Vail from Royal Oaks. We met at the annual homeowners' meeting."

Cherry's mouth, a slash of red lipstick, widened in a smile of recognition. "Oh, of course. You're the lady married to the cop. And don't you live on Alan Krabber's street?"

"We're his next-door neighbors. Say, can I buy you a drink? I'd like to discuss a few things about him."

"I'm afraid I have to—"

"I've reason to believe his death may not be a suicide," Marla said quickly before the other woman declined her offer. This might be their only chance for a private conversation.

"Well, I suppose I could spare the time." Cherry's eyes turned crafty. "But in exchange, would you agree to help with our community garage sale? We need someone to fill in for a volunteer who had to resign."

Marla figured she could fit in a few hours on a Sunday, and it might be a good way to get to know more neighbors. "Sure," she agreed. "I'm willing to pitch in."

"Great!" Cherry exclaimed as though relieved. "I'm in the mood to celebrate anyway." She headed for the parking lot.

"What's the occasion?" Marla scurried to match her pace. The woman had a brisk stride, arms swinging purposefully at her side as though she often did power walks.

Cherry glanced at her bracelet. "Oh, I guess you could say I got a bonus."

"Really? How nice. What sort of work do you do?"

Had Cherry just bought that piece of jewelry for herself? Or had it been a gift? Marla had seen fourteen-karat gold and diamond tennis bracelets range in price from just under three thousand to twenty thousand dollars in the department store ads. Cherry's bracelet had pretty large diamonds, although weight and quality could vary. Its brilliance contrasted to her chunky silver and turquoise necklace and earrings.

"Let's go to Bokamper's, and then we'll talk," Cherry said, inclining her head toward Marla. "Is that all right?"

"Sure. I just dropped my stepdaughter off for dance class, so I have some time to kill."

They got seats outside at the popular sports bar and grill. The outdoor area overlooked a waterway next to a busy intersection. Tuesday made for a quiet crowd, for which Marla was grateful. On weekends one could barely get space there, especially when special events centered around sports brought in more patrons.

Traffic hummed in the background while water splashed in a fountain in an adjacent pond. Tropical greenery graced the landscaping. The temperature, pleasantly in the seventies, benefitted from dry air and a descending sun.

Marla made small talk until they'd ordered. She decided to be generous, requesting a bottle of wine and offering to treat Cherry if she wanted something to eat. The woman placed an order for one of the restaurant's tastier flatbreads.

After their water and wine glasses had been delivered, Marla said, "We appreciate the work you're doing for the homeowners' association."

Cherry's shrewd eyes regarded her. "Sometimes it's a thankless job. People tend to blame us when they don't like how things turn out."

"That goes along with the territory, I guess. What kind of work do you do in real life? I'm a hairstylist and salon owner." She passed across her business card, ever mindful of possible new clients.

"I'm a history professor at Nova."

Marla arched her eyebrows. Nova Southeastern University in Davie was in the top tier of private schools. "Do you have a specialty?"

"Native American cultures. But that's no surprise considering my heritage, is it? My first name is actually Cherokee, although I'm half Immowakee," she said, pride filling her expression.

"Oh? I haven't heard of that tribe."

"Most people recognize the Miccosukee and the Seminoles, but not us. Before Europeans arrived in Florida, our state was home to generations of Native Americans. The Timucua, the Apalachee, and the Calusa were other early inhabitants. Anyway, I enjoy educating people about the rich heritage our tribes contributed to Florida's history."

Cherry took a large drink, nearly emptying her glass, and poured herself some more. "But tell me about Alan. Why did you say he might not have done himself in?"

Marla studied the other woman's straight ebony hair and cocoa brown eyes. "Some things didn't add up about his death."

"Is this public news or privileged information from your husband?"

"Nothing has been officially announced yet, but assuming it turns out to be a homicide case, who do you think might have wanted to harm the man?"

"Who didn't? No, really, I thought Alan did an outstanding job for our community. You have no idea how many hours he'd put in as a volunteer to ensure our association ran smoothly. I didn't always agree with his reasoning, but his decisions were sound. I'd back him in an instant, but not everyone felt that way."

"Like who?" *Besides my husband, I mean.*

"Well, there was that turmoil about the trees. Wallace Newberry got quite riled over our choices."

"This must have been before my time. What was that about?"

Marla leaned back as the waitress arrived with Cherry's flat-bread. The grilled vegetables made her mouth water despite her having already eaten dinner.

Cherry cut into the food with her knife and fork. "We voted to add plants in the median because it looked too bare, but we had to select trees that wouldn't go above twenty feet or they'd obstruct the power lines. Wallace, a master gardener, insisted that we choose native shrubbery. However, our options were limited by availability and cost."

"That sounds reasonable."

"You'd think so, right? Members couldn't agree on how much to spend. Some people thought we should pay eight thousand dollars for seventy trees, and other people wanted a minimal expense of five thousand dollars for forty-seven trees. Wallace said we should have a special assessment to cover more than a hundred new plantings. He got out of hand."

"What did the vote decide?" This didn't seem like a strong enough motive for Wallace to have offed Alan, but you never knew what might set off a normally mild-mannered guy.

"We went with the first option." She spoke in between bites. "Me, I can't stand the nitpicking. If I'd known that came with the job, I wouldn't have taken it. Then there was the speed bump issue. Mattie Nelson wanted them put on the main road to discourage speeders, but the majority voted her down."

Marla shifted in her seat, watching a motorcyclist zoom by on the roadway. The sky darkened to a deep sea blue. "These are probably normal issues by homeowner association standards. I can't see someone getting rid of Alan because of them." She paused. "At the meeting, you'd mentioned he had secrets to hide. Can you elaborate?"

Cherry choked, grabbing her water glass for a drink. She chased it down with another large chug of wine before pouring herself a new round. Marla, still on her first glass, stemmed her impatience. When was she going to learn something useful?

"I'm sorry, but I don't remember saying any such thing. However, I do recall Alan slinging some nasty remarks your way and your husband reacting to them. Is it wise for him to be involved in the investigation?"

"He's not. His partner is in charge. Dalton removed himself from the case since he knew Alan personally, and there might be a conflict of interest."

A small white lie, but it sounds better than "was removed."

"Oh, I see."

What I see is that you changed the subject and went on the offensive when I mentioned Alan's secrets. Did they by any chance concern you?

"So tell me, do you have any family in the area?" Marla asked. Cherry was nearly finished with her meal, and Marla didn't want her to dart off.

Cherry's long hair swung across her face as she bent to retrieve her napkin that had blown from the table. The breeze had picked up, a sweet-scented current of warm air.

"I'm divorced with two kids, both of them in college."

"That must be tough."

"I'm good at juggling our finances. At least they're grown and out of the house. I can't abide small children anymore."

"You and Alan both. He yelled at Susan Feinberg's kids for making too much noise in their pool."

"Yes, I heard them when I was . . . walking in the neighborhood."

Had she been about to say something else? Marla didn't recall seeing Cherry strolling down the sidewalk on their street, but maybe she walked during Marla's work hours.

"Dalton and I married in December," Marla confessed in an effort to encourage confidences. "It's a second marriage for both of us. He has a teenage daughter."

"Lucky you." Cherry's tone had a cynical edge. "Royal Oaks is a nice place to live. It'll get better as the trees mature and the empty lots get built out."

"I like the location. It's easy to go downtown, and we're near two malls plus the library."

"You'll be glad you volunteered for the garage sale, Marla. It'll help you get to know people. It's a popular event."

"Oh, yes, about that. What's the date?"

"It's the first Saturday in April. I hope you'll be in town?"

Marla nodded, a hank of hair falling across her face. She tucked it behind her ear. "When's the next committee meeting?"

"That's up to you to decide. I'll email you a list of members."

"Why is it up to me?"

"Why, my dear, you've just taken on the job of chairperson."

Marla's mouth gaped. "I-I did what? Oh, no, I can't possibly—"

"Gene will be relieved. He was so afraid we'd have to cancel, and it's a huge fundraiser for the community. We're hoping to use the proceeds to replace the carpet in the clubroom."

Marla's mind shoveled aside this new duty to focus on her original mission. "Gene is the vice president, right? Has he taken over Alan's position already?"

Cherry pursed her ruby lips. "Gene Uris has been chomping at the bit to be president, so he's leapt at the chance to fill the empty seat. He'll bring his enthusiasm and energy to the table."

How convenient for him that Alan is out of the way.

Wanting to pursue that train of thought but unsure what questions to ask, Marla poured the rest of the wine into Cherry's glass. "What can you tell me about Alan's personal life? Is anyone going to miss him besides his nephew?"

"Huh. He loved his computers more than anyone. I believe he was engaged years ago, but something happened and he never married the woman. He could have found someone else but remained single. Despite his abrasiveness, Alan could be quite charming to the ladies, so it wasn't from lack of choice." Cherry fell silent, her face sour as she gripped her wine glass.

"Do you know that from personal experience?" Marla ventured, sniffing garlic as the waitress carried a dish past them to another party.

"Who, me?" Cherry gave a braying laugh. "Let's just say the man could make a gal think she was hot stuff, but then he'd splash cold water on the relationship with his notions of purity."

Purity in what sense—a woman's sexual status or a racist viewpoint? Marla had experienced Alan's unwelcome advances as well as his religious bias. Maybe he liked to hit on supposed sinners in order to save their souls. He'd probably considered Cherry a half-breed with her mixed blood. It sounded as though her relationship with him had been bittersweet.

Yet he must have had charisma for people to elect him as president. Had he beat out Gene Uris in the election? Did the veep harbor any resentment toward him as a result?

"Did Alan have any friends in the neighborhood? Like, did he play golf or go out for sports with the guys?"

Cherry snorted. "He liked to eat. That was his sport. You've seen him. He sat in front of his computer all day and gained weight. He didn't like junk food, though. Mostly the man snacked on veggies, but he enjoyed his pasta a bit too much, if you know what I mean. And desserts . . . he couldn't pass them up."

And how would you know this? Cherry's conversation hinted at a more intimate knowledge of their neighbor, but the woman wasn't about to come out and say it.

"What did he do all day on his computer?"

"I got the impression he made money from his online activities. I didn't pry, but I'd wondered what might keep him so absorbed. Maybe he ran a gaming site. Don't players have to buy stuff to add to the world they're building for some of the more elaborate games?"

"I'm not familiar with those sites." Marla met the other woman's keen gaze. "Are you telling me this was the secret he was hiding?"

"Could be." Cherry shoved her wine glass away and picked up her handbag. "Let it go, Marla. Bigger things than a mere hobby could be at stake."

"Meaning what?"

"Why don't you ask Angela Goodhart? The two of them were

close. I suppose he considered her more acceptable to his standards."

Marla didn't miss the resentment in her tone. "I met her at the homeowners' meeting. Doesn't she have longish blond hair?" She recalled the woman who'd tried to excuse Alan's behavior.

Cherry scraped her chair back and rose. "That's right."

"What about Debbie Morris? The secretary was rather quiet at the meeting, although she spoke up to explain the line item for security." Marla signaled the waitress to get the bill and then rummaged in her purse for her wallet.

"Debbie is the type who always works in the background. She has her hands full with her family." Cherry stared at the traffic zooming past, while Marla glanced at her diamond bracelet that sparkled in the fading sunlight.

"How did she get along with Alan?"

"Oh, she basically followed his orders like a puppy follows its master. Alan could be a persuasive guy when it suited his needs."

"I suppose so. Thanks for taking the time to talk to me, Cherry. I'm hoping to make new friends in our community. Maybe we can do this again sometime."

"Sure, Marla. But a word of advice where Alan is concerned: Don't dig too deep, or you could stir things that are best left buried."

Chapter Six

"She's an odd duck," Marla said to Dalton later that evening, after Brianna had retreated to her bedroom. "Cherry offered all sorts of hints but didn't really say anything of substance."

Dalton stretched his arm around her. They sat on the sofa in front of the TV in the family room. The history channel was tuned to a program on war at sea. What was it with men and their love for sports and battles? Her ex-spouse, Stan, had liked documentaries about World War II.

At least Dalton watched the science channels. A puzzle lover at heart, he enjoyed delving into the mysteries of nature.

He tickled her bare skin. She'd already showered and wore a nightgown. He had on a pair of shorts and a black underwear shirt. "What did you talk about with Cherry?"

"She mentioned that she's part Immowakee. It's a lesser-known Florida tribe. Her real first name is Cherokee."

"So how does that play into things?"

"It affected her relationship with Alan Krabber. She seemed to have a love–hate attitude toward him. According to Cherry, he could be charming when it served his purpose but he had notions of purity."

"As in racial identity?" His fingers tightened on her arm.

"Certainly that makes sense, considering what we know about him, but he could have been referring to a woman's sexual history. Cherry didn't elaborate."

"How did she sound when she talked about him?"

"Like she wouldn't miss the guy, although she defended his decisions as Board president. It's as though the man had an uncanny ability to sway people to his manner of thinking."

"I could see that at the homeowners' meeting, except when it came to his personal abuse of the rules. Then he got voted down."

She noticed his smug tone. "His charisma seemed to extend more to women. The man was overweight and unattractive in my opinion, and yet Cherry seemed to have a flame for him. And so might Angela, if I understood her correctly."

"Who's that?" Dalton withdrew his arm and straightened.

Marla glanced at the TV and grimaced. It showed a ship taking on enemy fire during an air attack by the Japanese in the Pacific basin. "Angela Goodhart, another neighbor. Cherry said I should talk to Angela if I wanted to learn more about Alan because they were close."

"Close in the intimate sense?"

"She didn't explain."

Dalton watched the show, his profile stern. Marla gazed adoringly at his firm jawline with its evening stubble, his nose that was slightly out of alignment, and his deep-set eyes. She rubbed his arm, her affection surging.

He responded by giving her a lazy smile. "Where was Cherry Hunter the night of Krabber's death?"

His question dashed her ardor. "I didn't ask. That's probably information you could worm out of Lieutenant Minnetti."

"Like that's gonna happen. Who else did you discuss?"

She laced her fingers in her lap. "The other Board members. Cherry implied that Debbie Morris, the secretary, did whatever Alan told her to do. I guess that's another lady whom Alan charmed. She didn't speak much at the meeting."

"What about the veep?"

"Cherry said Gene Uris had wanted Krabber's position. I'll

have to ask someone about the last election. The rummage sale will be a good opportunity. Did I mention how Cherry roped me into taking over as chairperson?"

He glanced at her in surprise. "Huh?"

"She would only go for a drink with me if I agreed to work on the garage sale. She neglected to tell me, at least initially, that the job entailed taking charge. The other chairwoman had to drop out for some reason. Maybe Cherry will forget our conversation on that score."

"Let's hope so. You don't have a lot of spare time."

"Tell me about it. I met her coming out of a jewelry store by the dance studio. She'd been admiring a diamond tennis bracelet on her arm and said she had cause to celebrate getting a bonus."

"Oh? Isn't Cherry Hunter a history professor at the university?"

"Where did you hear that?" She hadn't mentioned Cherry's occupation. Had he been holding back on her?

"Kat is checking into the backgrounds of the Board members. I hear things now and then."

"I'm sure you do. Anything else you'd like to share?"

"Nothing useful. So Cherry got a bonus at her job and spent it on an expensive bracelet?"

"It appeared so, but I'm not exactly sure that's what she meant."

"It sounds as though she wasn't terribly forthcoming with information. Why did she go with you for a drink?"

"For one thing, the woman likes her wine. Plus, I sort of mentioned Alan's death might be more than a suicide. Probably she wanted to find out what I'd learned from you. Or else she just played me so I'd take on the garage sale."

His glance dipped to her mouth. "I can think of other ways to play you. Want me to demonstrate?"

She sensed his arousal. Her nerves responded by heightening her sensitivity to his every move. How easily her attention could be diverted.

"Wait, I'm not done." She raised a hand. "We discussed other residents who might have had grievances against the Board, but they were minor issues. Alan's secret vice was a bigger deal."

"His vice?"

"Cherry said he loved his computers more than anything. That's why he was putting in a standby generator, so he could keep the juice flowing to his machines in the event of a power outage. You know how self-righteous he was? What if he had an addiction to online gambling?"

He gave her a skeptical glance. "I believe that's illegal."

"People skilled with computers can find sites. Or maybe pornography was his thing. Either way, Alan would consider both of those activities to be sinful." She sat up straight. "Do you think that's why he killed himself? Because he was punishing himself for his lapse?"

"That's absurd. Krabber didn't kill himself."

"Still, it's worth checking out, don't you think? You're always telling me to investigate all the angles. Cherry thought maybe he ran a gamer site, like FarmVille."

"I'll pass along your ideas to Kat and have her look into them."

"Did the crime lab guys take Alan's computer?"

"He had several, and yes, they would have done so. However, scuttlebutt says his hard drives came up clean."

"You mean, clean in terms of showing nothing significant? Or do you mean formatted?"

"The latter. Even his emails were gone. Our cyber forensics team is trying to retrieve the data, but someone knew what to do." Dalton rubbed his brow, fatigue lines etching his face.

"Someone, but not Alan?"

"That's the assumption."

"Hey, maybe he wasn't into gambling, porn, or games. Do you think he could have signed up for one of those matchmaking services?"

"Anything is possible." Dalton reached across her and grabbed the remote to channel surf.

"Maybe the nephew can shed more light on Alan's hobbies. Detective Minnetti must have interviewed him. Isn't he the official heir?"

"Yes, Philip Byrd is a travel writer who lives in Boca. His mother, Krabber's sister, died from cancer two years ago." Dalton tuned in to a sports game and stared at the screen.

"And does Philip Byrd have a family?"

"No. He's in his mid-thirties and has never been married. Either he's still looking for someone, or else he's not interested in women."

"Maybe he just hasn't found Ms. Right. It isn't easy to meet people these days."

"That's why virtual dating services have become so popular." Dalton chucked her under the chin. "I'm lucky I found you."

She snuggled closer and rubbed against him. "We could continue this discussion in the bedroom. I'm getting tired."

He gave her a slow, sexy smile. "Perhaps we should."

The next day dawned bright and sunny but with a strong breeze heralding an approaching cold front. March could still bring variable weather to South Florida.

Marla sat down at her computer after Brianna left for school and Dalton for work. Her first appointment was at ten o'clock, so she had an hour to spare. She wanted to follow up with Angela Goodhart but didn't know the woman's phone number.

She accessed the community's website and the list of Directors. The Board members' contact info faced her from the screen. She'd bite the bullet and ask Cherry for the garage sale volunteer list. Maybe Angela would be on it. Or perhaps Cherry knew how to contact the woman. Marla didn't even have her address.

Glancing out the window in her study, she peered over toward Alan's house. A police car was parked at the curb. Hopefully, an officer was there to remove the yellow tape blocking the front door. She'd keep alert in case the nephew drove by. Was he even in town? As a travel writer, he must get around, unless his articles were confined to Florida.

After sending Cherry an email requesting the garage sale info, Marla lost time checking her own messages and adding an update to her Facebook business page. Luis had suggested creating one for the grand opening of their day spa, and Marla had thought it to be a great marketing tool for the salon. Mostly, she let him handle the online promotions.

She'd just grabbed her handbag in the kitchen when a shadow passed the front window. She snatched her keys, hurried into the dining room, and peered outside. The police car was gone and in its place was a silver Prius. Recognizing the vehicle as the one that had been parked in Alan's driveway the day he died, she rushed out the door in the hope of catching his nephew. As she approached, Marla noted the yellow tape was gone from the front porch.

A young man answered the doorbell. He had wheat brown hair that flopped forward onto his forehead in a tousled style, a faint moustache, and sad blue eyes.

"Hello, are you Mr. Byrd?"

"I am. And you are?"

"Marla Vail. I live next door." She gestured with her thumb. "I'm so sorry for your loss."

His face flushed. "Yes, well, thanks."

"I know it's a job when someone passes to take care of the house and all. I'd like to offer my help, if you need anything."

She floundered for something to say that might encourage him to talk.

"I appreciate that. I'm not going to rush into anything. First I have to deal with, um, Uncle Alan's final arrangements. He wanted to be cremated."

"I see. It can't be easy for you, having the police involved. I'm married to a detective on the force."

"Oh, really?" He examined her more closely. "Would you like to come in for a few minutes?"

Marla glanced up and down the street, and saw no one outside. Dare she accept his invitation? What if he had been the killer?

Nonetheless, she stepped across the threshold. "I'm on my way to work, so I can't stay long. I own the Cut 'N Dye hair salon," she explained. "I'll just tell them I might be a few minutes late." On her cell, she dashed off a quick text message to Dalton.

Byrd led her into a living room furnished with a worn sofa and armchairs, a marred coffee table, a couple of lamps on accent pieces, and an empty fish tank on a stand. Dirty socks adorned the soiled carpet. To the left rose a staircase.

Marla wrinkled her nose as her gaze lifted to the second-story balcony. A carved wooden railing bordered the edge. Her throat clogged as she imagined Krabber's body swinging there.

Philip noticed the direction of her glance. "That's where I discovered my uncle."

She swallowed. "It must have been awful."

"I don't believe he was responsible for taking his own life. The cops don't seem to think so, either. What's your husband's theory?"

"I imagine Detective Minnetti has already spoken to you about the possibilities." She watched him carefully, but he just hung his head sadly.

"Yes, she has, but she's looking at the wrong person if she thinks I did my uncle harm."

"Oh? What kind of relationship did you have with Alan?" At his invitation, she sank into an armchair near the door.

"I cared for the old coot. He had some strange notions about people, although I suspect that was due to his heartbreak."

Yes, now we're getting somewhere. "I heard he'd been engaged once," she said in a casual tone. "Is that what you mean?"

Philip paced the carpeted floor, hands folded behind his back. He took long, loping steps, like one would take to avoid cracks in a sidewalk. "Uncle Alan was in love with a woman many years ago. They were engaged and had started planning the wedding. But then her folks intervened and took her to Europe. You see, she came from a wealthy Jewish family, and they didn't want her to marry him."

Marla's mouth dropped open. "Alan Krabber was engaged to a Jewish woman?"

"I know, it's difficult to believe. When they returned, Uncle Alan tried to see her but she snubbed him. He never got over the feeling of betrayal."

That would explain a lot about the man.

"Your uncle didn't give his heart to anyone else?"

"He felt demeaned by the experience, as though he wasn't good enough. You could tell from his attitude. He started dissing on other people like they were below him." Byrd noticed her distasteful expression. "I gather you've been at the raw end of his remarks. Being rejected took its toll on his ego in a big way. Every now and then, he'd mumble about the end of the world and how he could save people's souls. I think he turned to religion as a crutch, using it to condemn anyone who didn't agree with him."

"Yet he was a successful businessman, wasn't he? I mean, he was able to retire in this nice house and was investing a chunk of cash on that generator. So whatever his personal beliefs, they didn't impair his relations with others, at least not in the business world."

Philip nodded. "He owned an insurance company that prospered despite the economy."

"Speaking of the generator, are you going to fill in the hole in his backyard? It's a hazard to children and pets. My dog got loose and fell down there the other day."

"So I've been informed. Sorry about that. I hope he's okay."

"Spooks had a slight concussion, but he'll be fine. Where is Alan's boat, by the way?"

"He'd moved it to the parking lot behind the clubhouse before he died. He told me he had to put up a fence to meet code regulations."

"He started to build one but neglected to do a survey or get a permit. And that brings up another point of contention between us." She leaned forward. "That swathe of stones leading around his side yard? It infringes on our property."

He plowed his fingers through his hair. "I know I have a lot of things to fix. I can't do it all at once with my job and all, but I'll get to them as soon as possible."

"We'd appreciate it a great deal. What kind of work do you do?" she asked, as though she didn't know.

"I'm a travel writer for the Global Rainforest Foundation. They sponsor my trips around the world. I write about rainforest preservation and send my articles to various publications." He plopped down on the sofa. "Rumor says your husband got into an argument with Uncle Alan over the property issues."

"That's right. They'd exchanged words about the fence and the stone path. I hope you'll think about planting those ficus trees somewhere else, too. Their roots are apt to grow into our property." Marla rose. "Anyway, I'm very sorry for your loss and again would be willing to help you any way I can." She sniffed the stale, foul-scented air. "I know a good housekeeping service if you need one. I presume you'll want to sell the house?"

Byrd leapt to his feet. "Eventually. I'll send my own maid over one of these days." He gave her a sheepish grin. "Can't abide housecleaning myself."

"Remember, I'm next door if you need anything, Mr. Byrd."

"Please call me Philip. Have you heard your husband's guesses about motives? I mean, why would somebody hurt my uncle? I know he could be snappish on occasion, but mostly folks realized he meant well."

"I'm sure Detective Minnetti is checking into his acquaintances. Are you his only relative in the area?"

"He has a cousin on the other side of his family, but we've never met. Would you know if the investigation has brought anything specific to light?"

"I'm afraid my husband isn't officially involved due to a possible conflict of interest. Even if he were, he wouldn't share confidential information with me."

The young man gave a nervous chuckle. "I get it. Marla, right? Thanks for stopping by. I'll probably see you around."

She'd just stepped outside when a delivery truck rumbled to the curve. Marla intercepted the driver as Byrd had already secured himself inside the house.

"Oh, is that for Alan? I'll take it to him." Grasping the parcel, she turned toward the door. On the way, she glimpsed the return address. The company name meant nothing to her, but she registered it in her brain to look up later.

"Your uncle got a package," she said to Philip when he opened the door at her summons. She handed it over. "He seemed to get a lot of deliveries." Could he have been one of those closet hoarders who ordered stuff off the Internet? Maybe he'd shopped on the computer all day.

Philip snatched the package. "Thanks. Likely I'll be sending this back and cancelling any other orders he'd made."

"I hope he made printouts of his transactions."

"I haven't had the chance to sort through his papers. That's another chore on my list." Philip stuck the bundle on a foyer table and then returned to the front door.

"Speaking of your uncle's papers, you might look for information on the workmen he hired to put up his fence." Marla slipped her foot over the threshold so Philip couldn't shut her out. "He'd promised to pay the guys that same day, but I'm wondering if he ever did since they never completed the job. Their truck had no visible license tag. The cops might want to question them if you come across their contact info."

A perplexed frown knitted Philip's brows. "Why? Do you think they returned to exact revenge on Uncle Alan for stiffing their fee?"

"It seems extreme, but you never know. By the way, I understand Alan spent a lot of time on the computer. What hobbies kept him so busy all day?"

"He was hooked on religious sites. I can't abide that stuff myself. I tuned him out whenever he got onto the subject."

Maybe you should have paid better attention. Nonetheless, that wouldn't explain the packages. Alan must have been ordering something on a regular basis.

Wait a minute. What if not all of those UPS truck stops had been deliveries but were pickups instead? Still, what did it mean?

"Maybe the cops will be able to pull some useful data off his computers," she said in a noncommittal tone.

"I doubt it. The lady detective told me his hard drives had been wiped clean. She asked if I'd done it. Huh, like I'd know how. Hey, I only stopped by now and then to see if he wanted anything."

"That was kind of you. Here's my card if you need to get in touch."

Turning away, Marla pondered how Alan Krabber could hibernate inside his house and hunch over the computer for so many hours. She barely had time to check her email, let alone sit in front of a monitor for amusement. There was more to life than devotion to one's machines.

Brianna wouldn't agree. The teen yearned for an iPhone and had pointed out several useful apps. But once she had one, Marla feared the device would prove an unnecessary distraction. The last thing they needed was for her to be answering the phone from behind the wheel when she started driving. But this wasn't about Brie or Marla's personal opinion. It was about Alan Krabber and how he'd spent his leisure hours.

In a crunch for time, Marla sped to the salon. She spared a moment to notify Dalton of her whereabouts before work filled her mind and obliterated any other thoughts.

Around noon, she got a text message from her mother. *Call me.* Her heart lurched. What now? Her mother rarely bothered her at work, and she almost never texted.

As soon as she had a break, she headed outside. Clouds scudded overhead, bringing sprinkles and cooler weather. Facing the parking lot, she sat in a chair provided by her salon. Some of the stylists liked to have a smoke in between clients. It wasn't a habit Marla encouraged, but she'd made an effort to accommodate her staff by setting out several inexpensive plastic chairs. Fortunately, the shopping center manager hadn't complained. A cast iron bench would have been better, but it cost more.

"Hi, Ma. It's me. What's going on?" She held her cell phone close to her ear.

"Oh, Marla, I don't know what to do!" Anita's voice sounded desperate.

"Are you sick? Do you need me to come over?"

"No, it's not that. Roger hasn't called."

Holy highlights, that's what had put her mother into a snit?

"Maybe you should contact his son and make sure he's all right."

"I did." A pause. "Barry said his aunt is in town, and Roger has been busy with her. Then he made a rude remark that I don't understand. You know how nice I've been to Barry. I had even thought he might be a good match for you before Dalton snagged your attention."

Marla rolled her eyes. She remembered her mother's attempts to fix her up with the Jewish optometrist. "What did Barry say?"

"Maybe it would be best if I gave his father some breathing space for a change. As though *I'm* the one who chases after *him*!"

"Barry could be driving a wedge between you and his dad on purpose. He might hold a grudge since I chose Dalton over him."

"That shouldn't make him interfere in my relationship with Roger. Perhaps it's the sister. Whenever Roger spoke her name, his face wrinkled like a prune. She's a bit of a snob."

"If Roger respects you, he wouldn't care about either of their opinions. He's not a true friend if he doesn't stand up for you."

"After all the good times we've had, I find his distant behavior worrisome." Anita's voice lowered. "You don't think he's found someone else, do you?"

Ugh, who would want the *fresser*? The glutton could eat his way through a buffet faster than anyone. "I doubt it, Ma. I'd let things alone for a few days. If Roger is interested in you, he'll call after his sister leaves."

"Oh, yeah? Well, if he does, just watch and see if *I* answer the phone. How are things with you and Dalton?"

"We're okay." She couldn't say more, having spotted her next customer pulling into a parking space. "I have to go back to work. I'll talk to you later."

She'd wanted to count inventory but didn't get the chance to do that, either. The hours flew by until she could pack up and go home.

Brianna sat at the kitchen table, doing her homework. Marla gave her a perfunctory kiss on the forehead, asked about her day, and set about glancing through the mail. Lucky and Spooks pranced about her ankles until she stooped to pet them.

She quickly sorted the bills from the junk mail, but one address caught her eye just before she slit the envelope open.

"Hey, look," she said to Brie. "This one came to the wrong street. I should walk it over there right now. Did you take the dogs out earlier?"

"Yes, I took them when I got home." Brie didn't bother to glance up, concentrating on her math problems.

"I'll go for a quick stroll, then. This is addressed to somebody named Alfred Godwin. That doesn't ring a bell, but he has the same house number as we do, on the next street over."

She changed into a sweater set and slacks before swinging out the front door. The sky had cleared and a cool breeze ruffled her hair. She strode briskly, enjoying the exercise and the smell of rain-slicked grass, until she rounded the next corner.

This street had a row of one-story ranch-style homes with manicured lawns. Marla approached the residence with a similar house number. Sculpted landscaping graced the front yard, highlighted by a sago palm. The home itself was sand colored with a red barrel tile roof and hurricane-impact windows. A couple of Adirondack-style white chairs sat on the front porch.

Marla pushed the doorbell, eager to get home and start dinner.

The door flung wide. "Why, hello Marla. What can I do for you?" Angela Goodhart, the neighbor she'd met at the HOA meeting, greeted her with a broad grin.

Chapter Seven

"Here, I received your mail by mistake." Marla extended her hand with the envelope.

"Why, thanks." Angela took the item and scanned the front. Her forehead folded into a frown. She wore a pair of jeans and a lavender, long-sleeved blouse and minimal makeup.

"It's addressed to somebody named Alfred," Marla said, hoping to learn more.

Angela peered at Marla from beneath her darkened eyebrows. Wisps of golden hair floated about her face. She'd pinned her hair into a twist but tendrils had escaped, softening her look. Her lips, shaded in rose, pursed as she considered her visitor.

"I have no idea who Alfred might be, but I recognize the return address." Angela propped a hand on her hip. "Our names must have gotten mixed up for some reason."

Or not, Marla thought, wishing she could glimpse inside Angela's house. Was the woman covering for someone who lived with her?

She pondered Cherry's insinuations that Angela and Alan Krabber had a relationship that went beyond friendship. Could Angela have been cheating on her live-in boyfriend?

"I want to thank you for being friendly at the homeowners' meeting," Marla said. "It helped soften the blow of Alan's words. I was stunned by his remarks. How could people elect him when his views were so inflammatory?"

Angela waved a hand in dismissal. "I told you he acts out

when crossed. At any rate, you won't have to worry about him any longer."

Marla swallowed a gasp. How could the blonde be so callous? "I thought you two were friends. It's horrible what happened to the man."

"Yes, it was." Angela's eyes narrowed. "Alan wasn't the only one who got riled at our meeting. I heard your husband confronted him out on the lawn."

"Word gets around, doesn't it?"

"Alan would have complied with the code. Mr. Vail shouldn't have threatened him."

"It wasn't a threat, merely a warning. How *did* Alan get elected to the presidency anyway?" she said to change the subject. "Did Gene run against him?"

Angela's face eased into a wry smile. "Nah, Gene knew he wouldn't win. Alan's skill was swaying folks to his point of view. That man could sweet talk you into anything."

"So now Gene takes over as acting president?"

"That's correct. And you can be sure he'll take advantage of the position."

"How so?"

"He'd like to move ahead on certain items that Alan had shelved. If you want more details, you'll have to talk to Gene about it. I'm not a member of the Board."

No, but you might have been close to the president when he was alive.

"Was the homeowners' meeting the last time you saw Alan?"

"Unfortunately, yes. The poor man. I can't believe he's gone."

"Do you know anyone who might have wanted to harm him?" Marla straightened her shoulders. She was getting tired of standing, but clearly Angela wasn't going to invite her inside. Besides, she had to get home to prepare dinner.

"No, why do you say that?"

"Because the police think it wasn't suicide."

Angela's face paled. "Really? When did they make this discovery?"

"Dalton's observations told him something wasn't right when he was called to the scene."

"I hope they're not relying on his assessment. He's obviously tainted."

Marla didn't care for her choice of words. "You mean biased, don't you? We both had an interest in seeing that Alan complied with city code, if that's what you mean. But Dalton wouldn't let personal feelings interfere in a case."

"I would hope not. I'm praying they let Alan rest in peace." Her gaze rose toward the heavens. "At least he won't be here for the apocalypse."

"Excuse me?" The drone of a lawn mower started from down the street, and Marla leaned forward to hear better.

"All of the signs are present, you know. Discord, pollution, hunger and poverty. The time is coming. Alan knew and tried to prepare us."

Perplexed, Marla said, "I'm not sure I understand."

"Aren't you a believer?" A moue of disapproval crossed her face. "Oh, I forgot. Of course, you're not. You might want to arm yourself since you'll be left behind. It'll be a struggle."

"Ah, sure Angela." Marla experienced a shiver of unease.

"That's how the Holocaust came about, you know, but this one will involve all of humanity. No one will be left untouched. The world is in a bad place, but those who believe will be saved."

Oh, no. Angela wasn't about to spout religious crap like Alan, was she?

"Sorry, I thought you were more tolerant of other views." Marla turned on her heel to go, but Angela's hand on her arm stopped her.

"I don't mean to sound that way," Angela said. "I just want

to help because you're a kind person. You deserve to be forewarned."

"Thanks, I appreciate it. Now I have to get home to fix dinner."

She walked quickly back home, proud of herself for doing a good deed in delivering the mail but puzzled over Angela's attitude. The woman seemed to want to mollify her at the meeting, and yet here she'd spouted language that could be construed the same way as Krabber's diatribe. Was she a closet bigot? Is this what she and Alan had in common?

Then where did Alfred Godwin fit in?

The cool breeze rustled leaves and whipped her hair about her face as she strode down the sidewalk. Spring poked its head up in the colorful blossoms gracing people's lawns. Dogs barked, competing with the whirr of the mower in the distance.

Doubts crept into her mind about their relocation. Maybe she and Dalton should have bought a resale house in an older part of town. Sometimes it was easier to get a feel for the neighborhood that way than in a new development.

The garage door was open when she reached her street, and Dalton's car was parked there. She caught him lifting grocery bags from his trunk.

"Hello," she said, giving him a peck on the lips. "I see you went shopping."

"We needed a few things."

She accompanied him into the kitchen. A bouquet of fresh flowers rested on the counter. Dalton put down the bags and lifted the cut blooms.

"These are for you, sweetcakes."

Marla grasped them in her hand and sniffed the carnations. She loved the colors, violet and purple and lavender mixed with white. "What's the occasion?"

"There isn't any. I just want you to know that I appreciate

everything you do for us."

Her heart swelled. "You're so wonderful." His thoughtful gesture warranted a lingering kiss until Brianna groaned with forbearance.

"Come on, you two, go to the bedroom. Or wait until later. I'm hungry. Are we having brisket again?"

"I froze the remainder. I defrosted some chicken cutlets for tonight. They won't take me long to make. We'll have them with asparagus and Israeli couscous. Dalton, will you fix the salad?" She knew he didn't mind chopping up the vegetables. She put away the perishables that he'd bought, glad he had remembered to get more cream for their morning coffee.

"Sure, just let me get cleaned up first."

He disappeared down the hallway while Marla tended to the flowers and then washed her hands. She glanced at Brie, whose crease lines between her eyes hadn't erased. The teen focused on a textbook and scribbled in a notebook on the kitchen table.

"Finished with your math?"

"Yeah. I'm on Spanish. It's harder in high school. Our teacher won't let us speak any English."

"You'll learn it better that way, and your job prospects will increase if you're bilingual."

"That's if I stay in South Florida."

Marla's heart lurched. *Lord save me, I'm not ready for this discussion. It's too early. I've just entered her life, and she wants to leave already?*

"Why, where were you thinking of going to college?"

"I dunno." Brianna's ponytail swung as she tilted her head to regard Marla. "I might want to see what it's like to live up north."

"You have a few years to think about it." What Marla saw was dollar signs rolling before her eyes. Nor did she imagine Dalton would be thrilled about his daughter moving so far away. With his overprotective instincts, he'd butted heads with the teen on more than one occasion, but Marla's influence had softened his attitude.

During dinner she brought Brie and Dalton up to date on her findings. Her husband didn't have anything new to add about Alan Krabber, but he seemed in a better mood. Maybe because he had a new case to work—a body had been found in a canal. But she knew it still irked him that he'd been removed from his regular team.

Wishing to do all she could to help him, she contacted the ladies on the garage sale list she'd received from Cherry and set a date to meet at the community center on Sunday. Marla had to get up to speed on what her predecessor had accomplished thus far.

Unfortunately, it wasn't much. When Sunday rolled around, Marla's heart sank as she regarded the piles of heaped clothing, bric-a-brac and housewares dumped in the clubhouse.

Oy vey, where do we start?

Once all ten ladies on her committee had filtered in, she introduced herself and requested clarification on their progress. They were glad for her leadership, having been left in the lurch when the former chair fell ill. Not a single person mentioned the association meeting, nor did anyone look down their noses at her as she'd feared. To her relief, the women were chatty and amiable. Amazed at how a young community could attract so many donations, Marla assigned a team to each category of goods and suggested ways to organize the items.

While the residents started sorting the goods, she sat down with pen and paper to work out a schedule, along with publicity for the event day.

A musty odor tickled her nose. Was it coming from the carpet or the old clothes? And why would the carpet give off an odor if it was only two years old? Was there a leak inside the clubhouse?

Cherry had mentioned applying the sale's proceeds to new floor covering.

"Marla, we really should tag everything." Debbie Morris wove her way through the tables in Marla's direction. The association secretary wore her strawberry blond hair in an attractive bob. "I can get the tickets if you want."

"What do you mean?"

The petite woman stopped by Marla's folding chair, a piece of luggage in her hand. She plopped the suitcase down and sank into the adjacent seat. Her earnest blue eyes fixed on Marla. "If you don't offer a price, people will make low bids. We should give them an idea of how much we want. Some folks have no idea of how much to pay."

Debbie wanted to tag each individual item? Was she nuts?

Marla scanned the room, overflowing with clothes and kitchenware and toys and sports equipment, not to mention a few containers filled with costume jewelry. Oh, and in that corner was a stack of books. They couldn't possibly label each one.

"That would be a lot of extra work." *Work that you're avoiding by sitting here.*

"Nonetheless, I've run garage sales at home myself, and I always make out well. Presentation is also important. We should group like items together in a tableau setting."

"Maybe you'd like to take charge since you have such wonderful ideas? I haven't done a garage sale before."

Debbie gave her a shy smile. "No, thanks. I'm not good at directing people."

You're doing just fine at the moment.

Marla searched for a way to take advantage of their tête-a-tête. "I feel kind of funny about holding a big sale like this right after Alan Krabber's death. He was our president. It doesn't seem respectful."

Debbie's head bent, and she tugged at her jeans. Gold flashed on her wedding band, reflected by the overhead lighting. "Poor Alan. He could be grating at times, but he had our best interests at heart. I can't say the same for Gene."

"The vice president?"

Debbie glanced over her shoulder and then leaned inward. "Gene had his reasons for wanting Alan to step down. Now he'll have his way since he's in charge."

"What reasons might those be?"

"You've only been here since January. It isn't rainy season yet, but watch out when it pours. You smell the carpet in here? That's because the windows leak. Unfortunately, the problem isn't limited to this building. Most of our homes are involved, and probably yours, too, even though it's newer."

Marla glanced at the beige Berber floor covering. "The earlier houses must have passed inspection. Are you saying they all have leaky windows? How is that possible? They're up to code, aren't they?"

"Oh, yes, they meet hurricane requirements, to be sure."

"So how can water get in? Aren't they properly sealed?"

Debbie's mouth turned down. She wore pink lipstick that complimented her fair complexion. "Ever hear of faulty components, dear?"

Marla's stomach somersaulted. She and Dalton had been so careful, checking for Chinese drywall and any other possible blots against the builder, but the man had come up clean.

"You'd mentioned Gene had his reasons for wanting Alan out of the way." She realized how that sounded when Debbie blanched. "I mean, he was ready to step up and take charge."

"Yes, because Alan's cousin, Beamis Woodhouse, is one of the suppliers for this development. Alan was trying to get Beamis to replace the windows, but Beamis says the problem isn't his fault. No wonder; replacements would cost a bundle of money. Gene suggested we get bids from other companies."

"It's better to get the guy who supplied the product to make good on his work, isn't it? Wouldn't this fall under our warranty from the builder if the windows are defective?"

"Not necessarily. I don't know the technicalities, but Alan didn't want to get the lawyers involved because of the potential cost to the association."

"That sounds reasonable. Hopefully, Gene will be able to follow through and get the issue fixed without us going to court."

Marla cast a glance at the area designated for linens. She hoped those donated throw pillows didn't come with bedbugs. This being a new community, that shouldn't be so, but people could have brought old goods with them from their prior homes.

"Hey, Debbie," called a heavy-set dark-haired lady, "are you gonna sit there all day? We could use your help over here."

"All right, I'm coming." The secretary turned to Marla with a wan smile. "Our resale values will be zilch unless we get the windows replaced. Let's hope Gene finds a solution fast."

Marla expressed her concerns to Dalton later at the local park, where they'd gone for a walk while Brianna visited a friend. The clouds had cleared and a cool, bright day ensued. She soaked in the sunshine as she strode beside him at a brisk pace. A sweet scent tickled her nose. At least she didn't have to worry about mosquitos this time of year.

"It could be the installation was faulty," Dalton suggested, a scowl on his face.

"If so, then the supplier would be in the clear."

"I'll see what I can find out. This sounds like material for a class-action lawsuit."

"Debbie said Alan didn't want to waste association funds on attorneys."

"Individual homeowners could file together. But perhaps the veep will come to an agreement with one of the contractors."

Marla returned to the foremost issue on her mind. "Do you

think the Board members are in the clear regarding Alan's death? I mean, what would any of them have to gain?"

"Other than Gene Uris stepping up to the presidency?" Dalton shrugged. "Kat is doing background checks but I'm not privy to her findings."

She heard the frustration in his tone. "I thought your pals were keeping you informed."

"Not lately, and besides, I've got my own case to work right now." He patted his pocket. "I'll have to go in if I get a call. Let's relax for now and enjoy the day."

They strolled in silence, while Marla's thoughts drifted to her own work-related issues. She'd had another incident with her recalcitrant stylist but hesitated to fire her. The salon would lose clients who were stubbornly loyal to the girl. What else could Marla do to bring her in line?

"Is everything set for Brie's birthday next weekend?" Dalton asked, regarding her with pride and affection.

Her heart warmed to this man she'd married. Throwing her cares to the wind, she proceeded to discuss their upcoming luncheon plans.

Monday found her going to the restaurant to confirm details for Brie's party and then meeting Kate, her mother-in-law, elsewhere for lunch. Kate and John had been renting an apartment until they could find a condo to buy. Dalton's mother had invited Marla to view several possibilities with her that afternoon.

"I love the location near the water of this one place," Kate gushed across the table from Marla at the Parisian Café on Las Olas Boulevard. They'd ordered their meals and sat sipping iced tea.

Kate's auburn hair was coiffed into a flattering style and her hazel eyes sparkled with excitement. She wore a teal patterned top and tan Capri pants. Gold jewelry and decorated flip flops completed her ensemble.

"How many rooms does it have?"

"Three bedrooms, which is great because we need space for John's stained glass studio. But I'm not sure I'd like living in a high-rise."

"It would be very different from your house in Maine."

"I know. John loves the ocean view, and we'd be directly east of you in Fort Lauderdale, but I'd prefer a place with more activities."

"Some of the fancy buildings by the New River have their own movie theaters, exercise rooms, and pools. Have you looked into those? They probably hold events for residents."

Kate shook her head. "It doesn't interest me. I've thought about Delray Beach. That city has a lot of cultural happenings along with interesting shops and restaurants. Plus, it isn't too far away from you." She paused as the waitress delivered their lunch plates.

Marla picked up her fork and speared a piece of lettuce. She'd ordered a salad with mixed greens, Gouda cheese, avocado, turkey, candied pecans and dried cranberries. Kate bit into her grilled chicken and melted cheese sandwich. They ate for a few moments in silence.

"How are the plans coming for Brianna's party? Does she have any idea her friends are invited?" Kate asked in between bites.

"If she does, she hasn't let on. I can't believe she'll be old enough for a driver's permit."

"Will Dalton allow her to get one?"

"We haven't discussed it. I plan to hire a driving instructor, though. I wouldn't want Dalton to give her lessons."

"A wise idea. John taught Dalton how to drive, and it was a nightmare." Kate chewed and swallowed. "I was planning to give Brianna money for her birthday unless you can think of something she wants?"

"She'd love to get an iPhone. We told her she'd have to save up for one herself, so cash would be welcome. Since Brie likes to read, we've bought her an e-reader."

"I'd still rather hold a book in my hand, but she'll like it."

A brief interlude ensued where they both enjoyed their meals. Kate's bracelets clinked on her arm. Marla eyed them surreptitiously, wondering what she could buy for her mother-in-law when it was her birthday.

"So tell me about this neighbor who ended up dead," Kate said.

Marla choked and sipped iced tea to chase the food down. "How much did Dalton tell you?"

"Just that the guy was a jerk, but he didn't deserve to die that way. He hanged himself?"

"Actually, Alan's death is being treated as a homicide case."

"Oh?" Kate arched her eyebrows, a lighter shade than her hair.

She should fill them in with a little brow pencil. Harnessing her thoughts, Marla informed Kate about their progress so far.

"Dalton is still irked that he's off the case," Marla concluded.

Kate's lips pursed. "Nonetheless, it's good policy to remove a detective who might be biased due to personal interests." She lowered her voice. "Dalton didn't get physical with the guy, did he?"

Marla stared at her. "How can you say that? You know your son. Usually he's the one who acts calm in a crisis."

"Yes, but this guy insulted you, and Dalton has a wicked protective instinct."

Marla stabbed a chunk of turkey with her fork. "Tell me about it."

"Did the nephew say he would remove the partial fence and the stone path?"

"He promised to comply with the code. We'll see if he follows through."

"Poor fellow probably has enough to handle."

"Alan was putting in a standby generator to keep his computers going in the event of a power failure. His gadgets were important to him. He also received lots of deliveries from UPS. I can't help feeling those things are related, but I can't figure the connection."

"I thought you said he was a retired insurance executive?"

"That's correct, and he made enough money to live comfortably. Then again, he didn't have a family to support."

"Had he ever been married?"

"No, he'd been engaged once to a Jewish woman. Would you believe it? Her parents disapproved and took the girl away to Europe. When she came back, I guess she broke off the engagement, because that was the end of their relationship."

"No wonder Krabber came down on you," Kate said. "He must have hated it when you moved in next door."

"His nephew said Alan didn't pursue anyone else after his broken engagement. It wasn't for lack of opportunities, either. According to Cherry Hunter, our association treasurer, Alan was quite the ladies' man." Marla repeated their conversation.

"So Krabber played around with women but didn't ever get serious again. Hmm, I wonder . . ."

"What?" Marla's teeth crunched on a candied pecan.

"Alan's fiancée was removed to Europe. It brings to mind the days when parents swept their unwed daughters off to the Continent because they'd gotten pregnant. Could this be why she disappeared off the scene?"

"But Alan meant to marry her. Why take her away if he'd make an honest woman of the girl?"

"In her parents' view, he might not raise a child in the proper religious tradition. What if their daughter had a son who needed to be circumcised? From what you've known of the fellow, can you imagine Krabber approving such a practice?"

"Maybe he'd have converted to please his fiancée. Alan might have married her even sooner knowing she carried his child. Her folks took that choice from him."

"Have you considered another possibility? He didn't know about the baby at all?"

CHAPTER EIGHT

"Thanks for meeting me here, Lieutenant." Marla wrapped a hand around her coffee cup and regarded Detective Minnetti, seated across from her at Starbucks. She'd chosen a couple of comfy armchairs away from the crowd lined up by the cashier.

Thursdays were her late day at work, so she had time in the morning to meet the detective. She'd been too busy the previous few days to follow up on her mother-in-law's notion. She decided to go directly to the homicide detective with her information. It could be something . . . or nothing. Minnetti could decide. Marla would mention it to Dalton later, if Minnetti felt her lead was worthwhile.

"What have you got?" Minnetti went directly to the point. She wore a pencil skirt with a cranberry blouse and black jacket.

Did she ever dress casually? Marla wondered how best to start.

She reported her findings to date, while expressions ranging from curiosity to surprise to disapproval flickered across the woman's face. Minnetti sipped from her cup of black coffee during Marla's recital.

"I can see how you've been helpful to your husband," Minnetti said with a slight smile. "Your theory is interesting, but I'm not sure we can trace this woman. Krabber was sixty-seven years old when he died. This would have been, what, forty years ago?"

"There must be something you can do to discover more about

her. Where did Krabber grow up? Can you interview people who knew him back then? Did he leave a school yearbook among his possessions? Or a collection of old love letters?"

The lieutenant assessed Marla with her shrewd brown eyes. "We've been researching anyone connected to him in his adult life. Old girlfriends, for example. Word has it that Cherry Hunter was interested in him at one time, but none of his flings led to anything serious."

"This goes further back into his past. Have you asked the nephew about memorabilia?"

The detective pursed her lips. "I can query him on the topic, but what's the point? Let's say the fiancée had a child while in Europe. She might have given it up for adoption."

"Or else she brought the baby home and married a guy who raised the kid as his own. Her parents were wealthy. They could have provided a financial incentive to this new suitor."

"Where are you going with this idea?"

"What if the child, once grown, was determined to find his biological father after learning he'd been adopted? He could have approached Krabber and been rebuffed. Krabber may not have cared about any offspring from the woman who rejected him."

"And then the kid killed Krabber out of resentment?" Minnetti shook her head. "That doesn't make sense. What would he gain?"

"Revenge? Maybe he believed Krabber had deserted his mother, and not the other way around. There wouldn't be any monetary incentive since Philip Byrd is the heir. Has anyone made a claim against the will?"

Minnetti cast her a startled glance. "I don't think so, but I'll talk to the attorney again."

"This may be a dead end, but it's worth pursuing. My husband always says to examine all the angles." Marla put her cup down and leaned forward. "I wish you'd trust him, Kat." She used the woman's first name on purpose.

"It's more a matter of him trusting me. He needs to let me do my job without sending you along as interference."

Marla stiffened. "Excuse me? Dalton doesn't know I'm meeting with you. I thought I'd give you the respect due your position and come to you directly with this information."

"And I appreciate that, but I also realize you're aiming to bring your husband back on the team. The chief is right to keep him out of it. He had personal feelings against the victim. Besides, he's working another homicide right now."

"The two of you are supposed to be partners. How will you watch each other's backs if you can't learn to work together?"

"That's not your issue." Minnetti's lips pressed together and her expression shuttered.

Marla sought a way to ease the tension that had sprung up between them. "Were you able to glean any data from Alan's computers, Kat? I'm curious as to what he did online all day."

"So am I. We're working on it. Meanwhile, do you have anything else to add?"

"What about the UPS deliveries? Have you tracked Alan's shipments to where the packages originated?" Marla heard a desperate edge creep into her voice. She wasn't going to learn any more from this conversation than going in.

Minnetti gave an exasperated shake of her head. "Let it go, hon. You know I can't discuss details about the case."

"Wait, I forgot to tell you that the fiancée who spurned Alan was Jewish. That might help you learn her identity."

"Actually, that is useful. It gives me an understanding of the deceased's attitude at the homeowners' meeting."

"See? I can be helpful."

"Oh, you've been helpful in more ways than one. But you're also meddling in affairs that shouldn't concern you. Focus on your family, Marla, and not on your husband's job. You never know when someone you love might be snatched away from you."

She rose and stalked away as Marla stared after her, wondering at the bittersweet tone of her last words. An urge to learn more about the woman grasped her, but it would be tough when Minnetti's emotional armor was so hard to penetrate.

Work occupied her time for the rest of the day, and then Marla got caught up in plans for Brie's birthday. She bought packs of flavored lip gloss as favors for Brie's friends. And then the day arrived, sunny and warm, a perfect Sunday for lunch on the Intracoastal.

Marla picked up her mother and headed over to the restaurant ahead of time. Dalton was bringing Brie after she finished her homework, or at least that was the excuse for their later arrival. Marla wanted to make sure enough seats had been placed around the tables. At final count, there would be sixteen guests.

"I'm sorry Roger couldn't make it, but at least he called you." She gripped the steering wheel while sparing a glance at her mother.

Anita hadn't said much, sitting on the passenger side with taut lips and a firm expression. She wore a canary yellow ensemble with green trim, reminding Marla of a parakeet. That made her think of Philip Byrd and his save the rainforests cause. How would he use his uncle's money? Would he put it toward his retirement savings? Buy himself a bigger home? Donate some of the funds to his nonprofit group?

Stop that, Marla, and focus on family. Minnetti was right; you never knew when happiness could be snatched away.

"So what did Roger say?" Marla probed, hoping to elicit a response and break through her mother's frost.

"He'd been busy with his sister who's in town. But when I said I'd like to meet her, he muttered an excuse." Anita's gaze lowered. "He sounded distant, as though he didn't care anymore. I think he called just so I'd stop pestering him."

"I'm sorry, Ma. But if that's his attitude, you're better off by yourself."

Marla aimed a few venomous thoughts in Roger's direction. She hadn't liked him all that much, thinking him loud and obnoxious, but he'd pleased her mother and kept her company. Now she'd be lonely, her days empty, unless she threw herself into some other activity.

It took them nearly an hour to reach Jasmine's on the Intracoastal in Hollywood. The last Sunday in March had brought out a crowd, but Marla found a parking space without a problem. Carrying her gift for Brianna and the box of bagged party favors, she entered the sprawling restaurant.

Marla nudged her mother toward the maître d' at the host stand. The dark-haired man's face brightened as he spotted her. He wore a sport coat over a tropical shirt and tan pants.

"Hello, Carlos, this is my mom, Anita Shorstein." Marla waited until they'd exchanged greetings. "Is everything ready? My daughter should be here shortly."

"Of course. Follow me, please."

With a grand, sweeping gesture, Carlos ushered them into a private room in the back. The space had an expansive bank of windows facing the famed waterway. A double-deck tourist boat plowed past, bursting with visitors. Across the glistening water, a mega-yacht parked at a dock by a private residence. Most houses facing the windows were mansion proportions by her standards.

Fort Lauderdale was known as the "Yachting Capital of the World." Most tourists didn't realize that the marine industry was the leading form of commerce there. Marla had read once that it contributed more than one hundred thousand jobs and over ten billion dollars to the local economy. With three hundred miles of waterways and plentiful marine repair facilities, Fort Lauderdale was a popular international port of call.

She took her dreamy gaze away from the windows and beamed at Brianna's friends, who'd assembled in readiness for the birthday girl's arrival. Kate and John hadn't arrived yet, nor had her brother's family, but it didn't matter if they encountered Brie on their way in. She expected them to be present.

Marla hugged each of the girls, complimenting their hair or clothes and generally making each one feel welcome. Then she checked over the table settings. The waiter chose that moment to zoom inside and ask if everything was all right. Marla reviewed her instructions with him as the girls resumed their chatting and laughter.

She glanced up when her brother Michael entered with his wife, Charlene. A grin split her face as she hastened over to greet them.

"Where are the kids?" Marla peered around her brother's tall frame, but Jacob and Rebecca were nowhere in sight.

"They're with my parents today." Charlene smoothed her sundress. Her tawny eyes brought out the golden highlights in her oak hair, which she wore straight down her back. "We thought it best not to disrupt the party with small kids. Besides, I could use a day off from children, if you know what I mean." Charlene, thirty-four, worked as an elementary school teacher and hoped to make principal one day.

"It's been a while since I've seen my niece and nephew. I'd looked forward to visiting with them."

"You can see them at Passover. Where are we doing it this year, anyway?"

"I thought I'd invite everyone over to our house. Cousin Cynthia hasn't seen our new place, and neither have you guys. Can you believe Cynthia's son is graduating college this year?"

"We're all getting older," her brother said. Having hit forty recently, Michael showed his age with graying temples. Otherwise, he shared Marla's brown hair and eyes.

"I'll discuss the Seder with Dalton, but I'm sure he won't mind. You'll have to lead the service, though."

"No problem."

"Excuse me, I'm going to put this gift down." Charlene headed to the table designated for that purpose.

"I should say hello to Ma." Michael veered away to greet their mother.

Kate and John joined the party ten minutes later. Kate approached Marla for a quick embrace and an air kiss.

"Hello, Anita," Kate waved to Marla's mother. "How are you?"

Anita strode over. "I'm just fine, thanks. How is your condo hunt coming?"

Stepping away, Marla skewed a glance at her father-in-law. John had meandered over to admire the buttercream birthday cake displayed on a separate table. With an inner wince, she recalled how her friend Jill's wedding had turned into a fiasco after Marla discovered the matron of honor dead under the cake table.

She shoved aside the memory to focus on this happy occasion. Dalton should arrive at any moment with Brie. However, the next person who shuffled inside the room took her aback. What was *he* doing here?

"Anita!" hollered Roger Gold. "Come and give me a kiss, lovey ducky."

Marla cringed, hoping her mother would tell him off so he'd leave. But no, Anita scurried to obey, her face bright with joy. Roger wore a gold shirt as befitting his name and a pair of green trousers. He'd combed his wheat-colored hair to cover the large bald spot on his head. His shirt didn't do such a comparable job with his girth.

"Heya, doll," he called to Marla, offering a wave.

Dalton's parents stiffened at his entry. She knew they considered him crass, but they acted polite for Anita's sake. It didn't look as though Roger had brought a gift, either, unless he planned to give Brianna some cash. Knowing the guy, she figured he had probably come for the food.

Marla summoned the waiter to remove one of the extra place settings since Michael's kids weren't there. Roger could have the other seat. In the midst of her preparations, she couldn't help overhear her mother's conversation.

"Why have you been ignoring me all week?" Anita asked Roger in a plaintive tone, her white hair making her appear senior to him although he bested her by two years. Anita had decided to go all snowy once gray hairs started to appear, so she had dyed her hair to a uniform color until her natural shade faded.

"But I did call about today, didn't I?" Roger's face reddened.

"Only after I left you dozens of messages. I realize your sister is visiting, but that's no reason for you to act like I don't exist."

Go, Ma! The shmuck deserved a put-down. Marla hovered nearby to hear his excuse.

"Well, Doreen left town early, so I could join you here after all."

"We have to talk about this, Roger." Anita's lips thinned. "I'm not sure we can just take off where we left things."

Taking her arm, he winked at her. "I'll make it up to you, *shaineh maidel.*"

Marla rolled her eyes. Calling her mother a beautiful girl wouldn't sway her.

"Surprise!" the girls yelled in unison when Brianna strolled into the room.

That put an end to Marla's eavesdropping. She bustled over to kiss Dalton and hug the girl. "Happy Birthday, Brie. I thought you'd like to have a few friends to celebrate with you."

"Awesome, Marla. You're the best." The teen threw her arms around Marla for a tight hug that brought moisture to Marla's eyes.

She'd been afraid of having children for so long, due to a past tragedy, that she'd missed out on the intense pleasure a family could bring. Maybe it was worth the agony of worry to experience the joy, but she still had enough to handle without bearing children of her own. That would be the *last* thing on her lifelong to-do list.

What amazed her was the delight in giving happiness to Dalton's child. Marla wouldn't have expected to gain so much from the simple act of trying to make the girl's life a better one.

Brianna looked pretty in a form-fitting maxi dress, making Marla realize how much she'd grown in the few short years they'd known each other. She was blossoming into a lovely young lady, mostly thanks to Dalton's upbringing after his former wife died. And while he tended to be overprotective, he had his heart in the right place.

She entwined her arm in his and smiled up at him.

"What?" he said, peering down at her with his smoky gaze.

"I love you." She savored his masculine scent and the spice cologne he favored.

"Love you, too." He disengaged to pat his stomach. "When do we eat? I'm starved."

Marla spread her hands. "Men! They're all alike. Speaking of eating, look who showed up. Aren't we lucky?"

Dalton cast a disdainful glance toward Roger. "So I see. What prompted his presence? I thought he and your mom were on the outs."

"His sister was visiting and monopolized his time, or so he said. I think Barry had some influence there. He must have soured on us since, uh, you and I got married."

Dalton's eyes darkened. "I hope your mom doesn't just lap up Roger's attention again."

"Me, too. Go greet everyone and then we can get started. Girls, you can take your seats. The menus are on the table. Order whatever you like."

They proceeded through the entrees while chatting and viewing the yachts passing by on the waterway. The water glistened in the sun's rays, a perfect day for the beach or boating. Weather in March could be variable, so they'd lucked out with the sunshine today.

Brie decided to open her presents before dessert. She exclaimed with pleasure over the e-reader from Marla and Dalton. The teen was a voracious reader of mystery novels, like Nicole at work. "I love it, thanks!" she said with a special smile just for them.

After opening all of her friends' gifts, she tore into Kate and John's package. Her eyes popped when she saw the box. "An iPad! You didn't! Oh thanks, Grams!"

"That's an expensive present," Marla muttered to Dalton with some dismay. It certainly outshone her gift, although e-readers and tablets did serve different purposes.

Nor was Anita to be outdone. Rather than giving cash, she'd splurged on a David Yurman necklace for the teen.

"It's beautiful." Brie held up the jewelry for all to admire.

Marla could get her matching earrings for the holidays. Then again, an iPhone might be less costly, and then Brie could sync apps between devices. Marla sighed with resignation. One of these days, she'd have to jump on the electronic bandwagon just to keep up.

She glanced around for the waiter. Some of the adults might want coffee, and she didn't see any birthday candles for the cake. Excusing herself, she hurried into the main dining room to search for the guy.

She'd just passed into the front section when her gaze caught on a familiar bearded face. Gene Uris, the homeowners' association vice president, shared a table with a red-haired fellow. Dressed in a suit and tie, Gene contrasted in refinement to his husky companion, who wore a sport shirt and jeans. Whatever they were discussing had made Gene scowl.

"Well, if it isn't Gene Uris, our esteemed V.P." Marla barreled toward their table with an enthusiastic smile. "Remember me? I'm Marla Vail, and I live in Royal Oaks." She stuck her hand out.

Gene shook it reluctantly. "Marla, this is Erik Mansfield. Marla's one of our residents," he explained to his friend.

Marla tilted her head. "You look very nice, Gene. Are you here for a special occasion? We're celebrating our daughter's birthday."

"Good for you. We're in a meeting, and then I'm going into work after lunch."

"Oh, I see." So he was there for business. A quick survey revealed a wedding band on his finger but their table appeared set for two. "Where do you work?"

"I'm manager over at Lemmings and Sons in Pembroke Pines."

"Nice." Actually, she'd heard the furniture chain wasn't doing so well. "Too bad you have to work on a weekend."

"It's part of the job." He turned back toward his friend, clearly dismissing Marla.

"I've heard about the faulty windows," Marla said, wanting to sound him out on the problem. "We've been living in our house for three months, but we haven't noticed any issues."

"That's because they only leak when it rains." He gripped his water glass. "I'm hoping Erik can clean up the mess that Ron left us."

"Who?"

"Ron Cloakman, the developer for the master community."

"Oh, I see." No, she didn't. Weren't there several different builders involved? "What do you do?" she asked his fiery-haired companion.

The man looked as though he'd be at home at a bar brawl. His nose was slightly out of alignment, as though he'd been punched in the face and his schnozzle had stayed that way.

"I'm in construction. We have one of the bids in for the playground. Gene is trying to persuade me to throw in the window extrusions for a steep discount."

Gene's shoulders hunched. "If he'll toss the window repairs into the deal, I'm sure the Board will vote for his bid. I'm convinced Erik is the best person for the job."

Marla glanced between them in confusion. "I'm sorry, but I'm not following."

"We didn't discuss this issue at the HOA meeting, because the Board didn't have enough information to present to residents. We'll send out a special notice when the time comes."

"For what? Am I missing something?"

"Really, Mrs. Vail, I'm on a time crunch, here. You can give me a call if you want to discuss things later. Or attend one of our Board meetings. Everyone is invited."

"Sure, I'm sorry to have bothered you. Nice to have met you, Erik." She stumbled away, wondering what on earth he'd meant.

Ruminating over their encounter, she signaled the waiter and got him to bring birthday candles for the cake. Lighting the wicks, singing "Happy Birthday," dessert and farewells took up the next hour. After Brie's friends departed, Dalton paid the bill while Marla shoved the gifts into a clean trash bag she'd brought for that purpose.

Kate and John said their goodbyes, on their way to more house hunting. Anita left with Roger. Marla watched them go with a grimace. He'd shown up at the last minute and hadn't even had the courtesy to give Brianna a gift. Heaving a sigh, Marla wished her mother would come to her senses and ditch the man.

It wasn't until much later that evening, when Marla was lying in bed next to Dalton that she brought up her conversation with Gene Uris.

"What was he talking about? What playground is up for a bid?" She turned on her side and smoothed her fingers along her husband's biceps. She liked to feel the contours of his muscles beneath his hair-sprinkled skin.

He hadn't gone to the gym this weekend and probably regretted the omission. Usually too busy during the week, he made time on weekends to work out. All of their activities of late had prevented him from following his routine. She vowed to lessen her demands.

"I don't know, and I don't care right now," Dalton said, a smile playing about his lips as he responded to her touch.

She recognized that look in his eyes. "I can always ask my garage sale volunteers. They're eager to share news about the community."

"You do that." He rolled to face her and brushed her lips with his. "I can think of better things to occupy our time."

Marla's mental wheels spun. "Yes, but what if Alan had harangued his cousin Beamis to fix the faulty windows, and the man decided to shut him up?"

"By killing him? It doesn't make the issue go away. Gene Uris has taken up the reins."

"He wants to get bids from other companies to do the repairs."

"Replacements are more likely." Dalton's brows drew together. "You said the other guy at the table with Gene was in construction?"

Dalton's face hovered inches from her mouth, his hot breath

caressing her cheek. Tempted to lose herself in passion, she clung to rational thought.

"That's right. Why wouldn't Debbie, our secretary, solicit bids from interested parties? I'd think it would be her job to make contact. It's odd for Gene to meet with this one contractor alone."

"How's this for making contact?" Dalton's hand reached down, and Marla's mind channeled along another path.

Chapter Nine

The weekend of the garage sale dawned bright and beautiful with temperatures in the low seventies and clear skies. Early that Sunday morning, Marla proceeded to the clubhouse to supervise her volunteers. More neighbors had offered to help, for which she was grateful. Even though it would be a busy day, she hoped to hear more about Alan Krabber.

The association treasurer had already unlocked the doors and set tables outside when Marla arrived. Cars with customers were lined up by seven o'clock. They'd billed the starting time for eight, but early birds always showed up to get the first look.

"Marla, shall I set up the cashier's desk at the far side of the parking lot?" Cherry said, hustling toward her inside the clubhouse. "That way, people can't slip past without paying."

"Sure, go for it." She wiped her hands on her jeans and contemplated where to start. "Angela, do you need any help with the bake sale?"

The blonde glanced up from the items she was adjusting on a platter. A glass domed cover sat on the kitchen counter next to it. "No, thanks, I've got it. You can put the sign on the door, though, so folks know to come inside to take a look."

Marla strode over and peered at the red, white, and blue frosted cupcakes and the decorated cake pops on a plate beside them. "These look fabulous. Did you make them?"

Angela beamed. "Of course I did. I love baking."

"You must have taken a cake decorating class to learn this precision."

Angela laughed, exposing even, white teeth. "You're absolutely right. I used to work at a supermarket bakery to earn money to go to college. Later, I'd find any excuse to bake a batch of muffins or other treats to bring into the office. I don't get the chance so much anymore since I've been working at home."

Marla put a hand on her hip. "What is it you do?"

"Graphic design." Angela's smile vanished. "Now if you'll excuse me, I need to start the coffeemaker. If you get hungry, we have refreshments for volunteers behind the counter. See? I made blueberry scones and lemon tarts just for us."

"That's very thoughtful of you. Tell me, is your friend coming over to help?"

Angela's brow furrowed. "Who?"

"You know, Alfred. I delivered a letter for him to your address."

Something flickered behind the woman's eyes. "Oh, that was a mistake. Someone got the names mixed up, but the mail was meant for me."

"O-kay." Marla glanced around. No one was near them, and the other volunteers were efficiently setting out the household goods and racks of clothing with pricing labels intact. "By the way, I ran into Gene Uris the other day," she said, lowering her voice. "He was talking to some guy who works in construction named Erik Mansfield. Do you know him? They were discussing association business."

Angela shook her head, waves of blond hair framing her face. "Can't say that I do." Her hands kept busy, putting the glass cover on the cupcakes and laying a cake knife next to an iced Bundt cake.

"Well, thanks so much for being here today, Angela. We appreciate your help."

Marla turned away. Was it her imagination, or did Angela prefer not to talk about her personal life? Maybe she'd been laid off from a job like so many people these days and had been forced to develop an at-home business. Or maybe she did something besides graphic design and didn't care to discuss the details. Whatever her issues, it was obvious she wouldn't say more about this Alfred person.

Had his name on the address been a mistake? Or did he live with her, and Angela didn't want to admit to having a lover? Who else could he be? Certainly not a son. People would have seen the kid going to school. But they'd also have seen a man coming and going from her house. So Angela was probably right about the mail having a mistaken name on it.

Anyway, Angela wasn't her focus. Heading outdoors, she scanned the group of women, wondering who she could ask about association business and Krabber's role in it.

"Marla, over here!" A woman waved. "Is this how you want things arranged?"

Marla bustled over to her section. "You should ask Debbie. She's the one who suggested the groupings, but this looks appealing to me." One table held silver items like serving spoons and candlesticks and bread plates. Another displayed dinner plates and bowls and miscellaneous dishware.

Someone jostled her arm as she roved by the kitchen gadgets. A heavy-set lady, sweat beading her brow, waddled past to peer at the display.

"Excuse me, but we haven't officially opened yet." Marla glanced at her watch. "Please get in line. It's only another ten minutes."

Oh, no. This lady wasn't the only crowd-buster. Others filtered in, nosing around the tables while residents struggled to finish setting up.

Her heart racing, Marla searched for the secretary's petite frame. Debbie wasn't anywhere in sight. Rising panic made her chest tighten. How would they manage when that influx of customers rushed them? Cars kept arriving, their occupants parking on the swale by the road and then emerging to join the growing crowd.

Cherry seemed cool and collected, manning the cashier's table. Wait, where were the shopping bags? Robyn Piper, one of the committee members, was supposed to bring them.

She spotted the woman wearing eyeglasses and a wide-brimmed sunshade and rushed in her direction. The slim brunette had taken charge of the designer dresses and accessories. Where had all this stuff come from? Marla felt overwhelmed. She'd been out here earlier in the week to tag more goods and didn't remember seeing all those Coach and Kate Spade items.

"Robyn, did you remember to bring plastic bags for the cashier?"

Robyn straightened from where she'd been arranging a display of belts and regarded Marla with amused brown eyes. "Relax, darling, I already gave them to Cherry. She probably put them underneath the table. You can't see because of the cloth."

"Whew, thanks for that." With a grunt of relief, Marla swiped her brow. "I can't help thinking I've forgotten something."

Robyn patted her arm. "Don't worry about a thing. You've done a great job, and we'll be fine. Each of us knows our stations."

Marla nodded to Susan Feinberg, over by the toys. Some were on tables while larger items were laid out on the lawn behind the parking lot. Susan's two kids played on the grass. And Jeanie from across the street had surprised Marla by taking charge of the shoes. Those were always one of the more popular stops at garage sales. Robyn was right. Everything seemed to be in order.

Marla took a deep, calming breath. Even when things were hectic at the salon, she never got this rattled. She was accustomed to that environment, while here she felt helplessly out of her element.

A thin, narrow-faced man approached her. "Excuse me, are you Marla Vail?"

"Yes, I am." Her gaze roamed from his receding hairline to his nervous dark eyes.

"I'm Debbie Morris's husband, Jimmy."

"Hello, it's nice to meet you." She glanced beyond him. "Is Debbie here? She's supposed to assist Cherry at the cashier's table."

"Debbie had to go take care of her sister. Poor thing has breast cancer and is having a bad time of it right now."

"I'm so sorry." Marla tossed a strand of hair behind her ear. The breeze was picking up, a godsend since the crush of bodies and rising temperature would soon raise the heat level in the parking lot.

"She sends her apologies. I'd stay and help, but I've got to watch the kids at home."

"Of course. Give her my regards and let me know if I can do anything."

She evaluated Cherry's situation. Could the treasurer manage the cash box alone? She'd taken a few steps in her direction when Robyn signaled to her.

"I forgot to mention it, Marla, but after this event is over and you're free, let's do lunch together. I'm always planning special events for my clients, and maybe we can work something out involving your day spa to give you some publicity."

"That sounds great, thanks."

She'd like to get to know the marketing expert better. Robyn, a single woman, must make a good income to afford a house on her own. Marla admired her independence, although she couldn't help wondering why Robyn wasn't in a relationship. Certainly with her looks and energy, it couldn't be from lack of male interest.

"Oh, look who's shown up." Robyn nodded toward a plus-size lady in navy pants and a cute patterned top. "It's Laura Ferret. You heard about her fiasco with the Board, I suppose?"

Anxious to move on, Marla hesitated. "No, I haven't. What happened?"

"She and her husband, Orville, built a second-story addition to their house and failed to get HOA approval. You know how it says in the rules we have to get certain improvements passed by the Board? Well, they neglected to do so. The Board cited him because his structure was too high."

"You mean the cost was elevated?"

"No, the height of the building exceeded allowable parameters. Alan threatened to put a lien on the Ferrets' property if Orville didn't fix it. The reconstruction cost and legal expenses set him and Laura back in mortgage payments big time. Now the bank may be moving to foreclose. Orville held Alan personally responsible for his financial troubles."

Marla gaped at her. "Did anyone mention this matter to the detective investigating Alan's death?"

"Why would they? Alan was despondent and hanged himself, according to what I've heard."

"You heard wrong. Alan was murdered. A public announcement should be coming any day now." Dalton had said it was okay to mention the case, which had been determined to be a homicide. The news had been released, but the broadcast stations hadn't covered it yet. Maybe the political scandals in Miami were more important.

"No way." Robyn scraped a hand over her face. She wore an

attractive shade of coral lipstick. "Do they know who did it?"

"Not at this point. Would you have any theories?"

"Huh. You're looking at her."

"You mean Laura?" Incredulity tinged her voice. Surely the woman wouldn't kill their president because he'd enforced association rules? Then again, it had cost Laura and her husband thousands of dollars in reconstruction, and vengeance could have filled their hearts.

After concluding her conversation with Robyn, Marla sauntered in Laura's direction.

"Hello, I'm Marla Vail, the garage sale chairwoman. Can I help you find something?"

Laura regarded her with violet eyes. She had ash blond hair teased in a bouffant style that had gone out in the sixties. "I'm just browsing, thanks."

"Well, take a look around. We have baked goods inside the clubhouse, too." Marla paused. "I'm relatively new to the neighborhood. Is there always this much drama?"

"Excuse me?"

"You heard about the murder, of course? Who'd have thought someone hated Alan Krabber enough to do him in?"

"What? I'd heard the terrible news that he had hanged himself, but not this."

Marla lowered her voice to a conspiratorial tone. "Oh, yes. I don't believe the news is all that widespread yet, but it's definitely a homicide." Hopefully, Laura didn't realize she was a police detective's wife. "Can you think of anyone in the community who might have wished him harm? Since the man was retired, it couldn't have been colleagues from work. And he didn't have that many relatives."

Laura's face flushed. "He had his fans, but he offended lots of people, too."

"You sound as though you're one of them."

"I'll say." Laura shot her a venomous glare. "We forgot to get Board approval for our two-story addition, and the Board sent us a citation that the structure was too high. They requested we tear it down and rebuild. Despite the potential cost, they wouldn't make any concessions."

"I'm sorry to hear that."

"Orville was furious. We had to extend our loan, and that's led to other worries. But neither one of us would go after Alan for it. The entire Board agreed with him. Did you know—"

"Marla, there you are!" Brianna rapped on her elbow. "How's it going? We came to see if we could help."

Marla twisted her neck to see Dalton bearing down on her. "Hi, honey. We've got everything under control, thanks." She smiled at her husband. "Dalton, I'd like you to meet Laura Ferret." But when she looked back, the woman was gone.

Bless my bones, what had the lady been about to say?

Marla pressed her lips together in frustration, but then shoved aside her musings and turned to her family. "Are you hungry? Angela baked cupcakes that look delish."

"No, I'm gonna check out the DVDs if you don't need me." Brianna skipped off, her ponytail bouncing against her back.

Dalton grinned down at Marla, admiration in his gray eyes. "You've done a bang-up job of organizing this thing."

"Thanks. How come you're not home doing the Sunday crossword puzzle?"

"It's too nice out to stay inside. We should go to the park later."

He'd solved his case and had been returned to his desk job. Marla was grateful he had weekends off again, but knew he got antsy. It was terrible to say it, but he needed a case to occupy his mind. His tomato plants, crossword puzzles, and household projects didn't take enough of his time. God help her if he ever retired.

"I won't be finished until three or so," she said. "The sale closes down at two and then we have to clean up this mess."

"Don't you have people assigned to that detail?" He shaded his face with his hand.

The rising sun made Marla wish she'd brought a hat. She fished for her sunglasses in the purse slung over her shoulder. "I'm chairperson, so I should stay. Everything that's left over gets picked up tomorrow by the Salvation Army."

"Okay. Why don't I take care of dinner for tonight? You'll be too wiped out to cook. You can do the salmon croquettes tomorrow."

"Good idea, thanks." She searched the throng for Brianna's familiar head. "Uh-oh. You'd better go supervise your daughter. She's looking at the jewelry."

As he walked away, Marla noticed how some of the residents steered around him or gave him the evil eye. *This, too, shall pass,* she thought. Eventually, the incidents of the fence and Alan's boat and even his untimely death would become old news and people would forget about Dalton's role. There, see? Some guy had stopped him and shook hands. They should realize the valuable insights he could bring to neighborhood security.

The morning wore on with a steady influx of customers. Marla had gone inside for a snack to still her growling stomach when she heard a steady thumping sound. What was that? Had someone turned on a loud radio?

Robyn rushed into the clubhouse, a frantic look on her face. "Marla, come outside. We have trouble."

She should have known. Didn't her mother always say, *A tsoreh kumt nit alain*? Trouble doesn't come alone. According to Anita, things came in threes. Alan's death and Marla's problems with Dara at work made two. Now what?

Stuffing the rest of a brownie into her mouth, she hurried outdoors. Robyn pointed toward the driveway entrance, where a circle of people held up placards. The rhythmic beating noise came from over there. Cherry had abandoned her post, leaving the cashier's table to an impromptu assistant. From Cherry's wild gestures, she appeared to be in a heated discussion with one of the demonstrators.

Marla approached, her dismay rising. The signs called for a boycott of their sale, saying the homeowners were desecrating sacred ground.

"What's going on here?" Marla addressed the treasurer, whose black hair hung in a braid down her back.

Cherry turned to her in exasperation. "Marla, this is Herb Poltice. We have to get him and his troop to leave. They're blocking the entrance."

"So I see." Wishing the community had a daytime security guard she could call, Marla pondered what to do. Several of the men pounded on drums, while the rest of the gang marched in a circle to the beat, waving their signs. For the most part, they wore loose-fitting shirts over jeans, but what struck her as peculiar was the war paint on their faces.

"Cherry, you can return to your post if you wish. I'll handle this, unless you can explain what the signs mean." Marla spoke in a mollifying tone, hoping to calm tempers.

"The spirits have summoned us," Herb intoned like a seer at a séance. "We cannot let this blasphemy go unpunished."

"Like you care what our ancestors might think. You're only in this for your own glory." Cherry glared at Herb, who shared the same raven hair and dark eyes. If glances could shoot poison arrows, he'd be dead by now.

Herb jabbed his thumb at her. "Oh, and you're not?"

"You promised me you would wait," Cherry said.

"You only told me to wait so you could verify the discovery." Herb's longish hair was bound in back, his face lined with crevices. Silver streaked his temples.

"What discovery? What is this about?" Marla felt as though she was intruding on a personal argument.

"Herb, keep quiet." Cherry's admonition seemed out of place when she had to raise her voice to be heard over the drums.

"The voices cannot be silenced any longer. We of the Immowakee must respect our heritage."

"That's what I'm trying to do, you imbecile."

He sneered at her. "On the contrary, you want to collect more evidence. In doing so, you are defiling the land."

Cherry put a hand on Marla's arm. "Can't you call your husband or something? He'd put a stop to this. They're disturbing the peace."

Gritting her teeth, Marla stepped back. If those drummers continued to make that racket, she'd end up smashing their instruments herself. Their presence wasn't deterring customers, however. People merely parked further along the main road and trudged over, giving the tribesmen curious glances. Maybe they figured this was some sort of entertainment.

Marla gave a startled glance at one guy who raised his cell phone in the air. Was he filming this protest? Great, all they needed on top of Alan's murder was to become the subject of another news feature.

"Herb, I'll have to ask you and your group to leave," she said, still unclear as to why the Native Americans were there.

"Oh, and who are you exactly?"

"I'm Marla Vail, chair of this garage sale and wife of homicide detective Dalton Vail. Do I need to call in reinforcements from the local police force?"

"Go ahead, Mrs. Vail. I'll tell them how this development is going forward with construction on consecrated ground."

Marla glanced between Herb and Cherry. Connections raced inside her head, like mental light bulbs popping on, one at a time, along a wire strung between poles. A theory took hold, one that would explain this little diorama and possibly Cherry's role in it.

"Aren't you barking up the wrong tree?" she said to Herb. "Shouldn't you be talking to the builders?"

"Heck, no. This started with her friend, the president. He should have reported his find to the authorities right away and not to you." Herb pointed an accusatory finger at Cherry.

Cherry stiffened. "He needed me to confirm his discovery. Herb, we've discussed this before." A pained look crept over her face.

"And see what happened? The spirits took their revenge on the man."

Marla leaned forward. While she wanted to learn more, she had to disband this group and get back to work. "If you're talking about Alan Krabber, my husband says the case is a homicide."

The man gazed at her with astonishment, but then his eyes narrowed. "Either way, he paid the price for his indiscretion. So will you," he told Cherry. "Nobody can disrupt the bones of our ancestors and not suffer the consequences. You should do the right thing and come clean."

"I need more time for my research."

"The longer you delay, the angrier the spirits will become. They'll take their revenge again, mark my words."

"Maybe I can help," Marla said. "Tell me your demands, and I'll relate them to my husband. He can see that the message gets to the proper person."

His glance scorched her. "We only learned of this site fairly recently. It hadn't been recorded in our annals. We must respect the dead and call a halt to any further building."

"Alan Krabber is with the spirits now. Why don't you ask him to intercede?" Cherry snapped. A vein pulsed in her neck, and her eyes blazed. She looked about to have a stroke.

"Make your choice, Cherry. You're either with us or against us. But be warned that the law is clear on the subject."

"Herb is the tribal shaman," Cherry said to Marla with a disdainful lift of her nose. "He considers it his job to commune with dead people. But he doesn't do it to bring harmony to nature. He does it for his own stature in the tribe."

Marla's gaze darted about in desperation. How did she get to be a buffer in this conversation? She needed help here. These people weren't going to budge.

The drums rose in crescendo. She glanced beyond the drumming circle toward the street and groaned. A local TV news crew had pulled up in a van, and a cameraman and a nattily dressed lady reporter spilled out. With eager expressions on their faces, they headed straight at her.

Chapter Ten

After the demonstration by the Native Americans, the arrival of the news crew, and the frenzy of the garage sale, Marla wanted nothing more than to sink into her bed and relax. But Dalton was preparing dinner, and she couldn't wait to talk to him.

She did spare the time to shower and change into comfy drawstring pants and a pullover sweater before entering the kitchen.

"Where's Brie?" She sniffed garlic and spices. A big soup pot sat on the electric range along with a covered saucepan. Her stomach rumbled. She hadn't eaten much all day and wouldn't mind an early dinner.

"She's over at Kim's house. I told her I'd pick her up at five."

Marla glanced at the wall clock. They had twenty minutes to spare.

"What are you cooking? It smells divine."

Dalton, standing by the sink, chopped up a red bell pepper for a salad. "Spaghetti and meatballs. I didn't feel like making the meatballs from scratch, so I used the ones from the freezer. The sauce is done. I put them in there to cook."

Marla gave him an affectionate smile. She thought he never looked sexier than when he worked in the kitchen with an apron tied around his waist. "Dalton, those turkey meatballs are already cooked. You could have heated them in the microwave."

He shot her a wry glance. "Well, why didn't you say so?"

"Why didn't you ask? Anyway, you can probably turn off the

burner for now." Bone tired, she sat on a chair at their round table in the breakfast nook. "You won't believe what happened at the garage sale after you left."

"Oh, yeah?" He tossed the diced red pepper into the salad bowl, then picked up a cucumber to peel. "Did you make a lot of money for the HOA? How much stuff was left over?"

"Cherry is still tabulating the results, but we did quite well. The turnout was great, especially when we hit the local news station."

That caught his attention. He whirled toward her, the cucumber upright in his hand.

"What? I didn't see anything on TV, but I was watching sports all afternoon."

She told him about the drumming circle and Herb Poltice's claims and his dialogue with Cherry Hunter.

"This puts a new spin on things," Dalton said with a thoughtful frown. Turning back to the sink, he carefully sliced the vegetable on a bamboo cutting board.

"It certainly does. What if Krabber's construction crew dug up more than dirt in his backyard?"

"How so?" The cucumber got added to the salad. Dalton couldn't put onions in; Brie wouldn't eat them, so he picked up a carrot.

"Herb mentioned bones. What if Alan halted the work detail, not because he was waiting for delivery of a propane tank, but because of what he discovered in that pit?"

Dalton's knife poised in midair. "You mean, he found human remains?"

"That's right—the ancient type, like you'd see in a natural history museum." Fired by the idea, she leapt to her feet. "I'm going to look this up on the computer. You can get Brie. I'll put the spaghetti on to boil while you're out."

"Okay, but we're not done talking about this." Dalton paused, looking adorable with a lock of hair falling across his forehead. "Do you want wine tonight? I've picked out a bottle of pinot noir."

"That would be great. I can use it after everything that's happened." She gave him a sly glance. "By the way, how are things going with Detective Minnetti?"

"She's handling the case. I'm not going to offer my advice unless she asks."

"But if we uncover new information, you'll tell her, right?"

He gave a noncommittal shrug. "If I don't, I'm sure you will."

Oh, so this was how he meant to play it. The fox hoped to scoop Kat on the killer. It wasn't the lady detective's fault she'd landed the case. The chief had made that decision.

Marla let the matter go and headed for their home office. It took a few searches until she discovered the Florida Department of State had a division called Historical Resources.

Florida had once been home to generations of Native Americans. Many tribal names had been lost to time, but most of the people followed specific burial practices. Unmarked human remains often originated from the era before European contact, more than five hundred years ago. These were usually found in burial mounds or prehistoric shell middens. Florida cemetery law had been revised to include these mounds or any monuments containing associated artifacts. Remains less than seventy-five years old fell under the jurisdiction of the Medical Examiner.

"Listen to this," she said to Brianna and Dalton as they sat eating at the kitchen table, forty minutes later. She'd brought the teen up to speed on her findings. "If anybody uncovers human skeletal remains while excavating, they have to halt operations, secure the site, and notify local law enforcement. If they fail to report their find, they face a second-degree misdemeanor."

Dalton sucked a string of spaghetti into his mouth. "So you think Krabber's construction crew dug up some bones, and he told them to stop working?"

"Either that, or the workmen said they'd have to report the find before they could continue."

"I don't think that's what happened. The authorities would have been scouring his backyard by now. It's possible Krabber discovered the bones himself and told the crew to wait until the propane tank was delivered."

"How would he know the remains were human, unless he'd found a skull? It could have been a small animal." Marla felt her eyes widen. "Hey, I get it. He wanted verification, and so he took a sample of his discovery to the one person he knew who might be able to provide validation—Cherry Hunter."

Brie waved her fork in the air. "She's a history professor, right?"

"At the university." Marla took a sip of dry red wine. "And Cherry specializes in Native American culture. She could have had someone in their labs test the sample."

"So why wouldn't she report it to the authorities?" Brie asked with a thoughtful frown. She stabbed a meatball and bit into it.

"Likely Alan told Cherry to bring her results to him, and he'd notify the proper people. They would send out a law officer, a Medical Examiner, and an archaeologist from the Florida Division of Historical Resources. This team would investigate the site to determine a course of action. That's what happens in cases like this. But Cherry went to the tribal shaman instead and spilled the beans."

"Why?" Dalton's single word punctuated the air.

"Maybe Alan had offended her somehow, and she wanted to go behind his back."

"How did he know her in the first place? Had they met as neighbors?" Brie asked. "Or did they have something going on between them?"

"Brianna, you're not supposed to know about such things!" Dalton gave her a disapproving glare. His statement lost its impact when tomato sauce dribbled down his chin. He dabbed at it with a napkin.

"Don't be a dork, Dad. I know everything. I'm old enough to drive."

"You wish. Anyway, Cherry and Alan were both on the HOA Board."

Marla picked up the thread. "It would have been logical for him to consult her. Cherry must have told Herb about the bones and the results of her preliminary tests. Obviously, the tribal shaman felt she wasn't doing enough, and so he brought his protest to the community to arouse public awareness."

"Did Cherry tell him out of loyalty to the tribe? You said she had Indian blood in her veins." Although addressing Marla, Brie cast a sullen look at her father.

"Could be. Or maybe Cherry wanted to claim credit for the discovery herself." Marla chewed a morsel and swallowed. "Think what a boost it would give her at work. She might even get promoted up the ladder."

"Krabber may have promised her the credit if she kept her mouth shut initially." Dalton speared his last meatball and stuck the whole piece in his mouth.

"But then why would she tell Herb? His little demo rained on her parade."

"There's only one option, Marla." Brie's eyes sparked. "You'll have to talk to Herb yourself and see what he knows."

"No way," Dalton said in a firm tone. "I'll pass this info along to Kat. It's her job to check out new leads."

Yeah, right. My bet is that you get to the guy first.

The next day at work, Marla discussed events with Nicole when they had a lag between clients. She'd cleaned off her chair and counter and stood holding a coffee mug while blow dryers whirred in the background, customers chatted, and water splashed in the shampoo sink. Marla inhaled the hairspray-scented air, enjoying this bustling atmosphere so much more than the garage sale frenzy.

Thank goodness that was over.

"And then the news crew came," she concluded. "It was chaos, but I'll have to say one thing. Sales were great. Cherry couldn't give us a final number yet, but she believes we made a decent profit."

Nicole gave her an indulgent smile. "Now maybe you can relax. I still don't see how you got roped into chairing that thing."

"Oh, you know the saying. Trouble follows me."

"So you think this Herb fellow can clue you in as to what Alan Krabber had discovered in his backyard?"

Marla drained the last of her coffee and put the mug down. "I do, but I don't want to tip Cherry off that I'm speaking to him. How do I find the guy?"

"You said he's a shaman, right? It can't be too hard to look up tribes in the area. If that fails, go visit the casinos. I'd expect he's in the area. It'll just cost you some legwork."

"Like I have the extra time."

"Did the nephew ever hold a memorial service for Krabber?"

"He had the body cremated, and since there weren't any other close relatives, he kept it private."

"Poor man," Nicole said, meaning the victim. "It must be sad to be so alone in your later years."

"Hey, did I tell you our other theory that he might have had a kid?"

Nicole's eyes rounded. "I thought Krabber never married?"

Marla told her about the fiancée. "How could I trace the girl, assuming she's still alive? I mentioned her to Lieutenant Minnetti and suggested that she examine school yearbooks or interview Krabber's old classmates, but I don't know if she followed through or not."

"Krabber might have kept his beloved's correspondence. Ask the nephew if he's come across anything. Once you have her maiden name, you can try looking her up on Facebook."

"Good idea. I'll have to watch for Philip's car next door."

"And you're doing this, why?" Nicole waved to her client who'd just walked in the door.

"To solve the case so Dalton can be put back on his team. I can tell he still resents Minnetti taking over his turf."

"They'll have to learn to get along."

"True, but it won't be easy for either of them."

Marla's next customer arrived, and her thoughts fled as she focused on work-related issues. That afternoon, she finally found time to count inventory. Back in the storeroom, she narrowed her eyes. Something didn't tabulate. Were they missing supplies that had been delivered last week?

She summoned Luis. It took him a good fifteen minutes to walk the gauntlet of customers, flirting with them along his way. He charmed the ladies with his dazzling smile, sexy innuendos, and suggestive body moves. Some of them came to the salon solely to snag the hot Latino's attention. So far, he preferred to play the field and remain unattached.

Facing Marla in the storeroom, he sobered quickly as she related her suspicions.

"I think you're right," he said after confirming her count. He stroked his trim beard. "Maybe we should install a security camera back here. Whoever is guilty will be hard to catch otherwise. She must be taking small items to fit into a purse."

Marla thought of the one stylist who had the largest bag, and her stomach pitted. That would be Dara, who always carried an enormous tote that would qualify as a piece of luggage. The stylist had made more of an effort to be on time lately, but she still mouthed off to the other girls. Marla would need evidence before confronting her, however.

"Please call our alarm company. See if they can install an additional surveillance camera back here. Do the same for the day spa."

"Sure, Marla." Luis shuffled his feet. "Look, I've been meaning to talk to you, but you're always so busy." He cast his gaze on the shelf holding coloring agents.

Lord save me, something says I'm not going to like what's coming next.

"What's this about, Luis? We have time now."

"I'm, uh, officially giving you my two weeks' notice."

"What?" She had thought maybe he'd ask for a raise.

He didn't look at her. "I've been accepted into Broward College for the summer term. It starts in two months, but I want to take some time off and travel."

"Oh. Well, that's wonderful news." *For you, it is. Not so much for me.* She swallowed a lump in her throat. "Our customers will miss you."

"I know. I'll stop by to say hello now and then."

Sure you will. "So you won't consider working part time, once you begin school?" How would he fund the tuition?

"I have money saved up. I'd rather take a heavy load and finish sooner. And if I do have to get a temp job, it would be in the I.T. field where I hope to work someday."

"Of course. I'll let the others know. We'll have to give you a going-away party."

He pumped his fists in the air. "A party, *si!* But I'm sorry to give you such short notice. I'll help find a replacement."

"I'd appreciate that, thanks."

Her cell phone buzzed. She grimaced as she read a text message to call her mother. Now what? Could this day get any more aggravating?

She waited until Luis left before contacting Anita. "What's up, Ma?"

"I don't understand that man. One minute he acts warmer toward me, and then in the next, he snubs me. What am I doing wrong?"

Marla raised her gaze heavenward. "What's Roger done this time?"

"I invited him to spend Passover with us. You know how he joins us for every holiday."

I know how he eats two portions at least. "Sure, so what did he say?" Hopefully, he'd refused, citing a feeble excuse. *Bad Marla. You should tolerate him for your mother's sake.*

"His son's girlfriend invited him to a Seder with her parents."

"For the first night?" That was when Marla planned to have her holiday dinner.

Oops, she'd forgotten about it in the turmoil of the past few days. She slapped a hand to her mouth. Was it too late to invite her cousin's family? Nor had she mentioned the event to Dalton yet.

"Yes, the first night," Anita said. "I already signed up for the Temple Seder on the second night."

"So we'll have one less mouth to feed if Roger doesn't come."

"Marla, that's not nice. This will be the first time he isn't joining us."

"Sorry. It sounds as though Barry's influence is stronger than yours. Maybe you're better off without Roger if he doesn't put your interests first."

"I don't know why I called you expecting a sympathetic ear. I've had a good relationship with him until recently. His sister must have poisoned him against me."

"Why would she do that when you've never met the woman in person?"

"*Ver vaist?* Who knows?"

Marla had her own theories. Barry had courted her at one time, but she'd turned him down in favor of Dalton. Likely, with his new girlfriend, he wanted to distance himself from her. And that meant detaching his father from Anita's strings.

"Ma, Roger isn't worth the effort if he acts inconsistent. You can't rely on him. If it were me, I wouldn't go chasing after him. Let him stew in his own pot for a while." Who knew she'd be advising her mother on relationships?

"We'll see. I don't want to keep you from work. I'll talk to you later."

Marla got busy and was unable to think about Luis, Dara, Herb Poltice, or any of the other things on her mind. That night, she broached the subject of Passover at the dinner table.

"How many people are we talking about?" Dalton asked, seemingly unperturbed about the religious significance of the holiday.

After Marla had counted them off on her fingers, Brianna said, "So that's at least fourteen people."

"We can add a folding table to the dining room set," Marla said.

"I have no objection," Dalton said, "but why don't we invite my folks, too? They've never been to a Seder."

"Do you think they'd want to come? I mean, would they feel awkward celebrating a Jewish holiday?"

"Not if they're included. Besides, you'll have Easter dinner the following weekend, right?" He grinned at her, the adoring look in his eyes melting her heart.

"Sure, if you wish. Our relatives have to get used to us honoring both traditions."

Having passed that hurdle, Marla told them about Luis leaving. "I can't afford to be without a receptionist. It'll be a zoo if we have to take turns manning the front desk."

She started interviewing candidates later that week. While she'd been on the Internet researching Native American tribes in the area, she'd also peeked at job-hunting sites. Plus, Luis had rounded up a few applicants.

The first girl was a walk-in who'd seen the sign in their window advertising the job opening. Marla sat outside with her in the set of chairs in front of the salon. Stacey wore a black bustier and mini-skirt with boots, spiked raven hair, heavy eyeliner, and a silver stud in her lower lip that drew Marla's fascinated gaze. Silver chains dangled from her neck.

"Can you tell me about your job experience?" Marla asked to begin the discussion.

Stacey plopped her hobo handbag on the concrete and crossed her legs. Her mouth worked a piece of gum. "Well, lemme see. I worked as a cashier for a few months, but it got boring. So I switched over to a food market for a while, but I didn't like shelving products. I tried a waitress gig afterward, but that didn't work out."

Marla folded her hands in her lap, reminding herself to be polite. "What are you hoping to gain from this position?"

Stacey gave her a bright smile. "Your place sounds like it could be fun. All I'd have to do is sit behind a desk and answer phones, right?"

"There's more to it than that," Marla said, thinking of the myriad duties Luis performed. "How familiar are you with computers?"

"I use them at the library sometimes. Why? Don't you keep track of things in, like, an appointment book?"

"Our programs are all online these days. Do you have a resumé you could leave with me?"

"Huh? A what?"

Marla winced inwardly. "Leave me your name and phone number, and I'll get back to you if we're interested."

"Oh, sure." The woman reached into her voluminous bag and withdrew a crinkled business card. "Here, I have this. It's from where I lived with my former boyfriend, so the address ain't right. But the phone number is still good."

Marla stood, not even bothering to offer her palm for a handshake.

Another candidate, a brunette, strode up to Marla inside the salon just after she'd finished a cut and blowout.

"Hi, I'm Amanda Stevens."

Marla gave her hand a quick shake. Amanda wore her hair in an attractive style, metal-rimmed eyeglasses on her nose. Marla liked the orchid color of her suit but she seemed a bit overdressed, unless this was one interview of many in her day.

"Let's go outside," Marla suggested, aware of several pairs of eyes glancing their way.

As soon as they were seated, Amanda pulled a stack of papers from her briefcase. "Here's my resumé, as well as details of several projects I completed for my former employer. I'm experienced in handling multiple phone lines, and I'm familiar with Microsoft Office, social networking, and other computer programs. You need someone to be proactive in this role, don't you? Consider me your Girl Friday. I have super organizational skills."

Marla shuffled through the sheaf of papers while a sense of overkill stretched up her spine. "May I ask why you are applying for this position when you're obviously so well qualified?"

"I could get my hair and nails done for free, right? It's not like I can afford these prices on my own. I'm willing to tackle anything." Her face colored. "Well, almost anything. I wouldn't want to sweep hair off the floor. Ugh."

Marla's lips tightened. "Thank you for coming by. I'd like to look these over, and then I'll give you a call back if I'm interested in going further."

Another strikeout, she thought glumly as she pushed open the door to her salon. Luis looked at her hopefully until she gave him a quick shake of her head.

The familiar noises and smells of her salon brought comfort as the afternoon progressed. She was walking to the front to search for her next customer when she spotted a familiar face at one of the nail stations.

"Susan, it's nice to see you again," Marla said to the woman who lived on the other side of Krabber's house.

"Likewise, Marla. I thought I'd try getting a manicure here."

Marla nodded at the technician. "Linnie is one of our best." She shifted feet. "Thanks for taking charge of the toys at the garage sale. I really appreciated your help."

"Oh, you're welcome. We made out great, didn't we?"

"I believe so, although Cherry hasn't tabulated all the results yet."

"No big surprise, since she was so busy talking to that guy from the protest, and then I saw her with Ron Cloakman later." Susan held out her other hand for the manicurist to tend.

Hadn't Gene Uris mentioned his name to Marla? "What business would Cherry have with him?" They had three different builders within the community. Ron was the master planner for the neighborhood. Part of their HOA dues went to his company.

"Something to do with our funds, maybe? As treasurer, Cherry is responsible for the budget."

"I suppose that's possible." Too bad Marla hadn't met the guy.

"Is anything new with our mutual neighbor?"

Marla glanced around to see who was listening besides the nail tech. "It's officially a homicide case. They finally announced it on the news."

"Scary, isn't it? I wish they'd hire our security guard for the daytime, too."

"Dalton would like to get involved on the committee. Maybe you could suggest it to the Board. Gene wasn't too enthusiastic about the idea."

"I'll do that, Marla."

Marla's next client arrived, and she stayed busy until four o'clock when her cell phone buzzed. Dalton had texted her to call him when she had a free moment.

"What's up?" she said, squinting in the afternoon sun. She'd gone outside to make the call in private.

"I have bad news." His deep voice sounded gloomy. "Cherry Hunter is dead."

Chapter Eleven

"Oh, my God. How did that happen?" Marla clapped a hand to her mouth.

"Her body was found inside her garage. She'd been bludgeoned to death."

"That's horrible. Susan Feinberg and I were just talking about her. Who discovered the poor woman?" She thought of Cherry's kids who would be called home from college. How terrible for them.

"The mailman who happened to be walking by and smelled something peculiar."

"No one heard or saw anything?"

Cherry's car headlights would have been on as she parked her vehicle. She could have seen anyone hiding in the garage, so the bad guy must have been waiting in the shadows outside. He'd crept in after she'd parked and rushed her when she came out the driver's door. But then she would have yelled for help, unless it didn't happen that way at all. What if she didn't call out because she knew the killer?

"Did you find the weapon?" Marla forced herself to ask.

"We searched through the tools in the garage but nothing stood out."

"*We?* Are you assigned to the case? Who's your partner?" Numbness claimed her. She kept seeing Cherry's dark hair, unseeing eyes, and painted red mouth open for the bugs to fly in.

"I'm reinstated to my team. The chief feels Cherry Hunter's

death may be related to Krabber's murder and that I can be a valuable asset."

"I'm glad for you, Dalton. It's about time Chief Williams realized you can be useful in that regard." She ran a shaky hand over her face as a couple of young women sidestepped her and proceeded along to Arnie's deli.

"You said you were just talking about the victim?" Dalton's deep voice sharpened her mind and helped her to focus.

"Susan is here getting her nails done. She said she'd seen Cherry talking to Ron Cloakman at the garage sale. Part of our HOA dues goes to his company."

"I vaguely remember noting that in our homeowner's documents. I'll have to check. Didn't you say Hunter could be related to that Indian guy who staged the protest?"

"Yes, but can we discuss this later? My next customer is pulling into a parking space."

"All right. I love you."

"Love you, too."

She stayed mute as she went indoors to prepare for her client. Her tongue itched to tell the news to Susan, but she'd have to wait until the police issued a public report. Sometimes it was tough having insider knowledge, but it came with the territory of being married to a cop. Dalton needed someone to confide in, and she served that purpose.

Maybe she could be more helpful. She'd wanted to talk to Herb Poltice, and now that mission became even more imperative.

The police would be sure to talk to the tribal shaman, especially after his altercation with Cherry and his protest in front of their clubhouse. He could be a person of interest in her death as well as Alan Krabber's. Marla didn't want to spoil their interview, so she'd have to wait until after Lieutenant Minnetti or Dalton spoke to him.

Now that her husband was back on the case, he might become more tight-lipped about their findings. But that didn't mean Marla had to be quiet. If she learned anything new after speaking to Herb herself, she'd pass on the info to Dalton. Likely Herb would only repeat what he told the detectives.

When Sunday rolled around, she broached the subject to Dalton during their morning walk. They'd driven down to Hollywood Beach to stroll the Broadwalk and shop in the organic farmer's market. Brie had gone to a friend's house to work on a school project.

Outside, the temperature had risen to the low seventies and the air was scented with the tang of the sea as they strode along the wide concrete strip bordering the beach. Roller skaters and joggers stuck to their designated lane while people of all ages walked the miles-long trail. One café after another sported customers wolfing down breakfast. Marla's mouth watered as she sniffed the aromas of bacon and coffee. In the near distance, the sun rose at the eastern horizon, casting jeweled sparkles on the water. Peace settled over her soul. While walking here, one could forget about daily concerns.

And that's precisely why she'd suggested they take a walk there today. Dalton could relax, and maybe he'd be more forthcoming about the case. She couldn't turn off her curiosity if she tried.

She brought him up to date on her attempts to find a replacement for Luis, making him laugh with her descriptions of the applicants. Then she segued the conversation toward her discussion with Susan.

"Did you ever speak to Ron Cloakman?" she asked.

"Very briefly." Dalton maintained a brisk pace.

"Where is his office located?" Marla dodged an older couple with a slow gait. She glanced to their left. A yoga class was performing stretches on the beach.

"He's in Miami at Brickell. His company owns multiple real estate holdings."

"Why did he stop by the garage sale? Was it specifically to speak to Cherry?"

"I'll find out on Monday. I'm planning to drive down there to talk to him."

Marla turned her brightest smile on him. "Can I go? I have the day off, and a nice drive would take my mind off things. We could do lunch after you finish your interview."

Well aware of her methods, Dalton gave her a searing glance through his sunglasses. "Kat is going with me. I don't think she'd appreciate having a civilian tag along."

"How about Herb Poltice? Have you spoken to him since Cherry's death?"

Dalton nodded, a lock of hair falling across his forehead. "Kat and I touched base with him. He didn't have much to add to what we already know. We're thinking of bringing him in for questioning."

"Have you found out where he works? I'd never heard of his tribe before." She knew of the Hard Rock Casino in Hollywood and the Miccosukee place on Sample Road. Those were the two main ones in Broward County.

They passed the concert shell on the left where people could come for open-air entertainment. Colorful art deco buildings bordered the walkway on their right. She cast an envious glance at a woman and young girl sitting outside on their own patio eating croissants. This beach was popular with French-speaking Canadian snowbirds who bought seaside condos.

"The Immowakee tribe has a smaller casino further west on Sample," Dalton replied, fast-walking past a slower fellow in Bermuda shorts and his bejeweled wife.

Marla broadened her stride to match his pace. "Oh? I've never heard of one out there. Why don't we swing by this afternoon?"

"It's Sunday. He isn't likely to be there."

"Isn't the casino open twenty-four hours? He might have a shift today. And if not, you can ask around where to find him."

"I don't think so. I'll follow up with Minnetti. You should concentrate on your salon problems and not on my business."

Marla tightened her lips. *Like that's stopped me before.* "Sure, honey. You're absolutely right. I have enough to keep me busy."

Knowing he'd be occupied in Miami the next day prompted her to call her friend Tally later that afternoon. Marla sat in the study with the door closed. Dalton was watching TV, and Brianna was on the landline in her bedroom. Marla intended to track down Herb Poltice and wouldn't mind having a girlfriend along for the ride.

"Hi, Marla. I've been meaning to call you." Tally's voice sounded exuberant.

"Really? I'm wondering if you want to meet me for lunch tomorrow. I'll pick you up at your store, if you can get away from work for a few hours."

"A few hours? Where did you want to go?"

"I'd like to drive to an Indian casino. I'm hoping to talk to the guy who staged the protest at our garage sale." She filled Tally in on recent developments.

"Holy smokes, Marla, you don't quit, do you?"

"It would help Dalton if I can find out more information. I feel awful about Cherry. That man might know something important."

"That's why you should let the detectives do their job. Anyway, I can't get away for that long. If you'd like to go somewhere local, I can meet you."

"It's the only time I have free, sorry." Marla hesitated. "Speaking of work, I'm having shortages of inventory. I told Luis to have surveillance cameras installed. Do you have them in your shop?"

"Not yet, although it's a good idea. With the prices today, I'm not surprised that some people pilfer things. Do you have any idea who might be involved?"

"There's one employee who's always giving me problems, but I'm not sure she's guilty. I don't want to make assumptions. On top of this issue, Luis is leaving. I've been interviewing candidates for a replacement. It's hard to find someone qualified to run our computer programs and who would be happy as a receptionist."

"No kidding. I'll keep my ears open in case I hear of anyone looking for a job."

"Enough about my problems. What's new with you? Are you feeling okay?"

"Oh, sure. Ken and I have been checking out baby supplies. You wouldn't believe the cost of strollers! A good one costs, like, over three hundred dollars."

"No way."

"One baby store sells cribs that convert into twin beds and changing tables that turn into full-size dressers. They're made from good-quality wood and are expensive. I don't want to spend that much! We'd rather get standard baby furniture and then buy a bedroom set later when Luke is old enough."

"Luke? You know you're having a son?" Marla's voice rose. This was noteworthy news.

"We found out on the ultrasound. Ken couldn't stand to wait, although I wouldn't have minded being surprised. This is what I meant to discuss with you. I wouldn't ask it of anyone else, but we've been close friends for so long. Will you give me a baby shower?"

Her jaw dropped. "Why, uh, I'd be honored."

"Don't worry, I'll help you with the plans."

Marla's thoughts collided, and she said the first thing that came to mind. "You'll register for gifts, right, in case people ask me what to get?"

"Of course. I'll pay for it, Marla, since this was my idea. It just doesn't look right for me to hold a shower for myself."

"Don't be silly. I should have thought of it first." Her face heated. If she hadn't been so caught up in sleuthing, she might have been more thoughtful. "Give me some potential dates, and I'll get to work on the arrangements."

"Super. I'm sorry I can't go with you tomorrow. Let me know what happens, and good luck on finding a replacement for Luis. He's a peach."

Marla gave up on her plan to visit Herb at his casino, deciding she should let Dalton and his partner do their job, until her mother called. Ten minutes later, she hung up with a smug smile on her face. Anita had asked Marla to accompany her to the Festival Flea Market on Monday. Marla agreed, if Anita would visit the nearby casino with her beforehand. Marla's mother hadn't needed any convincing to hit the slot machines.

"I wonder what kind of games they have," her mother said in the car on their northbound journey. "I've been to the Hard Rock in Hollywood but never to this place."

Marla kept to her lane on the turnpike. At eleven o'clock on Monday morning, traffic had thinned. "Those machines are beyond me. They're way too confusing."

She'd been to a Seminole casino once, and the flashing lights and general din in the slot machine section had thrown her into sensory overload. She couldn't spare the time to learn the games, including the Florida lottery, nor did she care to waste her hard-earned cash. She'd rather go shopping and have something to show for the expense.

She turned into a wide driveway lined with stately royal palms. At the far end rose a palatial white structure with garish neon signs. Locating the self-parking lot, Marla drove around until she found an empty space. It was crowded for a weekday, but tourists probably came here.

She slung her purse strap over one shoulder and exited the car. Warm air drifted her way, along with the aroma of barbecued meat. Her mouth watered. They'd eat lunch after Marla spoke to Herb Poltice, and then they would head over to the indoor flea market.

A bewildering array of slot machines faced them as they entered the spacious carpeted lobby. Anita wandered off to try her luck while Marla looked for an official to query. Displays of Native American artifacts stood about in glass cases or hung on the walls, properly labeled for the curious viewer. Marla strode past a painting of the Everglades on her way to the cashier. Maybe she could get the info she needed over there. Otherwise, she could always ask the bartender. A bustling bar nestled in the center was trimmed in gleaming brass and rich mahogany. It wasn't too early for the drinkers who sat on cushioned stools.

"Excuse me," she said to the woman behind the cashier's window. "I'm looking for Herb Poltice. He's a tribal shaman, and I've been told he works out of this location."

"Sorry, I'm with the casino staff, honey. You must be looking for administration."

"Are their offices elsewhere?"

"I really don't know. You might ask Tom Fairweather. He's head of security."

"Okay, thanks." Marla searched for someone in authority. For all she knew, these employees might have nothing to do with the Immowakee tribe.

After several more inquiries, she finally located the security chief. He was speaking to a uniformed guard in the doorway to a high-stakes game room.

"Oh, sure," he said upon her introduction. "Herb's office is upstairs. I'll take you there. Is he expecting you?" The man gave her a scrutinizing glance.

"Not exactly. I wasn't sure where to find him, but I need to discuss an important issue with him. We've met before at Royal Oaks."

"Why don't you wait here then, and I'll see if he's available."

"Tell him it's about Cherry Hunter." Marla paced the carpet, hoping her mother was occupying herself. She scanned the patrons at the slot machines but didn't see Anita's head of short white hair.

Her heart thumped in nervous anticipation. Would Herb be present and agree to see her?

Cherry's visage floated into her mind. Marla couldn't believe she was dead. What motive could someone have had to kill her? Was her death related to Alan Krabber's?

Her speculation was cut short when the security man hurried up to her, a look of approval in his eyes. "Herb will see you now, miss. This way, please."

Marla glanced around in awe as she followed the guy through a private door, up a flight of stairs and down a carpeted hallway. Glimpses of offices showed luxurious furnishings, comparable to those downstairs. Undoubtedly, the casino did quite well in terms of income if the elegant administrative wing was any indication.

Herb's sumptuous corner made her gulp in surprise. She hadn't expected a shaman to inhabit such plush surroundings, not when his practice relied on herbal medicine and the spirits to guide him. But what did she know about modern medicine men and their culture?

"Mrs. Vail, isn't it?" He came around the side of his desk to shake her hand.

"Yes, that's right. Thank you for meeting with me."

The security man left them alone, closing the door in his wake. Marla sat opposite Herb's wide mahogany desk, where tiger figurines were placed in various poses. Was that animal his spirit guide? Feathery ornaments decorated the walls along with paintings depicting nature scenes of cypress swamps and long-necked birds.

Seated at his desk, Herb picked up a black ballpoint pen and twirled it in his fingers. His dark eyes examined her from under his thick brows, while she studied the craggy lines creasing his face. He wore an aura of wisdom like a snakeskin—confidence combined with a certain cunning. She wondered how he saw patients if his office was here. Did he make house calls? Where did his people live?

He hunched his wide shoulders, encased in a loose-fitting shirt appropriate to the tropical climate. Putting the pen down, he folded his hands on the desk.

"So what brings you here, Mrs. Vail?"

Marla crossed her legs. "I presume you heard about Cherry?" She kept her tone noncommittal, watching for his reaction.

His eyes hardened. "Yes, I've spoken to the police."

"We were friends, and I'm trying to figure out who might have wanted to harm her. You seemed to have had an intimate discussion with her at our garage sale."

"That's right. She knew about the sacrilege and should have stopped it."

"You mentioned bones. Did she discover an ancestral burial site? I imagine that would be a boon to her career as a history professor." By pretending to know something about Cherry's affairs, Marla might get him to reveal significant information.

"So she hoped. He told her to keep quiet about it, but she couldn't help boasting about her claim to me. She should have known I'd urge her to do the right thing."

"*He* told her to keep quiet? Who do you mean?"

"Alan Krabber, of course. He's the one who asked Cherry to authenticate the find. When she agreed, he demanded her silence in return for promising that she could take credit for the discovery. At least he halted construction."

Marla's mind whirled. "So Alan *did* discover bones in his backyard when workers were digging a hole for his propane tank?"

"I thought you knew that." He assessed her with a suspicious gaze.

"I wasn't sure if he'd made the discovery or if it had been his workmen." She moistened her lips, uneasy under his scrutiny. "Both Cherry and Alan skirted regulations. They should have notified local law enforcement about the find. Why didn't you?"

"I'd hoped to convince Cherry to come forward, but she wanted me to be the one to rat on Alan."

"Why was that?"

"If you were truly her friend, you would know." Herb swept a hand over his wide forehead. He wore his longish black hair brushed off his face and tied into a low ponytail.

Marla sat upright. "I understand Cherry had a love–hate relationship with Alan. She'd been attracted to him at one time, but he turned her down."

"She always resented him after that, but couldn't turn against him. Telling me about his discovery was her way of getting back at him. She promised him she wouldn't tell the authorities, but didn't say anything about revealing his secret to me."

"Are the two of you related?"

"We're distant cousins."

"Did Cherry have any other extended family in the area?"

He shook his head, fingering a glass paperweight on his desk. "Cherry didn't embrace her heritage. She studied us like we were bacteria on a Petri dish. Our culture fascinated her but she didn't include herself as a member."

"She must have respected your beliefs if she taught others about them?"

"I believe she did, in her heart. But this dishonor for the spirits has cost her life. Now she is one of them." A sad, haunted expression crossed his face. "I pray for her to gain the peace she sought in this existence. I pray for the spirits to accept and forgive her."

"Do you think someone killed her and Alan Krabber because of the bones?"

"That's for the detectives to determine."

"Who do you suspect?"

He steepled his hands and leaned back in his chair. "You live in Royal Oaks. Who stands to lose the most if the neighborhood gets put under a microscope?" His dark gaze swept toward her as she sought a logical response.

"I don't know. The builders?"

"Good answer. This find could be as significant as the Miami Circle."

"What's that?"

"It's an archaeological site discovered in 1998 and believed to be nearly two thousand years old. A perfect circle is cut into the limestone bedrock."

Marla thought of crop circles mysteriously found in fields out west, presumed by some to be alien landing sites. "Who put it there?"

"Possibly the Tequesta. They were one of the first natives whom Ponce de León encountered when he set foot in Florida."

"How was the Circle unveiled?"

"An apartment complex stood on the property. A new buyer tore it down, planning to build a luxury condo building. According to Miami's historic preservation code, he had to conduct an archaeological field survey before starting construction. The excavation revealed a series of twenty-four holes arranged in a circle and cut into the limestone. They uncovered numerous artifacts as well."

"So what happened?"

"The developer wanted to relocate the circle and continue construction. Preservationists filed a lawsuit to stop further activity. Their injunction was denied, but the builder agreed to wait until the archeologists finished their work. In the meantime, the Miami–Dade County Commission filed a lawsuit to take ownership of the property. The developer agreed to sell and ended up making a profit on the deal."

"Sounds like it worked out well for everyone involved."

Herb's lips spread in a half-smile. "The developer got paid off in 1999. By 2002, the site was listed on the National Register of Historic Places."

Marla shifted her position. "This is fascinating, but what does it have to do with Alan Krabber?"

"Similar regulations apply. Any site with human remains has to be examined by an archeological team."

"Was the Miami Circle a burial site?"

"No evidence was found to that effect. The holes were believed to hold posts supporting a structure on stilts, possibly a religious building."

"So what's there now?"

"It's a park. The circle itself lies buried."

"Do you think Alan shared his find with anyone else besides Cherry?"

Herb's eyes gleamed with a peculiar light. "Oh, I know he did."

Before Marla could ask another question, a knock sounded on the door and it pushed open. "Sorry to intrude, shaman, but a guest isn't feeling well. We need you downstairs," said a man wearing a casino logo shirt.

"I'll be right there." Herb shoved his chair back and stood. "Mrs. Vail, I hope you have a better understanding of how vital it is to preserve our history and the memories of our ancestors.

Our tribe isn't as renowned as others. This will help us gain recognition."

Along with some federal grants, perhaps? What was in it for him and his tribe, exactly?

"Here's my card in case you think of anything else," she said, rising. "I appreciate our little chat, Herb."

He took her business card and dropped it on his desk. Then he collected a suede sack from a cabinet and hefted it over his shoulder.

"I can show you the way back to the bingo hall, if you wish." Stepping toward the door, Herb allowed her to precede him into the hallway.

"My mother is playing the slot machines."

"I thought you came with Angela."

She rounded on him. "Angela Goodhart? Why, is she here?"

"She's a regular player. I figured you must have driven here together."

The fellow who'd come for Herb tugged on his sleeve. "Will you please hurry? We don't want a fiasco like the last time when someone got sick and you weren't around."

"I'm on my way, aren't I?" Herb hustled along beside Marla. "I hope you'll spread the word about our burial ground. We regretted having to disrupt your garage sale, but it's our duty to ensure proper respect for the ancestral spirits."

He spoke in a loud tone, making Marla wonder about his status in the tribe. Did he hope this discovery would boost his personal clout? What fiasco had the other guy referred to that involved Herb?

Wishing she knew more about tribal politics, she hastened downstairs. Herb led her past the bingo hall, where a glass wall allowed her to peer inside. Sure enough, she spotted Angela, head bent, eyes focused on her playing cards.

Herb knew about her neighbor's presence here. Were they

more than casually acquainted? Was Angela the person Herb had been about to name earlier, the other person to whom Alan had related his discovery?

Marla's head spun with possibilities. Shaking away the labyrinth of her thoughts, she hastened forward to collect her mother.

Chapter Twelve

"I'm worried about our investment in this house," Marla said to Dalton later that evening in their bedroom. "What if Herb's tribe presses the government to take back our land? We're right next door to a potential historical site."

He'd just emerged from the shower. Wearing boxers, he towel-dried his hair. Marla's fingers itched for a blow dryer and hairbrush. Her gaze roamed to his broad shoulders, and her body stirred. She'd never tire of admiring his virile form. He sported hard muscles, unlike her ex-spouse Stan, whose softness had been the price for sitting in a law office all day.

"I doubt anything that drastic would happen," Dalton said. "Herb's people might petition for a memorial park to be built somewhere in the development." He glowered at her, but the effect was lost as she apprised him in his underwear.

Marla offered a wicked grin in return and sashayed closer. She'd put on a silk nightgown. Her heart rate accelerated at the flare of interest in his eyes.

"This could hurt business for the developer. How did your interview go today with Ron Cloakman?" She'd been dying to ask, and this presented the perfect opening.

"He's fairly confident that he could stop any attempt at an injunction."

"But what if the entire site is riddled with bones? Herb might want to get the property declared a National Historic Landmark, depending on what the archeologists uncover."

"I doubt the range is that extensive, but the issue could easily end up in court."

"I'm sure Herb will press the issue." She hesitated. "I spoke to him today, and he seems to be using this discovery to further his personal agenda with the tribe."

Dalton dropped his towel and stepped toward her. "You did what?"

She raised a hand. "Don't get upset. Ma wanted to go to the Festival Flea Market so we stopped off at the casino first. She had a good time playing the slots. Herb happened to be available, and we had a little chat."

"Marla, I warned you against interfering in my investigation. The last thing I want is for Kat to view you as a meddling wife."

"You know I've given you valuable information over the years. People say things to me that they're afraid to reveal to the cops."

"I may understand as much, but Kat sure as hell wouldn't see it that way."

"Well, I'm so sorry that her opinion counts more than mine." Marla drew back the comforter on her side of the bed.

"Hey, I'm the one who's sorry. I didn't mean to sound harsh." He approached and turned her around, peering down at her with contrite eyes.

She sniffed his clean soap scent and her tension ebbed. "I want to help, that's all."

"I know, sweetcakes." His tone softened. "So what did you learn?"

"I got a hint that Herb is in disfavor with his tribe. He's going to play this matter for all it is worth to gain stature in the eyes of his colleagues."

"We know he's distantly related to Cherry Hunter, and they were seen talking together at the garage sale. Did he say anything about her death?"

Marla nodded, her skin tingling where he stroked her arm. "Alan did consult Cherry about the bones he dug up in his backyard. In return for confirming their historical value, she wanted credit at the university for the find. But she wasn't about to keep quiet. Angry at Alan for spurning her in the past, she told Herb about the bones. Herb indicated that Alan might have revealed his secret to someone else."

"Did Herb say who it was?"

"No, and at first, I thought it might be Angela. Did you know she plays bingo at his casino? Anyway, now I'm thinking Alan must have told Ron Cloakman. Susan spotted him at the garage sale speaking to Cherry. It stands to reason Alan approached the man. Ron's revenue might be adversely affected by an injunction." She sucked in a sharp breath. "What if Alan blackmailed the guy in return for his silence?"

"That's a distinct possibility. Cloakman denied any role in either of the murders, though. But then again, they all do." His mouth curved in a cynical smile.

"Ron's company would stand to lose millions if the government intervened. Or, if they purchased the land like the Miami Circle, Ron could profit same as the guy who owned that property." Marla explained about the site further south. "But here's the thing—why was Cherry talking to Ron? Did he know about her role?"

"Cloakman is definitely a person of interest." Dalton's fingers trailed toward her neck and dipped into her cleavage. "Anyway, can we put these problems aside for now?"

She lifted her face. "Sure, what did you have in mind?"

"This." He lowered his head and kissed her.

Marla pushed away her deliberations until she was walking the dogs the next morning before work. Dalton had already left the house and Brie had caught the school bus. A sense of peace settled over her as she strode down the sidewalk, admiring the sculpted landscaping at the neighboring houses and the fresh scent of spring. The air was delightfully cool for a stroll. As she passed an empty lot, she wondered what would happen to their community.

Ron Cloakman wouldn't be the only person affected if construction had to stop. The three builders involved would also take a hit. And what about the fiasco with defective windows? Which builder had contracted with the supplier, who happened to be a cousin of Alan Krabber? Was Beamis Woodhouse to blame for the problem?

She was so lost in thought that she didn't notice Angela pruning her shrubs until she walked past and Angela hailed her.

"Hello, Marla." Angela straightened from trimming a bougainvillea bush, her face red with exertion.

Marla reined in the dogs. She didn't want them doing their thing on the woman's lawn. "Hi, Angela. I saw you at the casino the other day."

Angela's eyebrows lifted. "Oh?"

"I was visiting Herb Poltice to discuss the protest he'd staged at our garage sale. I didn't know you played bingo."

"It's a hobby of mine. I go twice a week. It gets me out of the house." Her eyes scrunched. "What did Herb say?"

"Alan had dug up some bones in his backyard and asked Cherry to authenticate them. Cherry believed the remains might belong to their tribe. Herb is a distant cousin."

Angela's mouth formed an *O*. "You don't say? Bones, is it? Not recent ones, I presume."

"Cherry was an expert on Native American cultures. That's why Alan consulted her to verify his find."

"That woman had no business interfering."

Now it was Marla's turn to stare in surprise. The sun hit her eyes. She should have worn sunglasses. "What do you mean?"

"Cherry got involved in too many things. Look at the terrible price she paid."

"She was seen talking to Ron Cloakman at the garage sale. Do you know what that was about?"

"Likely it had to do with her role as treasurer. She was responsible for sending our dues over to the master corporation. Someone should have a talk with that man. If anyone had a motive to kill Alan and Cherry, he'd be the person I'd suspect."

"Dalton has interviewed Ron, but so far he hasn't reached any conclusions." The dogs tugged on their leashes, and Marla moved forward a few feet. "I need to get going. Nice seeing you again."

Angela pointed at her. "There's still hope for you, Marla. I can help."

Uh, oh. She'd better pretend ignorance. "I have no idea what you mean."

"The time is almost here. You'll be left behind if you don't embrace Him."

"Ah, thanks. I'll keep that in mind." She bit back the retort searing her tongue and hurried on.

What was wrong with Angela? Maybe her relationship with Alan hadn't been intimate in the carnal sense like someone had suggested. Maybe they had belonged to the same evangelical church.

Not wanting to go there, Marla focused instead on Angela's remark about Cherry and Ron. Had they been discussing the burial site, or something relating to the HOA? Maybe Cherry had discovered that Ron knew about the bones, and she was arguing her case for taking credit. He could have been imploring her to keep silent. Or maybe he'd offered to pay her off.

She should tell Dalton about these theories. But then again, he'd already interviewed the real estate developer.

She'd really like to talk to Ron Cloakman, who might have not wished to air his dirty laundry in front of Dalton and Kat.

But how could she see him without driving all the way to Brickell in Miami?

During a break at work later that day, Marla phoned his office. As she'd hoped, a secretary answered the phone. Marla never did understand why that moniker had gone out of style. Today people were receptionists or administrative assistants.

"I need to talk to Mr. Cloakman about his Royal Oaks development. I'm in Palm Haven, and I hate to drive into Miami with the traffic on I-95," Marla said in a coy tone. "Will he be coming to Broward any time soon?"

"Actually, he's giving a presentation to the county commission on Thursday morning. Shall I pencil you in for an appointment while he's there?"

"Sure, I can pop over to see him. Where exactly is this meeting?"

"Downtown in Fort Lauderdale. Your name, please? I'll notify him to expect you."

Marla gritted her teeth. "Downtown where? At the county courthouse?"

The assistant shuffled papers in the background. "I'm sorry, but I can't be more specific unless you identify yourself."

Look on your caller I.D., lady. The woman couldn't be that brainless, could she? It's the first thing Marla would have done.

"Never mind," Marla said, scratching her arm. "I'll make my own arrangements."

Did a mosquito just bite her? With the front door opening and closing on clients all day, she couldn't keep insects from getting inside the salon.

Marla tucked her cell phone away and frowned at the shelves in the storeroom, where she'd gone to make her call. Had things been shifted around?

Her next client arrived before she could investigate.

It wasn't until Wednesday night that she spared the time to

look up public hearings on the computer. Cross-referencing with Cloakman's company website allowed her to find a commission hearing downtown in Fort Lauderdale at nine-thirty the next morning. That was perfect. Thursdays were her late day at work, and she didn't have her first customer coming in until one o'clock. She'd planned to get in early to consult Luis about the inventory, but it could wait. This might be her only chance to meet the developer.

She caught him on Thursday just after eleven as he walked out of a government building. He carried a leather briefcase and wore a harried air. Marla identified him from his photo on the Internet. The man had silver hair neatly combed back from a wide forehead, steel gray eyes, and quarterback-wide shoulders.

"Mr. Cloakman? I'm Marla Vail." She grinned and stuck out her hand.

He glanced over her attire, a skirt and silky top with a strand of matching beads and earrings. She'd gone to pains to appear professional, as though she were one of the governmental minions scurrying about the courthouses. Business culture downtown, while more laidback than up north, was still dressier than elsewhere in Broward.

He shook her hand with obvious reluctance. "Have we met?" He surveyed her, his eyes matching the slate gray of his vested suit.

"Um, not quite, although I saw you at a distance the other day. I live in Royal Oaks."

His gaze darkened and his lips pressed together. "If this is about those windows—"

"No, it's not." She strode beside him as he headed toward the parking lot. A gusty breeze blew her skirt about her legs. The air smelled from car fumes and refuse. "I want to talk to you about Cherry Hunter."

He halted, looking chagrined. "Poor woman. I can't imagine who would hurt her."

"A neighbor saw you speaking to her at our rummage sale. Did you come all the way from Miami just to see her that day?"

He resumed his walk. "What business is it of yours?"

"I'm married to Detective Dalton Vail. We live next door to Alan Krabber's house."

"I told the cops everything I know."

"Really? Alan informed you about the bones he uncovered in his backyard. Did he also tell you he'd consulted Cherry about them?"

He shot her a startled glance but quickly washed an impassive expression over his face. From his beginning jowls and mature crease lines, she'd put him in his early fifties. His shoulders raised and fell in a shrug meant to show his disinterest.

"What about it? The police know about the discovery."

"Now they do, but you would have had reason to keep the news quiet before then."

"Of course I'm upset that construction in Royal Oaks has to wait until an archeological team investigates. I'll lose money in the process. But that's the law when human remains are found."

"Is that what you told Alan when he confided in you?"

"Look, Mrs. Vail, I don't know where this is going, but it doesn't seem to be any true concern of yours. Why don't you let your husband do his job?"

He stopped in the parking lot beside a black Lexus and clicked open the door with his remote. Opening the passenger side, he tossed his briefcase onto the leather upholstery.

Marla tried a last tactic as he shut the door and strode toward the driver's side. "Why did you come to see Cherry that day? Had you heard about the protest?"

Cloakman rounded on her. "I wasn't happy about that, but

no, it wasn't the reason why I needed to see her. If you must know, my accounting department noticed some irregularities in our payments from the Association. The percentage of income didn't tally with the number of units sold. Cherry Hunter was responsible for making those payments to our parent company."

"What are you saying?" She kept her voice on an even keel.

"Miss Hunter may have been diverting funds. I didn't say anything about this to the detectives because it's only speculation. I am hoping you won't go and spread rumors. But maybe you can be useful."

She became aware that they were very much alone in this spot. A mahogany tree provided shade while she stood her ground.

"How so?" She shifted her handbag, resisting the urge to glance around for other people. If he shoved her inside his car, no one would notice.

"Two members of your community are dead," he said. "Despite what you might think, I had nothing to do with their deaths. But since this involves the HOA, it concerns me. I don't want any further taint on our property than what's already there with this Indian mess."

Oh, it's all about you, is it? I'll bet you don't even care about the victims.

"So what is it you want me to do?"

"Put a bee in your husband's ear to investigate the other members of the Board. My accounting team will be tracing the funds from our end. Something isn't right."

"Dalton and his partner are already checking into everyone's background." Including yours, she added silently.

Cloakman opened his driver's door and hesitated before ducking inside. "He might want to take a closer look at the HOA's books."

After buying more time from the parking meter, Marla called

a friend who lived in the area. Fortunately, Wendy was free for lunch and they met at Mango's. Thus she had an excuse later that night when speaking to Dalton about the encounter.

"You'll never guess who I ran into downtown when I was having lunch with Wendy."

She plopped down beside him on the sofa in the family room, where he sat flipping between TV channels on the remote. He smelled of fresh soap, having just come from the shower. Marla tapped his arm.

"Ron Cloakman. Imagine! I gathered he had business in Fort Lauderdale."

Dalton's mouth twisted in a wry grin. "And of course, you couldn't resist probing him about the murder cases."

"Naturally, why pass up such a good opportunity?"

"Spill it, Marla. What did you learn?"

"Ron said he didn't kill them."

"So say most murderers. He still has one of the best motives, and he can't provide a solid alibi for the night Krabber was hanged."

"Ron is well aware of the laws regarding discovery of human remains. An injunction against further construction would mean less income for his company. Maybe he was guilty of paying hush money to Alan, but that doesn't mean he murdered the guy. Ron suggested you should take a closer look at the HOA's bookkeeping practices."

"Why is that?" Dalton switched to a station reporting a drop in stock values and grimaced.

"Something doesn't jive regarding the percentage his company is receiving. Cherry would have been responsible for payments to the master corporation."

"Maybe Cherry was dipping her fingers into the pot."

"And maybe Alan found out. She killed him, and then . . . what?"

"Exactly. Why was Hunter killed? It's too much of a coincidence that two Board members from the same community ended up dead without their murders being connected."

"Maybe Ron Cloakman is just trying to throw suspicion off himself, and there's nothing wrong with the bookkeeping."

"That's always a possibility," Dalton said in a noncommittal tone.

She jabbed him. "Do you know something I don't?"

He put the remote on the coffee table. "Well, there's still the faulty window issue, plus the contractor bids for a new playground. Any one of those matters could play into the case."

"You'll put the pieces together. You always do. Did you ever find out what medication Alan took the night he died?"

"He had an elevated level of diphenhydramine, a common antihistamine, plus codeine. And he'd ingested alcohol, likely with dinner. Remnants of a meal were in his stomach. The man had a sweet tooth judging from the cake in there."

"Ugh. I can do without that image, thanks. I suppose you looked for cold, cough or allergy medicines in his bathroom?"

"He had some prescription bottles in his medicine cabinet, but they were nearly full."

"Still, that combination of drugs would have made him drowsy."

"It's not unusual for suicides to take pills or alcohol before they do the deed."

"And then he hanged himself? Maybe someone else slipped him the drugs, knowing he'd have his favorite cocktail with dinner."

"That's a distinct possibility, and it's one we are definitely considering." Dalton raked her over with a slow, sexy smile that derailed her thoughts. "How are things going at the salon? Did you take care of your issues?"

"Dara continues to cast a pall on the place with her rude

behavior, yet I hate to lose her clients. For some reason, they follow her like sheep. The woman is skilled, I have to admit. But the disharmony she causes makes me think it's not worth keeping her."

"It's always hard to let someone go."

"Tell me about it. I think she may be responsible for pilfering our supplies. It could be her way of getting back at me for reprimanding her."

"Did you get the surveillance cameras installed?"

Marla nodded, wishing their Board members would listen to his ideas on security as well. "Luis is taking care of it. We should have full coverage throughout the salon then. Lord save me, what will I do without him?"

"You still haven't found a replacement?"

"Nope. Finding a receptionist isn't as hard as finding someone with his computer skills. Most people with those qualifications don't want to work in a salon."

"Keep at it. You'll discover the right person."

She grinned at him, glowing in the warmth of his faith. "I found you, didn't I? What could be better?" And she devoted the rest of the evening to showing him her gratitude.

Chapter Thirteen

On Monday morning, Marla detoured by the community clubhouse to hand in their monthly HOA payment.

Angela's words from their last encounter flared in her mind as she entered the office. Did that woman share Alan's bigoted beliefs? Marla had meant to sound out other neighbors, but she'd been too busy over the weekend to think about Alan Krabber or Cherry Hunter, and Dalton had avoided the topic except to point out the nephew's car on Sunday. The poor man must be sorting through Alan's things, she'd surmised.

"We don't need a manager." Debbie Morris's strident tone reached Marla as she entered the clubhouse.

The office was directly to her right. On her left was a small room that served as a library and conference room. Straight ahead was the meeting/party room with its wood-planked dance floor, raised stage, and adjacent kitchen area. The space looked a lot less cluttered than during the garage sale.

"It was always our plan to hire a management company," Gene Uris said from the inner office. "We're almost built out enough."

Marla paused just inside the entrance, hesitant to disrupt their conversation.

"It's unnecessary for a community this size. Why go to the expense when I can be here? That's my job as secretary."

"You don't get paid for this voluntary position. Plus, it takes time away from your commitments as a real estate agent.

Wouldn't you rather have the free hours and not be stuck here three mornings a week?"

"We'd have to change our lockbox agreement. It would mess up the record keeping."

"Hiring a manager would ease things for all of us. John Hardington has stepped up as treasurer until we hold elections. I'll ask his opinion."

"Oh, and mine doesn't count? Listen Gene, I know what you're doing with the playground bids. You need to let me keep my job."

"You'll still be secretary. That won't go away."

"You know what I mean. If you hire a manager, he'll examine the budget and look for ways to cut expenses."

"That would reduce our monthly dues. This community is getting too big for us to handle on our own."

"Says who? Are you afraid of Ron Cloakman, is that it? Do you hope to create some smoke for your deal?"

"Be quiet, Debbie. You don't know what you're talking about."

"Oh, I know very well. I'll bet you have things all sewn up with Erik Mansfield."

"I don't care for your insinuations." Gene's tone edged with anger. "Watch what you say, or I might call for an audit. You wouldn't like that very much, would you?"

Erik Mansfield? Wasn't he the man with whom Gene was having lunch the other day at the restaurant on the Intracoastal? Marla backtracked so as to make a noisier entrance. Gene peeked out in response to her rap on the door.

"Oh, it's you," he said. "I was just leaving. Debbie, we'll talk more about this later. I have to go to work."

After he left, Marla handed over her check to the association secretary. "Here's our April payment. Sorry it's late, but I got busy with our daughter's birthday and forgot to turn it in."

"You're still within the grace period, so don't worry. How are things?"

"Good, thanks, except I was shocked to hear about Cherry Hunter. Her death must be another blow to the Board. I'm so sorry."

Debbie bent her head, a lock of strawberry-blond hair falling forward. "It's unbelievable. I'm beginning to think we're cursed."

"We are, if you listen to Herb Poltice. He's the guy who staged the protest at our garage sale."

"Oh, Lord. That was a nightmare."

"What's happening with the development in regard to a potential archaeological site?" Marla asked with wide-eyed innocence.

Debbie lifted her gaze to meet Marla's. "Further construction is halted for now. I don't know what will happen. I can't believe Alan didn't come forward with this news instead of keeping it to himself."

"He told Cherry about it. I suppose he wanted to make sure those were human remains and not animal bones before he called in the authorities."

"How did he even know the bones were old and not recent? Alan should have gone through proper channels."

"That's true." Marla shifted her purse to her other shoulder. "So Gene is acting president now, right? I understand he has an interest in getting the new playground built. Won't that project also be affected by a construction delay?"

"I suppose, but that might be beneficial. It's going to cost us a special assessment. We need to know how much so we can send out a letter to residents."

"Doesn't the cost depend on which bid we accept?"

"Gene means to give the job to Erik Mansfield's company so he can get a kickback." Debbie slapped a hand to her mouth.

"Oh, gosh. Don't tell anyone I said that."

Marla lowered her voice. "I heard him mention hiring a management company. Wouldn't an outside firm examine our financial records?"

"Sure," Debbie said in a wary tone. "Why?"

"Well, if they discover any discrepancies, they'll be sure to report them."

"I'm not sure I understand."

Marla leaned forward, her hands on the desk. "I spoke to Ron Cloakman. He hinted that something isn't right in the association's books."

Debbie's face paled. "Is that so? I wonder where he gets his information. Maybe you should ask Cherry, our treasurer. Oh wait, she's dead."

That's a bit harsh, pal. "Cherry would have been responsible for keeping track of dues payments, right?"

"Yes, I just collect the checks. It's not my job to do the entries into the books."

"Don't our payments go to some lockbox in Tampa? I was under the impression that you sent our checks there and they make the deposits."

Debbie's lips pursed. "Just so."

"And it was Cherry who made this arrangement? Why don't residents mail their payments directly to the lockbox instead of going through you?"

"It's easier to send them bundled together." Debbie shoved her chair back. "Listen, Marla, I have work to do. It takes time out of my own schedule to be here, and I don't get paid for these hours."

"All right, I have some errands to run anyway. Nice talking to you, Debbie."

As Marla headed for the front door, Robyn Piper breezed inside. The brunette paused upon spotting her.

"Hey Marla, how's it going?" Robyn brushed her hair off her face. The marketing executive wore designer sunglasses and carried a Michael Kors bag.

"I'm great, thanks. And you?"

"Not so good, actually."

"Oh? What's happened?" A flush of guilt assailed her. Marla had been meaning to call Robyn. She felt the two of them would click. Sometimes you could tell when you met a person that you were on the same page, and Robyn struck her as the goal-directed type.

"My position got eliminated. I'm getting laid off."

"That's awful! I'm so sorry. What will you do?"

"Hold on a second while I turn in my dues. I almost forgot about it." A moment later, Robyn returned. She pushed her sunglasses further up on her nose.

They walked out together. Already the sun had warmed the morning air, but at least the humidity was low. Marla rummaged in her bag for her own shades and took out her car key as well. She beeped the remote.

"I'm not sure where I want to look for another job," Robyn said. She wore skinny black jeans and a cranberry top. "I'm tired of the usual frenetic pace. Fortunately, my mother left me an inheritance, so I have a decent income that covers the mortgage."

"You're lucky in that regard." *More so than most people.* A germ of an idea made her pulse race. "Say, can I buy you a cup of coffee, or are you in a rush to get to work?"

"Like I care if I'm late. Let's go to Starbucks. I'll meet you there."

Ten minutes later, they sat across from each other and nursed cups of strong-brewed coffee. Marla savored the aroma, sipping carefully so as not to burn her tongue.

"I'll have to update my resumé," Robyn said. "It's been a

while since I've gone on job interviews. I hate the process."

"Where will you start?" Marla surveyed her new friend's narrow face and straight cut hair. Robyn could use an update to her hairstyle as well.

"I'll check out sites online."

"Will you stay in the area or consider a move?"

"I don't want to relocate, but I need to make enough money to cover living expenses, plus taxes and insurance. Hopefully, I'd still have some left over to save for retirement, not to mention vacations." Robyn's shoulders slumped.

"How are your computer skills? Are you familiar with social networking sites?"

"Sure, who isn't? It's essential today to know that stuff." Robyn grinned, and it transformed her face into a younger, more energetic person; someone she could be under the right circumstances.

Marla noted her chin and the angles of her face. A layered cut and shorter length would do wonders for her.

"I have an idea. It's not your field and it won't pay nearly as much as you're expecting, but I'm looking for a receptionist. It involves more than just answering phones. I need somebody who can manage everyone's schedules, update our websites, design ads, connect with other merchants in the area, and help with special events. Believe it or not, I'm having trouble finding qualified applicants."

Robyn gripped her coffee mug. "That's not quite what I had in mind."

"I understand, but maybe you know someone who might be interested."

"Do you need this person right away?"

"Luis still has another week to go, and then my stylists will have to take turns manning the front desk until we hire someone."

"I'll think about it." Robyn fingered her hair. "I've been meaning to change my style. Maybe I should make an appointment to come in and I can check out the place while I'm there."

"That sounds great. I'll give you a discount as a first-timer."

Robyn gathered her purse. "Thanks for the coffee, Marla. I've got to run. I'll be in touch."

Oh, crap. Marla had forgotten her other purpose in inviting Robyn to chat. She'd wanted to inquire about their association Board members. Now she'd have to think of another way to coax information from her neighbors.

That opportunity came when she ran into Gene Uris at the grocery store on Tuesday afternoon. The bearded director was pushing his shopping cart down the health food aisle.

Marla trundled up to him, ostensibly searching for her favorite brand of cranberry juice. "Hey, Gene," she said with a wave. She put a couple of juice bottles in her cart.

Recognition flared in his expression before a look of displeasure crossed his face. "Mrs. Vail. How nice to see you." His flat tone said the opposite.

A mother pushed by, her toddler wiggling his legs in the shopping cart made up to look like a cartoon car. Marla sidestepped around them.

"I'm wondering if there's going to be an election soon?" she asked in a cheery voice. "I mean, we have two Board positions vacant. Or do we only hold elections once a year?"

He drew back his lips, showing his large front teeth. "Our bylaws account for successions in the event a director's chair is vacant. Since I've become acting president, a volunteer has filled my prior spot as veep, and John Hardington has stepped in as treasurer. We won't have to hold elections until the regular time next year."

"But we just had the annual meeting. Isn't that a long time to wait?"

"Not necessarily. We'll see how it goes. An interim election may be held but then you've got the ballot printing and mail-outs. It gets expensive."

You don't seem worried about expenses where the playground is concerned.

"I see. Speaking of the treasurer's position, I've heard rumors about our bookkeeping practices. Has there been an audit in recent times?"

His eyes bulged. "What have you been hearing, and from whom?"

She shrugged. "I have a reliable source. This person believes the master corporation should be getting more income based on our dues. Debbie collects the checks every month, right? And it's her job to record each payment and send the checks to the lockbox?"

"That's right. Debbie set up the lockbox arrangement. She's the one who recommended the financial company to the Board."

"Debbie did so, and not Cherry?" The secretary had let Marla assume otherwise. "Why can't residents make deposits directly into this account?"

"You'd have to ask Debbie. This set-up seemed efficient when she presented it to us. It saves time for our treasurer." He glanced down the aisle as though eager to escape.

"You're telling me Cherry didn't enter into the equation at all?"

"Oh, sure she did. She'd get a report from the financial company every month."

"Let me see if I've got this straight. Debbie accepts the checks each month. She mails them to the lockbox. The financial company deposits them and then sends a report back to Cherry." She gulped at her mistake. "Or the report goes to the acting treasurer."

"Correct." He selected a nonfat plain soy milk carton and

put it in his cart. "I don't know how Debbie manages. Between her three kids and her sick sister, she has her hands full. Our Board positions are voluntary, mind you. There's no compensation."

None that's evident, Mr. Acting President.

Did Ron Cloakman suspect Cherry was cooking the books? Was that why he'd confronted the treasurer at the garage sale? If so, he appeared to be barking up the wrong tree.

Gene knew it, too. She recalled his exchange with Debbie. Were they protecting each other's secrets?

Later on at dinner, she related her news to Dalton and Brianna.

"Do you think Cherry suspected Debbie of embezzling funds, and Debbie killed her to shut her up?" She forked a salmon cake—or a croquette, as Anita called it—onto her plate, followed by a heap of spaghetti and tomato sauce.

"We've examined the Board members' bank accounts," Dalton said between bites. "Debbie Morris has some hefty expenses."

"I'd imagine so, with her family obligations. Does she have any unexplained income?"

"There's one paper trail we're following. I'm expecting Kat to call with the results. So far, I'm putting my bet on Ron Cloakman as the killer. He has the potential to lose thousands of dollars with construction shut down."

"What about the builders, Dad? Won't they be affected as well?" Brianna had been listening intently.

"They haven't invested as much as Cloakman. That reminds me, I want to interview Beamis Woodhouse, the guy who supplied the leaky windows, to assess his role in this game."

"Isn't he a cousin of the dead guy?" Brie asked, reaching for another salmon cake. She studiously avoided the freshly cooked broccoli.

"That's right," Marla said. "He's tangled up in this somehow. Alan was trying to get him to replace the windows. If I recall, Gene would rather bypass him and get bids from other companies."

"That doesn't make sense if he's responsible."

"Beamis denies it's his fault. He could just be a middleman for the manufacturer."

"Or he could have bought a cheaper product than specified in his contracts, in which case he cheated on the builders," Dalton suggested.

Brie jabbed her finger in the air, her face intent. "Maybe Mr. Krabber found out and threatened to expose this guy to the licensing bureau."

The dogs had been roaming at their feet. They suddenly raced to the other side of the house and started barking.

Dalton wandered off to investigate. "I didn't see anybody walking by outside," he said upon his return. "Must have been a squirrel."

"We really have to get our yard fenced in." Marla took her empty dish to the sink. "Lucky and Spooks need the freedom to run around back there."

Dalton added his plate to the dirty pile. "What are we waiting for? I thought you were going to call for estimates."

"I haven't had time." She hadn't the heart either, not after their dispute with Alan.

I guess that doesn't matter now. The nephew would sell the house once he disposed of Alan's goods. That shouldn't affect their plans to erect a fence.

"Brie, are you almost ready for dance class?" Marla asked as the teen rose from the table.

Brianna plopped her dish by the sink. "Give me five minutes. By the way, I think this is my last year. I've been going for ages, and I want to do other things."

Both Marla and Dalton spun to stare at her.

"Like what?" Dalton asked in a surprised tone.

The teen's eyes flashed with enthusiasm. "I want to try out for the drama club next year. And you promised I could take acting classes, remember? I'm kind of liking soccer, too. Maybe I can get on the girls' team. And then there's a charity drive that a friend of mine is organizing."

"Whoa." Dalton held up a hand. "This is all great, but when would you have time for homework?"

"Really, Dad? My GPA is 3.8, and you're worried?"

"You have to prepare for college," he said with a pleading glance at Marla.

Marla wiped her hands on a dish towel. "I think it's wonderful for you to branch out. Colleges will look at extracurricular activities on your application. I'd suggest focusing on a few things, sticking with them, and doing them well."

Brianna nodded, her ponytail swinging. "I knew you'd understand. I'll get my bag."

As soon as she'd left, Dalton pulled Marla into his arms and kissed her. "As always, you know just the right thing to say. I have to admit, though, it pains me to see Brie give up dancing."

"She's not a little girl anymore. Get used to it."

He gave a resigned sigh. "I can take her tonight. I want to run by the hardware store for some longer screws so I can fix that cabinet in the bathroom. And then I have to stop by the station. There's something I was having the boys check out that I'd like to follow up on."

"Okay, but don't forget to return for Brianna. Call me if you get stuck at work. Meanwhile, I'll catch up on email for a change."

She got engrossed on the Internet after their departure and, at first, the sound outside didn't register. But then she heard the dogs barking again and the sound of a truck rumbling by.

Rushing to the window, she glanced out at the budding night. It was getting dark earlier, but she could see a delivery truck pulling up to the curb next door. Surely they weren't still making deliveries to Alan's address. Yet as she watched, a uniformed driver holding a package approached the house. A few minutes later, he returned, empty-handed.

He must have left the item on the front stoop. Should she go over and pick it up in case the nephew wasn't around? Maybe Dalton had his phone number, and they could notify him.

She hastened to the hall closet, pulled on a sweater, and grabbed her house keys on the way out. After locking her front door, she tucked the key ring into her jeans pocket. She'd changed after work, not wanting to wear her skirt ensemble while cooking dinner.

A breeze stirred her hair as she scurried across the grass onto her neighbor's property. The nephew still hadn't removed the stone walkway. Although she hated to bother him, she'd have to complain. Or perhaps he'd give her and Dalton permission to remove it. She wouldn't mind shouldering the cost if it solved the problem.

She shivered in the cooler temperature. Other than her dogs barking in the background, the street was quiet. Overhead lamps cast a surreal glow at set intervals, while shadows played in the recesses. A sense of unease crept up her spine at the eerie stillness.

Her breath hitched as she stepped up to Alan's bare front stoop. Where had the package gone? The glass paneling on the front doors was too high for her to see inside the house. Was Philip Byrd here without his car?

What if the dogs had barked earlier not because someone had strolled by on the sidewalk, but because someone had been walking around the mutual side of their houses?

Marla trod around to the eastern edge of her property. She

scanned Alan's residence, but all windows appeared secure. Hoping none of the neighbors were watching, she patrolled all the way around his house but noticed no open windows or cut patio screening. Was she imagining things in believing someone might be inside?

And then she smacked herself on the head. *Schmuck! Why don't you ring the doorbell? If Philip is here, he'll answer the door.* He would have let himself in with a key.

Marla rang the bell. No response. So much for that theory. But then her initial question returned. If not Philip, who had accepted the package?

Something stung her ankle, and she bent down to scratch her skin. Damn bugs.

As she bent over, she sensed rather than saw a movement behind the front curtain. She wasn't alone! But who was inside?

Patting her pockets, Marla cursed herself for forgetting her cell phone. Should she run home to call Dalton, or wait to see if someone left? She moved to the side of the covered portico, wondering how to proceed. This person must have gotten in the house somehow. Could one of the windows or doors be unlocked? Or what if the killer had his or her own key?

When living in her townhouse, Marla had given her next-door neighbor a spare key in case she ever forgot hers or needed him to check the place while she was away. Alan might have done the same. Had Dalton said how the killer might have gained entry? She didn't recall.

Keys only worked at regular doors. She jimmied the front door knob, but it was securely locked. Since this one was secure, that left the patio doors, the laundry room door, or the side garage entry. The latter served as an escape route in case hurricane shutters were up and other exits were sealed.

She stepped onto the soft grass and strode around toward the garage side door. The knob twisted easily in her grip, but she let it go. She'd head home and phone Dalton while watching the house safely from a window.

She turned on her heel to leave but had only taken a few steps when she sensed a movement from behind.

Something smashed into her head, and all went black.

CHAPTER FOURTEEN

Awareness seeped into Marla's brain. A cold, hard surface lay beneath her. Where was she?

Fog enshrouded her mind, rendering her immobile along with a throbbing, pounding headache. The raspy sound of her own breathing reached her ears.

Her limbs twitched. At least she could move, she realized, testing her arms and legs. She cracked open her eyes. Darkness met her confused gaze. Why did she feel as though mud encased her brain?

Her eyelids fluttered closed.

Wake up! Alarm bells clanged in her head. For some reason, it was imperative she regain full consciousness.

With a moan, she twisted sideways. The movement produced a rumbling vibration. Or had that been there before? She froze, listening. Yes, the sound came from somewhere outside herself.

Her eyes snapped open as a shot of adrenaline clarified her mind.

She'd surprised an intruder by Alan's garage who must have hit her on the head.

And—dear Lord—that rumble was a car's engine turned on, if she wasn't mistaken. The intruder must have dragged her inside the garage and shut the side door.

She folded her legs but lacked the strength to push herself upward. Thank goodness she hadn't been trussed up like a chicken meant for the oven. But what was wrong with her? Her body felt so heavy.

A single, clear thought pierced her like a hairpin—carbon monoxide, the silent and odorless killer.

She was meant to absorb the fumes. That's why her brain felt like mush and her limbs seemed weighted down.

She squinted and discerned a faint outline of light. That would either be the window or the side door. She'd only need to reach that wall to find an escape route. The garage door would have a manual override, but she could never manage it in her weakened condition. Nor could she make it to the car to turn off the engine.

Her breathing slowed, her peripheral vision narrowing. She had no time to lose.

Dalton and Brianna need me. Get moving, girl.

Inch by inch, she dragged herself toward the meager light. When her outstretched hand met something solid, she summoned her energy. With a desperate shove, she pushed to her knees. Her fingers grappled along the wall until she grasped a knob.

She twisted the cold metal, and the outer door swung open. Thank God it hadn't been sealed shut.

She rolled outside onto the grass, her legs still partially inside the garage. Clean, cool night air filled her lungs. She sucked in desperate breaths, eager for the oxygen to displace the toxic gas in her system.

Her mind cleared and she set a new target. She had to reach a telephone.

Mouth open like a beached fish, she staggered to her feet and stumbled toward her house. If only she could stop that painful symphony in her head. She reached a hand to her hair and touched something wet. That wound would heal. The blood in her cells wouldn't fully recover until she got help.

She made it across the expanse of lawn that seemed to have

expanded into a football field. Her stomach heaved as nausea rose up to greet her. She swayed, tempted to topple over and let darkness overtake her. The steps to her porch wavered in her vision.

The image of Dalton kept her going. She made it to her front door and all the way inside to the kitchen.

Surprisingly, the dispatcher on the other end of the phone understood her garbled message and sent the paramedics.

She still had the oxygen mask on when Dalton arrived home at her urgent summons. His white face loomed in her sight.

"Marla, what happened?"

One of the medics, writing out a report, signaled to him. "Your wife suspected someone was inside the house next door and went to investigate. She ended up with a bruise on her head and lying on the garage floor. A car engine had been left on. She's lucky to have made it back outdoors."

Another EMT monitored her blood pressure. She recognized him as Kevin Jones, the same man who'd saved Spooks. Were the rest of the crew the same guys who'd responded then, too? They must talk amongst themselves about the excitement in this neighborhood.

During the first man's recital, Dalton's expression changed from incredulity to disbelief to fury. He rounded on her, huddled in a kitchen chair.

"How could you?" he said, his jaw muscle twitching. His eyes darkened, and his mouth stretched into a taut, firm line. "If you saw something, you should have called me, not gone over there yourself. You know the dangers."

She worked her lips to respond but it took too much of an effort. So she stared at him in mute contrition. Finally, she managed to get one word past her dry tongue.

"Brianna."

"Christ, I forgot all about her." He glanced at his watch. "I can't leave you. I'll call Arnie to pick her up."

"No, wait." She didn't want him to explain to their friend, but it was too late. He'd strode away, his cell phone plastered to his ear.

She slumped back as the throbbing in her head eased. The uniforms had cleaned her wound but she'd refused their offer to take her to the hospital.

Dalton could drive her if she had any further problems. The oxygen was doing its job of filtering her blood. They'd put the air-conditioning down, so cool air circulated throughout the house. She'd be all right after a while.

She needed assistance getting to the couch, though. The room still spun too much for comfort, and her stomach hadn't quite settled. But she supposed that much was to be expected after her ordeal.

Feeling fortunate to be alive, she didn't want to consider who'd assaulted her or what it meant that she hadn't been killed outright. Cherry Hunter had been bludgeoned to death with a blunt instrument in her garage. If the murderer was in Alan's house, why hadn't he finished the job instead of leaving her to asphyxiate?

Because he'd wanted it to appear as an accident? Or because it might be a less messy way of disposing of her? It had been a close call. Marla shuddered, chills racing up and down her spine.

Dalton conferred with one of the EMT guys, casting occasional glances her way. She knew his anger masked his concern. He'd be right to condemn her behavior. She should have called him rather than going next door by herself.

"Marla, you really should go to the E.R. to be checked out," he said, scuttling back to her side. "They need to check your blood gases and your head injury."

"Fine, but you can take me. I won't go for an ambulance ride and rack up a bill." It was bad enough that the neighbors would see a rescue squad truck in front of their house.

"I'll tell Brie what's going on. She'll be worried sick."

A flush of remorse washed over Marla as he made the call. She hadn't thought about the repercussions of her actions. If she'd suspected someone was inside Alan's house, she should have called Dalton at once rather than lingering nearby. Everything she did affected her loved ones. It was both a burden and a joy she'd have to learn to accept.

Hours later, Marla returned home after an endless visit to the emergency room. Her hemoglobin had checked out okay and her head wound had been superficial. Still wobbly on her feet, she didn't protest when Dalton led her to bed.

Exhaustion claimed her as she settled onto the mattress, but she wasn't allowed to get a good night's sleep. Dalton woke her at intervals to check her level of awareness and her pupils as instructed. His manner might be solicitous, but she could tell a storm was building from his curt responses. Lacking the energy to deal with him, she accepted his ministrations without protest.

In the light of morning, though, he let her have it.

"How do you feel?" he began after she emerged from the bathroom in her nightgown. Already dressed for work in a clean dress shirt and trousers, he stood facing the mirror to knot his tie. He glanced at her, his expression unreadable.

She put a hand to her head, the heaviness making her feel as though she'd imbibed several drinks the night before. Whether from lack of adequate sleep or a leftover from her ordeal, a headache persisted. "I'll live. I need a cup of coffee."

"Maybe you should go to your doctor for a follow-up exam."

"No, I'll be fine." Or so she hoped. Getting up and moving around was better than lying in bed all day, and her clients wouldn't care that she'd been banged up. At least her hair would cover the injury, which wasn't as big as she'd thought.

"I find it hard to believe you acted with such reckless

disregard for your safety." Anger laced his tone as he wheeled around to face her. His eyes darkened to slate.

"I'm sorry, okay? I was on my way home to call you when I got attacked. I'd meant to take the package for Alan's nephew but it was gone."

"What package?"

"Didn't I tell you? The UPS truck stopped at Alan's house. I saw the guy bring a package toward the front stoop. When he returned to the truck, his hands were empty. I figured he must have left the item on the porch. Who knew when Philip Byrd would return? I went over, planning to keep it here until we could give him a call, but there was nothing at the door."

"Did you look under the mat?"

"No need. It was flat. At that point, I wondered if maybe Philip was there and had accepted the delivery. But no one answered the doorbell. Then I thought I saw the curtain flutter, as though someone was inside watching me."

"You're certain you saw the delivery man carrying a package? I can contact UPS to trace its origins."

Dalton had gone next door earlier, letting himself in the garage through the unlocked side entrance to look for clues as to who had assaulted her. The rescue people had turned off the car engine after their arrival the night before, and he'd hoped to lift some fingerprints off the shovel found on the ground or the door handles.

His gaze grew thoughtful, while Marla inwardly breathed a sigh of relief. Once his mental gears got going, he wouldn't focus on her blunders anymore.

She moved closer, until she stood inches away. Her face lifted toward his, and she rose on her tiptoes to peck him on the mouth. "Forgive me? I promise I'll leave the investigating to you hereafter. No more antics on my part, okay?" She stroked his arm.

He smiled, despite his ire. "Why do I not believe you?"

"I have enough to do at my salon. No more snooping, I swear. Oh, did I tell you about Robyn Piper? She might be perfect for my receptionist job. Her marketing position got eliminated, and she's being laid off."

Marla rattled on about work issues as she picked up a hairbrush. She proceeded to fix her hair, careful to hide the wound that was sensitive to touch.

Dalton stooped to kiss her neck. "Don't hesitate to come home if you feel unwell today. You can be stubborn as well as impulsive, and while endearing at times, these traits can also be your undoing. I'll check in with you later."

"Gee, thanks for the compliments."

Brianna meandered into their room. "Are you okay?" she asked Marla with a concerned glance.

"Yes, thanks, I'm fine. I should have woken you earlier. You'd better hurry, or you'll be late for school."

Appreciative of her family's care, Marla vowed not to worry them in the future. She reached for her clothes. By the time Brianna finished in the shower, she'd pulled on a maxi dress with a matching sweater and low-heeled shoes.

Dalton entered the kitchen as she was drying the breakfast dishes. The dogs danced around his ankles. He'd taken them out while Brie was getting ready. Now Marla refilled their water and food containers, marveling at how her family had expanded. She scratched Spooks behind his ears and then gave Lucky a pat. Truly she was blessed.

"I put a tracer on Krabber's package with UPS," Dalton said, his keen gaze assessing her. "Maybe we can track down the sender."

"That would be helpful. Alan got a lot of deliveries. I'd love to know what he ordered all the time. He wasn't a hoarder, was he? Did you see anything unusual when you searched his house?"

"He had a lot of hurricane supplies."

"What do you mean?"

"His closet was crammed full of survival gear. The man must have been paranoid about natural disasters. Hence the generator in his backyard, too."

"Maybe he went through Andrew," Marla said, mentioning the disastrous hurricane that had driven people north from Homestead and Miami.

Dalton poured himself a glass of orange juice and downed it, while Marla unplugged her cell phone from the charger. Stocking up for a hurricane wasn't something she'd have to do for a few more months. The season didn't start until the first of June.

"I'd say Krabber was being more than cautious from the stuff crowding his shelves." Dalton regarded her steadily. "Not only did he stock up on nonperishable food items and paper goods, but he had water filtration kits, first-aid supplies, lanterns and camping gear, solar energy kits, and even respirators."

"Wow, he was nothing if not prepared. Philip did say his uncle talked about the end of the world. Maybe he hoped to survive."

"The guy was methodical. His items were stacked in alphabetical order."

"No kidding? And you don't consider that a bit extreme? Obsessive labeling of his possessions and collecting so many goods could be indicative of OCD."

"Or, like you said, Krabber had been through a disaster himself, and it spooked him. I don't understand the mailing supplies, though. He had enough boxes and package tape to open his own post office."

"It's my theory that not all of those UPS stops were for deliveries. Some were for pickups."

Dalton shrugged. "Let's see what I can find out from the delivery people."

They each left for work with plenty of thoughts to chew on throughout the day. Marla told her mother about their latest discovery when checking in with her during a break at the salon. She carefully left out any mention of her near disaster.

"Maybe he was preparing for the end of the world," Anita said. "Some nutcases out there preach that stuff, you know."

"Living in Florida would have given Alan enough reason to be cautious." Speaking of nutcases, what was happening with her mother's beaux? "By the way, how are things with Roger? Have you seen him lately?"

"We went out for dinner last night. I was surprised when he asked."

I'm surprised you accepted after the way he's treated you.

"How nice," she said instead. "I suppose he hasn't changed his plans for Passover?"

"No, and I really don't care. Who else is coming to your house?"

Marla related the guest list. "It should be interesting with Dalton's parents there. It'll be their first Seder."

"I imagine your brother will lead the service?"

"Yes, and I've already told him. I have the Haggadahs. Our friends Arnie and Jill are coming with their kids, too."

"Oh, good. I haven't seen them since your wedding. What would you like me to bring? Shall I do the chicken soup?"

"That would be great, thanks." Marla sucked in a deep breath. "Dalton expects me to host Easter dinner the following weekend. Would you like to join us?"

"I suppose I'll have to get used to you celebrating both holidays." A pause. "All right, I'll be happy to come." Anita made it sound as though Marla needed her for moral support. "What will you serve? Not pork or ham, I hope."

"Certainly not." They were having brisket and chicken for Passover. She should do something different for Easter dinner. What else might be a traditional dish? "I'll have to think about it. Maybe I'll do turkey."

Passover would be the first time she and Dalton entertained in their new home. Then again, other than Arnie and Jill, what mutual friends did they share?

An epiphany burst inside her like a cascade of fireworks. A newlywed couple had to build new relationships. Accustomed to being single, she'd been seeking out other women for friendships. But now she was part of a family, and that meant she should look for couples with whom she and her husband could both socialize.

"What's the matter?" Nicole asked when she returned to her chair from the back storeroom where she had made her private call.

Marla related her observations. "I never thought of marriage in those terms, but we're establishing a new life in more ways than one. It's a different *megillah.*"

"No kidding, sister. And don't forget your teenage stepdaughter. It would help if you could meet parents with kids her age. Then you can compare notes on college applications and all that stuff." Waiting for her next client same as Marla, Nicole glanced toward the front desk. "I need to bring Eddie up to snuff, or it's going to be too late for me to have children."

"Yeah, and how's that going?" This was a frequent refrain for her fellow stylist. Eddie, an electrician, was happy with their casual relationship.

"I don't want to scare him off, Marla. If I give him an ultimatum, that's what will happen. He'll skitter away like a frightened rabbit. The man is allergic to commitment."

"You can't go on forever this way if you really want to tie the knot, although lots of couples these days aren't getting married."

It was a sad reflection on western society that so many young people lived together without taking the next step. Now that women were financially independent, did they prefer to keep their freedom rather than submit to the bond of marriage? Yet living together brought along its own set of responsibilities.

She could understand an older couple not wanting to risk their estates being taken from their children, but a pre-nup could take care of that worry. Young adults didn't have those concerns. Although not a religious person, Marla did believe in certain basic tenets. According to her faith, the Lord sanctified marriage. Was modern society straying so far from this doctrine? Was Angela right in that the end was near because, like in Noah's time, people had lost their way?

"Yo, Marla, your two o'clock is here," Luis called from the front desk.

She shook herself from her reverie and strode ahead to greet her customer. After applying the highlights and setting the timer, she turned back to Nicole, who had just applied a coloring agent to her client. They both had about twenty minutes free, having a lull in their schedules.

"Let's continue our discussion outside." She signaled to Nicole to follow her to the rear where they could go out the back door and talk in private. "What are you going to do about Eddie? Just let things slide like always?"

Nicole leaned against the outer wall. "I'm afraid of losing him if I push too hard."

Across a canal, the back of another shopping center faced them. To the left was the meter room, which held unpleasant memories for Marla. Maybe that's why she didn't come out here too often. Fortunately, none of the other stylists were here having a smoke.

She inhaled a deep breath of warm, dry air. The odor of sun-heated trash came her way along with the more enticing scent of roasted garlic from Arnie's deli a few doors down.

"Why are you so concerned with how Eddie feels?" she asked Nicole. "Shouldn't it be the other way around? Maybe he should be afraid of losing you."

Uncertainty rode in Nicole's brown eyes. "Maybe he doesn't care."

"Then is he the right person for you? You deserve better, hon. I say, put him to the test."

"How so?" Nicole flicked a strand of raven hair behind her ear. She'd cut and straightened it into a chin-length bob that flattered her oval face.

"Make him jealous. He doesn't have any hold over you. So date other guys."

"I'm not interested in anyone else."

"How do you know? You've gone with Eddie for so long that you've forgotten what's out there. There's a cute guy in the fire department who might be right for you, and I think he's single. I didn't see any ring on his finger."

"Oh, yeah? Where did you meet this fellow?"

Marla watched a long-necked white bird alight on the grassy slope by the canal and peck around for food. A breeze whipped hairs about her face. It was a day more worthy of a walk in the park than work.

"Good heavens," Nicole said after Marla told her about the incident next door. "And you have no idea who attacked you? Man or woman? Any special clues you remember? Shoes, smells, anything?"

"I got hit as soon as I turned around to head back to my place. But you're changing the subject. We were talking about you. Dalton and I should hold a barbecue after the holidays are over, maybe on Memorial Day weekend. We can invite you and the EMT guy. Heck, we'll invite the whole team who saved me so it doesn't seem odd."

Nicole gave her a severe look. "You shouldn't have needed rescuing in the first place. Are you telling me your husband hasn't found the neighbor's killer yet?"

Marla had told Nicole that Dalton was back on the case. She shook her head. "Lots of people have motives, but there are still too many loose ends to follow."

"What does Dalton say about the suspects? Surely, he must have eliminated some of them based on their alibis by now. So who's left?"

Marla stared at her. "Good question." Dalton's willingness to share the details was limited, however.

"Means, motive, and opportunity," said Nicole, raising a finger for each term. As an avid fan of whodunit fiction, she knew the finer points of homicide investigation. "You haven't done your homework."

Without a backward glance, Nicole strode inside the salon. Marla lingered to dial Dalton's number. She had to clarify this issue right now. If he'd knocked off some suspects from his list, he hadn't told her.

"Marla," he said upon answering. "I was just going to call you. Are you feeling okay?"

"Yes, I'm fine, but—"

"We've located Alan Krabber's former girlfriend, the one who left him to go to Europe? Lucky for us, she's alive and well and lives on Marco Island. Want to take a drive to the west coast?"

Chapter Fifteen

"Tell me again what you know about the woman." Marla shifted in the passenger car seat on the following Sunday. Dalton drove, his gaze fixed on the road. They sped along Alligator Alley toward Florida's west coast.

Brianna sat in the back, texting friends on her cell phone. Dalton had been delayed during the week with other issues, and Marla had been busy at the salon, so they'd agreed on Sunday for their excursion. Alan's former flame owned a boutique and had agreed to talk to them.

"Her name is Gayle Lindberg. She's married with three kids who are grown and out of the house. She and her husband lived in Massachusetts until five years ago when he retired and they moved to a condo on Marco Island."

"Wasn't she from Florida originally? She was only a teenager when she met Alan and they had their torrid affair."

He inclined his head, a lock of hair falling forward. "It wasn't merely an affair. He'd planned to marry her."

"What happened, Dad?" Brianna piped up from behind.

"They got engaged and even started planning the wedding, but she was Jewish and Krabber wasn't. Her parents disapproved of him. They lived in Miami at the time, and social circles were tight in those days."

"Her folks hustled her off to Europe, where she wrote Alan a letter to break off their engagement," Marla said. "After her return, she mailed his ring back and refused his attempts to see her."

Dalton shot a wry glance her way. "She married a Jewish lawyer who had two children. Not long after their wedding, they had a baby son."

"How long afterward?" Brianna asked.

Marla twisted her neck to peer at the teen. "Are you thinking the baby might not have been the husband's child?"

Brianna nodded, her long hair fixed in a ponytail. "The girl's parents whisked her away to Europe, not only to get her apart from Mr. Krabber, but also because she was pregnant. It seems to me her lawyer husband needed a mother for his kids, and she needed a man to raise her son. The marriage worked out for both of them."

"From their many years together, I'd assume it was a good match in the long run," Dalton remarked.

Marla grinned. She saw that expression often whenever she and Brie dominated the conversation. He didn't like to be left out.

"What are you hoping to gain by your interview?" Marla asked, appealing to the investigator side of him.

"I'd like to learn the boy's location and if he knows his true parentage."

"You're not certain he is Alan's son, are you?"

"It's just a theory at present. If he isn't related, I can eliminate this angle. But the ex-girlfriend might be able to give us more insights into Krabber's character. Who knows, maybe she followed his activities through the years. It's worth a shot to see her."

"And it gives us a great excuse for a beach weekend. I'm glad you suggested that we stay overnight, although I'm not pleased Brie is missing school tomorrow."

"It's going to be a boring day anyway, Marla. I won't miss

anything important."

"Just make sure you get your assignments from one of your friends. Hey, why don't you put your cell phone away and look at the scenery? Let's play Count the Gators."

Brie gazed at the canal bordering the road. "I don't see any. It's probably too warm out."

"Well, look at the birds then. There's an anhinga." She pointed to a gray bird with a large wingspan sitting on the bank.

They'd already passed the river of sawgrass with its unending view stretching to the horizon. Having entered the cypress preserve, she knew it took an hour to reach Naples at the other end.

The divided highway had moderate traffic so they made good time. Fluffs of white clouds floated overhead in a clear blue sky. Marla couldn't wait to get to the beach. It had been ages since she'd taken an entire day off to relax. She gazed at the egrets and herons and other birds as they drove along, a forest of cypress trees bordering the road.

They turned south on Collier Boulevard, an eighteen mile stretch that led them toward a network of islands strung out below Naples. The shrubbery lowered from tall trees to scrub brush and palms.

Marla consulted the directions she'd printed out earlier. They'd locate their hotel first before going to their rendezvous.

Upon arriving at the front gate, Dalton told the parking attendant they were checking in, and he waved them through.

"You know the room won't be available until later," Marla said. "We're too early. We could get lunch and then head over to Gayle's store."

"Let's go inside and do the paperwork," Dalton suggested as he pulled into a parking space. "I'd rather stash our luggage at the hotel than leave it in the trunk."

They trundled into a spacious lobby with floor to ceiling

glass windows overlooking the pool area and the sparkling sea beyond. Marla hung back with Brianna while Dalton approached the front desk.

"Man, I can't wait to lie out." Brianna pointed to the sunbathers.

Marla was more interested in food. Usually Dalton was the hungry one, but she'd only eaten a blueberry muffin and yogurt that morning.

While eager to enjoy the resort facilities and take a much-needed break from her routine, she hoped this mission would prove fruitful. What could they hope to gain by talking to Alan's old girlfriend? Would she even admit it if her son belonged to him?

Several hours later, Marla fortified herself with a deep breath before entering the clothing boutique for their interview with Gayle Lindberg. Her stomach felt satisfied after a delicious meal of baked stuffed shrimp at a scenic restaurant overlooking the water.

Inside the boutique, racks filled with colorful beach clothing tempted visitors. Caribbean music played in the background, lifting her mood with its bouncy beat, while citrus scented the air-cooled interior.

"Look at all this cool stuff!" Brianna wandered off toward one of the clothing carousels.

Marla plastered a smile on her face as she and Dalton approached the cash register. "Hi, we're here to see Gayle," she said to the tanned woman in a sundress behind the counter.

"That's me. You must be the folks who called about Alan." Gayle had short, bleached blond hair, a trim figure, and a ready grin.

Marla would put her age in the early sixties. A round of introductions followed, wherein Dalton confirmed his identity as a police detective.

Her gaze caught on a pair of turquoise cropped pants and a host of matching shirts. With effort, she wrenched her attention away from temptation. Another saleslady had gone over to assist Brie, who already had an armful of outfits to try on. Marla could shop later.

"I was so sorry to hear about Alan." Gayle leaned an elbow on the counter. "It's hard to believe someone would want to harm the poor man."

"Did you ever think about getting in touch with him?" Dalton's broad shoulders stretched the fabric of his malachite green polo shirt.

"Of course not. My Donald wouldn't have it. I promised him I wouldn't ever attempt to contact Alan. He insisted on this vow as a condition of our marriage, and I'm not a person who goes back on her word."

"Donald knew about your former engagement?" Marla asked.

"It wasn't any secret. My mother informed him of my situation right from the start. His young wife had died from cancer, you see. He'd been heartbroken and left with two children. One was barely a year old."

"He must have been lost with grief," Marla said, trying to understand. "Why would he jump into a new relationship so soon?"

"Donald was entering a new law practice, and he didn't have time to raise the girls. He didn't really want to date again, not for a long while. He was afraid to love someone else for fear of losing her like his first wife."

"Did he consider hiring a nanny, or couldn't he afford one?"

"Oh, no. He wouldn't hear of it. Elise, the toddler, went into daycare. He found a neighbor to watch the baby during the day. It was a difficult time."

"You were pregnant when you met him?" Dalton said with a sidelong glance at Marla.

She liked how he sought reassurance from her presence and gave him an encouraging smile in response.

"You know about that?" Gayle said in a choked whisper.

"We know you fled to Europe after you got engaged. We met Alan's nephew, Philip Byrd, and he told us some of the story. You wrote Alan a 'Dear John' letter."

"That's true. My parents felt he wasn't good enough for me, but mostly they didn't approve because he wasn't Jewish. That mattered more back in the day, you know? It didn't matter that Alan was hard working and in love with me. He may not have had an advanced education, but he crawled up the ladder and made a success of himself."

"How did you know? Did you follow his activities?" Dalton drew imaginary doodles on the counter surface.

Gayle glanced away. "I still held him in my heart. I felt so bad about what I had done that I wanted to see if he could find happiness. Knowing he did well in life was important to me."

"And yet he didn't ever marry." Marla avoided any hint of censure. She'd done her share of turning away suitors. Someone always got hurt, but when you were young, you were callous about those things. Girls had to kiss a lot of frogs before finding their prince.

"Alan stayed single, but he dated around. It wasn't my fault he didn't settle down. I figured I'd done him a favor by cutting him loose. We were way too young to get married or to truly know our hearts." Gayle paced the small area, standing aside when the other saleslady came to ring up a customer.

Marla glanced around the interior, seeking Brianna's familiar dark head and not spotting her. She must be in the dressing room.

"And yet you wed Donald not so long afterward," Dalton said after the saleswoman went back to the floor. When Gayle gave a curt nod but didn't elaborate, he reminded her, "Alan

Krabber was murdered, ma'am. Anything you tell us may be helpful in bringing his killer to justice."

"Of course." Gayle gave a deep sigh, as though unburdening her soul.

Maybe it would bring her comfort to tell us what had transpired so many years ago, Marla thought. In any event, Dalton was right. An item that seems insignificant now might be important later to the case.

"Our parents thought we would suit each other, and I could be the mother Donald needed for his children. After losing the woman he loved to a painful death, he wasn't interested in sentiment. Fortune smiled upon us when we grew to care for each other."

"And your baby?" Dalton asked. "How did that work out?"

"My father wanted me to have the baby in Europe and give it up for adoption, but I refused. So this was the solution they found for me. Donald agreed to raise the child as his own. Actually, he was delighted to have a son."

Marla gasped. Gayle had almost admitted she'd given birth to Alan Krabber's baby.

"Did you ever tell the boy about his true parentage?" Dalton said, stroking his jaw.

"Ethan found out by accident. I'd taken all the children at one time or another to visit our safety deposit box, so they'd know what to do if anything ever happened to us. Riffling through the papers, Ethan discovered his birth certificate in the vault. I'd given Alan's name as his father. I had to tell him the whole story then."

"How did he react?" Marla's pulse accelerated. This angle might affect Dalton's case.

"How do you think? He'd been raised thinking Donald was his father, and then to find out he wasn't . . . it hurt him to the core. But he realized Donald loved him as his own son, and that took some of the pain away. He had a harder time getting over my betrayal."

From the corner of her eye, Marla glimpsed Brianna over by the shoes, trying on pairs of flip-flops. Brie had given the saleswoman a bundle of clothes to reserve for her. They were lying on the counter in a pile as high as the bill Marla was going to get. From her attentive face, Brie was keeping track of their conversation.

The background music stopped, and Gayle strode over to a console and twisted some dials. A lively tune from a steel drum band started up again, making Marla want to tap her feet. A blast of hot air came their way as the front door opened and closed. Two women entered, carrying bulging shopping bags and laughing at a private joke.

"Did Ethan try to locate his biological father?" Dalton rolled his shoulders as though they'd gone stiff. His face wore a patient expression, which she'd seen before when he interviewed people. However long it took, he'd stay until he got answers.

"Not at first," Gayle said, her gaze following the two women who roamed the store. "Ethan let it go, or at least he didn't seem interested in his birth father right away."

"When did Ethan start asking questions about his background?" Marla wanted to get to the point and move on. She shifted feet, tired of standing. It would have helped to be seated during their conversation. A lounge chair by the pool would feel good right about now.

"He met a girl, and suddenly it became important. You see, she wasn't Jewish. Donald and I are a lot more liberal than my parents in their time, but it mattered to Ethan. He wanted to learn about his mixed blood, so to speak."

"Go on." Marla cast a warning look at Dalton not to intervene. The woman was responsive, but she might clam up if they came down on her son.

"I told him Alan's last known whereabouts, and Ethan traced him from there."

"Did they ever meet?"

"I don't know. Ethan went to check Alan out. I think he wanted to see what kind of man he was before revealing himself."

"Did Alan know you were pregnant when you went to Europe?"

"He had no clue, or he would have followed me. We let him believe I'd jilted him for another man. I think he always regarded Ethan as Donald's son, that is, if Alan kept track of me at all."

"So if Ethan exposed his origins, it would have been a shock to Krabber?" Dalton asked.

"I'd say so, but I think Ethan chickened out. He didn't say much when he came home. Maybe he was disappointed in his birth father, or maybe he just didn't want to disrupt the status quo. We never talked about it after that time."

Marla hesitated to ask her next question, but finally said, "Could Ethan have revealed his identity to Alan, and Alan rejected him?"

Gayle shrugged. "As I said, we avoided the topic. Donald loves him so much, and he's the only son we have. I couldn't risk alienating him. It was bad enough that Donald kept nagging the boy to make something of himself."

"Oh?" Marla straightened. "What do you mean?"

"Well, you know Donald is an attorney. He's retired now, but he had a successful firm. He would have liked for Ethan to follow in his footsteps, but the boy hadn't the head for a college education."

"What does Ethan do for a living?" Dalton asked.

"The construction industry appealed to him. It used to be better, before the recession, but he's doing well now." Her chin lifted with pride. "He runs his own company. He's over on the east coast. At least he's still in Florida," she added.

"How did your husband react to Ethan's discovery about his father?" Dalton said.

"Oh, Donald was terribly upset, mostly because he was afraid Ethan might turn against him. But Ethan would have no reason to blame the man who'd taken him in and loved him as his own. His sisters accepted the news with barely a blink."

"So did he resent anyone? Like, did he blame Krabber for turning his back on you all those years ago?"

"How could he fault Alan, who didn't even know he existed?"

"Alan might have pleaded his case stronger with your parents and gone after you to Europe. Ethan might have not understood the conflicts involved."

"He could also have blamed my parents for separating me and Alan, but he didn't."

"How do you know what your son felt?"

"Why does it matter, detective?" Gayle met his gaze squarely.

Dalton spread his hands. "You don't know if Ethan actually met with your former fiancé or not, and if so, what might have transpired."

"That's true, but—"

"Where does he work?"

Gayle's face flushed. "He owns a company called Steers Industrial Supply."

"That rings a bell. Let me text my partner for a minute."

As he turned away, Marla said, "Do you mind if I have a look around? I see some tops that I like."

"Please, go ahead. This conversation has been a strain anyway."

"We're sorry for troubling you. However, as Dalton said earlier, your information might help bring Alan's killer to justice."

"Do you have any suspects?" Gayle's eyes widened. "I hope

you don't suspect Ethan—"

"Oh, no. Dalton has to check all the angles, you understand. This is just a loose end he needed to tie up."

Brianna sauntered over. "Aren't you going to shop, Marla? I've seen a few things that would look great on you." She poked Marla in the ribs and spoke in an undertone. "Don't forget to ask for the kid's contact info."

"One more thing," Marla said to Gayle. "Do you have an address or phone number for Ethan? Dalton may want to ask him some questions about Alan."

Gayle scribbled down the data on a piece of note paper and handed it over. "Here, take this. I hope you won't bother him too much. Alan is a sore subject for him now. I'd rather he focus on the good in his life: a family who loves him."

Let's hope he does. "Thanks so much, Gayle."

Marla wandered off, aware of Dalton punching buttons on his cell phone in a corner of the store, other customers gushing over the wares, and the steady beat of background music.

She'd just come out of the dressing room after trying on a bunch of outfits when Dalton accosted her.

"I was right," he said in a soft tone, pulling her aside. "Ethan's company is the same one that supplied manufacturing materials to Beamis Woodhouse. Kat said it's not the first time Steers Industrial has had a problem."

Marla plopped the clothes she'd chosen on a nearby folding chair. "It's awfully coincidental that Ethan would be involved with Alan's cousin."

"Listen to this. Steers Industrial was sued in the past by Myers Aluminum, who accused the company of breaching its warranties by selling defective polyvinyl extrusions." He read the info from notes on his cell phone. "The District Court concluded that the bowing of Steers vinyl occurred due to heat deformation caused by poor manufacturing techniques. The court awarded twenty-eight thousand dollars to Myers Aluminum."

"So Ethan's company produced faulty materials. He didn't lose his license over it, though."

"No, and the first incident happened a while ago. He must have gone back to his bad habits to make more money. Or else he's done it all along, and the building supplier got blamed. Beamis Woodhouse has been right in saying the leaky windows are not his responsibility."

"Someone should tell Gene Uris who's at fault."

"I'd like to have a talk with Ethan myself first. Maybe he got involved in our community on purpose."

"Why, to get back at Alan? Our neighbor was only elected president recently."

"Yes, but Krabber moved here when the first houses went up. He might have done a preconstruction sale. Maybe Ethan was keeping an eye on his movements."

"What for? Did Ethan reveal his identity to Alan, who wanted nothing to do with him, and that set the guy off? So he decided to get his revenge by sabotaging the community?"

They locked gazes as a sudden chill raced up Marla's spine. Either way, Ethan Lindberg had become someone Dalton needed to interview.

Chapter Sixteen

Refreshed from the getaway on Marco Island, Marla bounded into the salon at ten o'clock on Tuesday morning. Normally, this was a slow day, and she was grateful. Passover was next weekend. She still had to do the food shopping, set out the extra table, and find the Seder plate and matzo cover, among other things.

After waving a greeting to Luis and the other stylists, she headed for the rear to toss her lunch—a turkey sandwich—into the refrigerator. A frown creased her brow. Luis's time there was almost up, and she hadn't found a replacement. She should ask her staff if they knew anyone who was job hunting. Robyn hadn't gotten back to her, so Marla assumed the marketing exec had other interests in mind.

"Hey, Marla, how was your weekend?" Nicole said from the next station when Marla strode over. Nicole's first customer had just left, her gray hair elegantly coiffed.

Marla glanced at the schedule Luis had printed out for her. She had a cut and blow dry at ten-thirty, a touch-up at eleven with a wash and blow, and then a highlights. Hopefully, in between treatments she could take a break to eat lunch and catch her breath.

"We went to Marco Island," Marla said while plugging in her instruments. "The hotel had a fabulous restaurant overlooking the beach where we ate breakfast, plus we found a neat seafood place for dinner on the water." She winced. "The only downer was the bill we got from boutique shopping. Our one little excursion cost nearly five hundred dollars."

"Ouch. Did Brianna go with you? If so, what else did you expect?"

"It was worth the money. Dalton interviewed the boutique owner in regard to the case he's on. Oh, before I forget, we're holding our barbecue on Memorial Day. You're invited, without Eddie if you don't mind. We asked over the EMT team that responded when I got knocked out. It's our way of thanking them." *And I can introduce you to the hunk, Kevin.*

Marla had verified that he was single. Her blood surged at the notion of being a *shadchan* or matchmaker. Hey, it might be more fun than solving crimes—and far less dangerous.

Oh, no, I'm turning into my mother.

Ma could use some fixing up, too, now that she thought about it. Marla would be happy to see Roger get the shaft. Anita deserved better than that jerk.

"How come Dalton took you and Brianna to interrogate the suspect and not his new partner?" Nicole queried with a raised eyebrow. She looked sleek in a halter top and skirt.

"Your *pipek* is showing, hon." Marla pointed to Nicole's exposed navel. Her friend yanked up her waistband. "Gayle isn't a suspect, and anyway, the trip made for a nice family excursion. Plus, Kat was following up on another lead."

"Like what?"

"The paper trail for our HOA. Ron Cloakman, the developer, suggested someone is siphoning funds from the accounts. We need to determine whether the secretary or treasurer is involved."

Nicole sipped from a mug of coffee. "Isn't your treasurer dead?"

"Yes, but that doesn't automatically point the finger at Debbie Morris."

"How do you know Cloakman didn't mean to throw you off his trail? Maybe he killed Alan to keep him quiet about the burial ground, and Cherry found out so he did her in next."

"And then he knocked me on the head outside Alan's garage?"

"Who else could it be?"

"The nephew, although he had no motive to get rid of Cherry. Besides, his alibi checks out. So does Gene's."

"Who's he?" Nicole asked.

"The HOA vice president, who is filling in for Alan's position. I saw him having lunch with one of the potential contractors for our community's new playground. Gene favors this guy's bid. When I spoke to Debbie, she blurted out that the contractor promised Gene a kickback."

"Oh, yeah? That reminds me of a case in New York in the nineties. Over fifty property managers and co-op board members were indicted for taking millions of dollars in payoffs from contractors and suppliers. Investigators found fake receipts and forged contracts among their files." A grin split her face. "At the time, I thought it would be a great basis for a mystery, but my attempts to write one went down the drain. I don't have the talent, so I'll just remain a happy reader."

"There's nothing wrong with that." Marla glanced toward the front desk, but her next customer hadn't arrived yet.

Nicole propped a hand on her hip. "What other leads is Dalton following?"

"Remember I told you about Alan's lost fiancé? Well, we found her. That was the lady we interviewed on Marco Island. She admitted her son was Alan's, who hadn't known he was a father. The kid discovered his birthright and went to seek his natural parent."

Nicole's cocoa eyes widened. "Do you think he's involved in Krabber's death?"

"He isn't ruled out yet. Dalton and Kat are going to follow up and talk to the guy. But that wouldn't explain Cherry's death."

"Maybe they're unrelated."

"I don't see how, unless Herb Poltice got to her. You'd think the tribal shaman would be grateful. After all, Cherry told him about the bones."

"What motive would he have?" Nicole put her mug down and pulled up her waistband. Her skirt kept falling below her belly button.

Had she lost weight? Marla examined her with a critical eye. She did look thinner, come to think of it. And shadows sunk under her eyes. She hoped Nicole wasn't too stressed over her situation with Eddie. That guy should either come up to snuff or bug off. It wasn't right of him to keep Nicole dangling, and she was too afraid of losing him to give an ultimatum.

"Maybe Herb considered it a sacrilege that Cherry handled the sacred remains of his ancestors, and he killed her to appease the spirits," Marla said.

"You're grasping at straws. Do you really believe that's the case?"

"People's belief systems can make them do bad things. Look at the lessons learned throughout history. That reminds me. Did I tell you I saw Angela Goodhart playing bingo at Herb's casino? You could have knocked my socks off. She talks about religion and then goes gambling. What a hypocrite."

"Well, it should be interesting to hear what Alan's son has to say."

As the day progressed, Marla wondered if Dalton had been able to interview Ethan Lindberg. Had he met his biological father, or had their trip to Marco Island led to a dead end?

Jennifer, one of the other stylists, pulled her aside in a spare moment.

"Marla, my can of spray mousse is missing."

"What do you mean?" She glanced toward the rear. The shampoo assistant was busy with a client at her sink, and the storeroom door was shut beyond.

"I had Luis order the brand I like. It's not on the back shelf where I left it, and Dara is using a can with the same label. No way could she have ordered the same one. I asked her about it, and she said the spray had been shelved among our other supplies. She's lying! I'd put that can aside myself."

Marla gave a heavy sigh. She couldn't accuse Dara without proof, and while their surveillance cameras had been mounted, the security company still had to activate them.

"Did you check with Luis on the order?"

Jennifer nodded, some blond hairs loosening from her twist. "He only requested the one for me. It supports what I'm telling you. When are you going to get rid of her, Marla? None of us like her. She's rude and inconsiderate and steals our stuff. If she stays, I don't know how much longer I can tolerate it."

"All right, we'll have to be more diligent to catch her in the act." Marla glanced at the stylist with spiked black hair and a nose ring. Dara, busy blow drying a client's hair, shot visual daggers her way.

Marla recognized the customer as a regular. How many people would they lose if she fired the girl? Then again, would her other staff start leaving if she didn't take action?

First, she had to have grounds for dismissal. After authorizing Jennifer to reorder her item, Marla returned her attention to her clientele.

When the next person was ready for a wash, Marla escorted the woman to the shampoo station.

"Juanita, can you use a different shampoo on Abby today?" she said to the assistant. "She's complained several times now that her scalp itches. I'm thinking she must be sensitive to our standard product."

"Of course, my dear," Juanita said with a heavy Hispanic accent. "I have some of this other one we can try. I test on skin first." She always appeared with her face expertly made up, hoop earrings on her ears, and a smile on her face. She was also old enough to be Luis's mother.

"Hey, Marla," called Zoey, another stylist, as Marla was walking back to her chair. "Do you remember how to do a perm? I have a lady coming in for one in an hour."

Marla still did about two perms a year. "Sure, it's like riding a bicycle. Once you learn, you never forget. You'll be fine. Just ask your customer how tight she wants it. That will dictate the rod size."

Zoey was fairly new at the business, having graduated cosmetology school six months ago. Her only experience with perms might have been in training. Marla should keep an eye out for her technique in case it needed finessing.

Finally finding time to go to lunch, she steered toward the back room. When she entered, she spied Dara sitting on a folding chair eating a sandwich—*her* turkey sandwich!

"Where did you get that?" Marla zoomed to the fridge and popped it open. Her lunch bag was notably missing.

"Oh, I saw this inside there and figured no one wanted it." Taking another bite, Dara shot Marla an insolent look.

"You thought wrong. That was my lunch. You stole it, just like you stole Jennifer's spray mousse from the shelves. And what's that?" She pointed to Dara's open purse, where something white gleamed out. "Toilet paper? Don't tell me you bring your own to work."

"Don't be so uptight, Marla. We have plenty of supplies. They're ours to share, right?"

"They are not yours to take without permission, and nothing from here should walk into your bag and go home with you.

Other items have gone missing, too, and now this. I've had enough complaints about your behavior. You're fired." Marla knew her voice quivered with rage. "You can see your clients for the rest of the day, but clear out your station when you're finished. I'll cut you a check for the remainder of your pay."

As though meaning to spite her, Dara dumped the remaining sandwich into the trash.

Marla stared after her as Dara stomped out of the room and went back to her post.

The stylist's chutzpah astounded her. How dare she steal from them? Her rudeness was bad enough, but this was definitive proof that Dara didn't belong on her staff. Glad the deed was done and the girl would be gone by tomorrow, Marla mentally reviewed possible replacements. Getting another stylist was easier than finding a front desk person.

Running a shaky hand over her face, Marla lingered in the back room until she could regain her composure. Now what? She needed something to eat and a shoulder to lean on.

She strode through the salon, exited the front door, and headed down the shopping strip to Bagel Busters. Inside, she waved to the proprietor behind the cash register. Arnie Hartman walked around to greet her. He had receding dark hair peppered with gray at the temples, a trim mustache, and kind eyes. As usual, he wore an apron over his dress shirt and belted jeans.

"Marla, my *shaineh maidel,* how are you?" he said, patting her on the shoulder. His knowing gaze scoured her from head to toe. "You look upset. What's happened?"

"Everything. Can I order a sandwich? I'm starving, and I don't have much time."

"Sure, what would you like?"

"I'll have turkey and cheese on challah with mustard, lettuce and tomato."

He clucked his tongue at her nonkosher combination but

wrote up the order and placed it with his cook. A customer arrived to pay her bill. Arnie resumed his post, but signaled for Marla to come over after the woman left. "So what's going on? Is your family okay?"

"Yes, they're fine. How about Jill and the kids?" She hadn't had much time to catch up since their weddings last year. It had been second marriages all around. Arnie and Jill's nuptials had been scarred by the matron-of-honor's death. Marla shuddered at the memory of finding the woman's body under the cake table at his reception.

"We're doing great, thanks. Talk to me."

Her mouth watered as she sniffed garlic and pickles. "Should I start with the murders in my neighborhood, the girl at work I just fired, or the fact that Luis is leaving and I'll need a new receptionist?"

"What, Luis quit on you?"

"He's been accepted into Broward College. He plans to work in computer technology."

"Good for him. He's talented in that field. So where have you looked for a replacement?"

"I've put signs up, searched the job sites online, and asked around. It's not hard finding someone to man the front desk, but getting a person who's also qualified to run our computer system and manage our websites is more difficult. Do you know anyone who's looking for that type of job?"

"Not offhand. Let me think about it and get back to you." His concerned gaze raked her. "You said something about murders?"

Marla filled him in on recent events.

"Oy vey, you're up to your usual shenanigans. Lucky you weren't hurt worse. You need to be more careful."

"Thanks, I've already had that lecture from Dalton."

"Who does he suspect?"

"Just about everyone. I'm sure you'll get an earful on Passover."

"Oh, yeah. What would you like us to bring? We can do the desserts so you don't have to bother. I'll have several ones kosher for Pesach at the deli."

"That sounds great." The cook signaled that Marla's order was ready. "I'd better run. We'll talk more next time. Thanks for listening, Arnie."

"Always." His dark eyes gleamed as he regarded her with affection.

On her way to the salon, she passed the day spa. Ducking inside, she spoke to the front desk girl.

"Traci, I should have asked you this earlier, but do you have any friends with computer skills who are looking for a job? Luis is leaving, and I'm having a hard time finding a replacement."

Traci, an attractive brunette who wore her hair in a shoulder-length, layered cut, shook her head. "Sorry, I don't know anyone who's job hunting. I could always come over to help, but this place is crazy busy so I wouldn't have much time."

"Thanks, but we'll manage somehow."

Marla glanced at the customers in the waiting area and at the extra hair stations she'd added beyond for overflow from her salon. Further down was a hallway lined with private rooms for the various treatments they offered. Business had boomed since they'd opened their doors a few months ago. With the soft lighting, wood furnishings, and rich paintings on the walls, Marla had meant to provide a pleasant, relaxing experience. New Age music induced a state of calm along with a soothing eucalyptus scent.

With a wave, she left to return to her salon. Luis signaled to her as she entered.

"Marla, someone brought these cupcakes for you. A kid dropped them off and said you should bring them home. They weren't to share with your staff."

In a bakery box with a clear window on top, Marla spied an assortment of red velvet cupcakes with swirled vanilla icing. A candy heart decorated each top center. There appeared to be a dozen of the mini-sized cakes.

"Who sent them? Is there a card?"

"*Nada.* Maybe I should taste one?"

"I'm not supposed to share, remember? That's an odd request, but I suppose it's a personal gift."

"You must have a secret admirer." He winked. "Are you sure it wasn't Dalton? Is today a special occasion you've forgotten?"

"Heck, no. I'd better refrigerate them. Write me a sticky note that no one is to touch these." She lowered her voice. "I've given Dara her notice. She's to clear out her station at the end of the day. Make sure she doesn't walk off with this box in her bag."

The handsome Latino's brows furrowed. "It's about time. No one will be sorry to see her go. You did the right thing."

A pang of sorrow for his imminent departure hit her. She hadn't realized how much she relied on him. Oh, gosh. She'd forgotten all about a farewell party. How could she plan one plus get organized for the holiday?

Luis raised his index finger. "Marla, I forgot. The kid who delivered these said you could sample one about an hour before you left work. That way, the sugar rush wouldn't kill your appetite for dinner."

"I'm not in the mood for sweets, but Dalton and Brianna will enjoy them."

Marla gestured for her waiting client to get shampooed while she refrigerated the cupcakes in the rear and devoured the turkey sandwich from Arnie's deli. Coffee mug in hand, she returned to her station and quickly filled Nicole in on her plans.

"Thanks, pal," she said when Nicole offered to arrange a

going-away party for Luis. "If I add one more thing to my slate, I'll *plotz.*"

As she cut and blow-dried her customer's hair, Marla wondered how Dalton was making out on his investigation. Had Kat learned anything new? Glancing in the mirror, she examined the spot where she'd been injured outside Alan's garage. Her hair covered the bruise but it still hurt when she touched it. An urge to call Dalton nagged her during the afternoon. She must have had a sixth sense because he phoned her as the clock struck four.

"Sorry to bother you, but I have a couple of questions." His deep tone resonated through her, singing to her nerves and sparking her energy.

"It's okay. I've just applied a coloring agent to my next customer, so we have a half hour to wait. I don't have anyone else scheduled until then."

Holding the phone to her ear, Marla strode toward the front and outside. Nobody occupied the chairs in front of the salon so she claimed one. She crossed her legs, wincing in the bright sunlight as she faced west.

"Did Alan Krabber's nephew say anything to you about his uncle's estate?" Dalton said.

"No, why? He *is* the heir, isn't he?"

"Undoubtedly. But Byrd gave me the impression that he only expected to inherit a modest amount."

"Krabber made his money in the insurance field. He must have invested it wisely. Certainly, he had enough money to pay for that expensive generator."

"That wouldn't explain the regular monthly deposits into his checking account. They're for different amounts each time. He had a considerable nest egg."

"Really? Were you able to trace the source?"

"Yes. Krabber had been receiving funds from a business account belonging to StayTrue Ministries."

"What's that?"

"Some kind of church, I assume. Did Byrd mention this organization to you? I'm wondering if he knew anything about his uncle's involvement."

"Philip said that Alan favored religious sites online. What do you know about this ministry?"

"They're registered with the state, follow all the proper protocols, and have a popular website that gets thousands of hits."

"Strange. You'd think Alan would be giving donations to a ministry instead of getting money from them. Do you think he sold them an insurance policy and those deposits were commissions?"

"On what? There's only a post office box listed for the business, not a physical address."

"Alan may have sold them a liability policy or performed another service for which he was reimbursed." Marla bit her lower lip, considering the man's passion for computers. "Maybe he created and maintained their website."

"That's always a possibility."

"Whoever established the ministry's post office box could be the same person who set up their bank account. Do you know the signatory for either one?"

"Kat is investigating that angle. The post office is local so this ministry must be in the area."

"What if Philip Byrd knew about Alan's financial status and hoped to cash in on it? Have you examined his accounts?"

"That's one of the first things we did. He has a decent balance without any irregularities, plus he has a solid alibi for the night his uncle died."

"And he didn't have any reason to do Cherry in, either. That's assuming their deaths are related." A moment of sadness afflicted her for the woman's children. Pushing aside those unhappy thoughts, she drew in a breath full of humid air in an attempt to focus. "What about Ethan Lindberg? Weren't you and Kat supposed to interview him?"

"We did see him as scheduled. He didn't speak about Krabber with any fondness."

"So he admitted to a relationship? Did he visit Alan in person and reveal his identity?"

"Ethan was nervous about talking to us at first. I think he was afraid we might cite him for fraudulent business practices. When I mentioned Royal Oaks, he was quick to deny any responsibility for the leaky windows."

"Despite his being hit with a lawsuit for the exact same thing in the past?"

"He said the installers were at fault and offered to give us a tour of his factory."

"Oh, joy. So what did he say about Alan?"

"Ethan used Gayle's name to meet Krabber at a bar. The young man revealed himself as Gayle's son and Krabber's as well. At first Alan didn't believe him, but then Ethan showed him a copy of his birth certificate. He said Krabber hit the wall and nearly had a stroke. Then he started spouting anti-Semitic remarks that shocked Ethan and drove him away."

"That must have created a scene."

"Get this—it happened a while ago, before Ethan sold his vinyl extrusions to Beamis Woodhouse for the Royal Oaks development."

"Really? I'd gotten the impression from Gayle that Ethan went to see him fairly recently."

"Apparently not. It makes me wonder if Krabber's rejection and the disparaging remarks about his mother caused Ethan to snap."

"So you're theorizing that Ethan killed his own father out of hurt and rage?"

"It's been known to happen."

"Do you think he purposefully sabotaged the construction materials to get back at Alan? And if so, why wait until now to do him in? And why kill Cherry? Did you find any DNA linking the cases?"

Before Dalton could reply, Luis poked his head out the door. "Marla, come quickly. *Aiyya.* Something is dreadfully wrong."

Chapter Seventeen

"I have to go," Marla said to Dalton before she accompanied her harried receptionist into the salon. "What's the problem?"

"Dara is passed out in the back room." Luis hustled Marla toward the rear. "And I'm afraid I have worse news. She ate your cupcakes."

Marla noticed the curious glances of her staff as she hurried past the hair and nail stations, the shampoo sinks, and the laundry room to the back storeroom.

Inside, she spied the black-haired stylist sprawled in a chair, her head lolled back. Vanilla icing smeared her lips. On the counter, the bakery box lay open as proof of her guilt.

"Oh, Dara, how could you?" She must have stuffed herself and then fallen asleep. But when Marla prodded her, Dara failed to respond. Her nose ring didn't so much as quiver, alarming Marla all the more. "Hey, wake up."

"What's wrong with her?" Luis narrowed his eyes. "Do you think she's taking drugs? I wouldn't be surprised. Maybe your firing her pushed her over the edge. I hope she didn't accidentally O.D."

Could she have overdosed? Marla studied Dara's chest, which rose and fell in a slow, regular pattern. And her pulse was strong.

Her glance skewed to the open box. Dara must have eaten four of those mini-cakes, she judged from the empty spaces.

Marla's blood chilled, and she felt the color drain from her face. Good God. She'd been meant to ingest them.

"Luis, what did the messenger say who brought these cupcakes? That I shouldn't eat any until an hour before I leave work?"

His mouth gaped. "Surely, you don't believe—"

"I'd have been driving home. Imagine if I passed out at the wheel. It could have caused an accident."

"But there's no guarantee you would have eaten one."

"No. But if I didn't, it's a certainty that Dalton or Brianna would have tried them." She snapped the lid down with the side of her hand. "Get me a bag. I'm giving these to Dalton to send to the lab."

"What about Dara?" He pointed to the recumbent stylist.

"She might sleep it off . . . or not. I hate to call the paramedics, but we don't know what she's ingested. It could be a harmless knockout drug or something worse."

"Are you seriously suggesting she was poisoned? By eating *your* cupcakes?"

"That's correct. Drugged or poisoned, what's the difference? I'll ask Dalton what to do." She had a feeling it would mean a call to the rescue squad again. On the good side, maybe the hunk she wanted to meet Nicole would show up. "I'll tell Nicole what's going on and have her take charge up front. You stay with Dara and make sure she doesn't convulse or anything."

Luis gulped, his Adam's apple visible. "Make it fast, okay?"

Marla trembled at this latest crisis as she strode to her station. She hoped Dara was just asleep and would wake up later, none the worse for wear.

Nicole was busy teasing an older lady's hair in the next chair. Marla approached, crooking her index finger. "Listen, I need you to watch the front desk for a few minutes. Luis is doing something for me in the back. We have a situation."

Marla leaned over to whisper in her ear. The stylist's eyes widened at her news.

"No way. You'd better make that call, girlfriend."

Marla nodded, already half out of the salon. Once again on the front sidewalk, she called Dalton on speed-dial.

"Call the paramedics," he said. "I'm on my way. Stay put until I get there."

"Dalton, come around through the back door, okay? I don't want to cause a commotion in the salon." She gave the same instructions to the dispatcher.

They arrived within fifteen minutes. Marla didn't see the guy she had in mind for Nicole, but she recognized one of the other team members.

"Brett, isn't it? I think Dara ingested something that knocked her out."

She stood back while they brought in their equipment to assess Dara's vital signs. Luis, relieved of his duty, scampered back to his post.

Dalton pulled up in his sedan behind the rescue truck. Catching sight of him made Marla yearn to run into his arms. Quickly filling him in on what she knew, she sagged against a wall. This was one instance where she was glad to let her husband take charge.

Several hours passed before she could go home. She was clearing away the dinner dishes while Dalton lingered over a glass of wine at the kitchen table. Brianna had gone to her room to talk on the phone with friends.

"Those cupcakes were meant for you," Dalton said, regarding her with a hooded expression. He'd changed into jeans and a polo shirt that stretched across his broad chest.

"For all of us," Marla said, gesturing with a dish towel in hand. "I'm glad Dara will be all right." The stylist would eventually wake up, according to hospital personnel. Meanwhile, Dalton had sent the cupcakes to the lab for analysis.

"You're sure Luis had never met the kid before who delivered the box?"

"Nope. Someone must have paid the boy." Marla stood by the sink, rinsing the plates and loading them into the dishwasher.

"Obviously you've ticked someone off. First the incident by the garage, and now this."

"Yes, but my getting hit on the head next door happened because I surprised an intruder."

"An intruder looking for what? We'd already combed the place."

"I don't know. Maybe your team overlooked something significant. Have you gone around to the backyard lately to see if any new holes have been dug in Alan's lawn?"

"Why would I do that?" Dalton glanced down at Lucky who nudged his ankle.

"Herb Poltice could be snooping around, hoping to discover more ancestral bones. Did you find any connections between Alan and Cherry's deaths?"

Dalton swirled the remaining dregs in his wine glass. "We're still working on it. I can't help wondering what the intent was in giving you those cupcakes. To knock us all out? And then what?"

"I think I was meant to eat one before leaving work so I'd fall asleep at the wheel."

"Potentially causing an accident? You might not have been hurt, though. So it appears this incident is merely a warning."

"Not necessarily. Look at Dara who ate four of them and is out cold. What if I'd eaten more? In a higher dose, it could lead to respiratory depression."

"I don't believe the drug is that strong. It causes deep sleep but isn't lethal."

"How reassuring. We'll know more when you get the lab report."

"Maybe some other evidence will show up from that box." Dalton rose and brought her his empty glass. "By the way, I have a fence guy coming on Thursday for an estimate."

"Oh, good. With all that's been happening, I'd forgotten about it. I wish we had the enclosure already. It'll be annoying to have the dogs underfoot on Passover."

"That's when, on Saturday night?"

"Yes, and I'm going food shopping tomorrow. My mother said she'd bring the matzo ball soup." She reviewed her mental list of other ingredients. Roast brisket with prunes and sweet potatoes was the main meal. She'd bake some chicken breasts for those guests who didn't eat red meat.

"How many people total are coming?"

"We're up to eighteen including everyone's kids." She ran down the guest list for him.

"You're kidding? Eighteen? This is Tuesday already, and we haven't done anything."

"Don't worry, we'll manage. Just make sure work doesn't interfere with your being here for the entire Seder. See if Kat can take calls. Oh, what time is the fence person coming on Thursday? Luckily that's my day to work late."

"He'll be here early, between eight and nine. I told him to bring samples but said we'd probably go for the white."

"Aren't we getting a chain link fence? I want to be able to see the shrubbery."

"Wood fences give more privacy. I don't want someone else looking into my yard."

Spooks yawned and stretched upright from his favorite spot in a corner. The poodle gave Marla a forlorn look and barked. The dogs had already been out, so what did Spooks want? Did he sense her growing agitation?

She didn't want to argue with Dalton, but the type of fencing should be a joint decision. "We'll talk about it later. Oh, remind me to stop by the front office in the morning. I have to turn in my final report on the rummage sale. The Board wanted to know what kinds of things sold best, so we'd have an idea for next year."

Wednesday morning on her way to work, Marla spotted Debbie Morris's car parked by the community center. Another vehicle was there, too, so she'd quietly drop off her summary. As she approached the entrance, loud voices sounded from within the office. Its door stood partially ajar. Reluctant to intrude, Marla hung back.

"Residents will know something is wrong," Gene Uris said, his pitch raised. "If anyone questions the expense, we'll all take the heat. I'm not gonna let that happen."

"We'd need an assessment anyway, Gene. This bid is too high. Don't think for a minute that I'm not aware of your machinations. That detective who lives here suggested we get sealed bids from different contractors. You're pushing us to accept Erik Mansfield's company because you'll benefit personally," Debbie replied in a shrill tone.

"There's nothing wrong with him giving us a show of appreciation if he wins the contract."

"Giving you, you mean. How much money did he promise you?"

"Don't go there, Debs, or I'll tell people about your sister. You hear me?"

She sniffled. "At least my motives aren't selfish."

Marla shifted her feet, uncomfortable with eavesdropping. She should make her presence known.

Loudly clearing her throat, she rapped on the door frame.

The door swung open so suddenly, she sprang back. Gene snarled upon glimpsing her. "Oh, it's you."

"I hope I'm not interrupting anything." Marla breezed inside, waving her folder. "Hi, Debbie. I brought the report on the garage sale that you requested."

Debbie cast the acting president a resentful glance. "Gene was just leaving."

Gene glared back at her. "I hope I can count on your support, Debs. It'll benefit us both." And without another word to either woman, he swept out the door.

Marla handed her papers to the petite secretary. Debbie's strawberry blond hair looked sadly in need of care. It hung in limp tendrils about her face.

"You seem upset," Marla said in a kindly tone, hoping to inspire confidences. "It must be difficult dealing with association issues after two deaths on the Board."

"You have no idea." Debbie swiped at a tear trickling down her cheek. "And it doesn't help that your husband keeps asking questions."

"That's his job, Debbie. How is your family?" she asked, changing tactics.

"Oh, the kids are great and Jimmy is always busy. There aren't enough hours in the day for all of the things we have to do."

"Tell me about it." Marla propped a hand on her hip. "You're a real estate agent, aren't you? How do you manage to fit that in?"

"I'm only here three mornings a week. And I often work at my regular job on weekends, when I don't have to be with Hannah."

"Is that your sister? I'd heard she was ill."

Debbie's shoulders sagged. "She has cancer, and the treatments are so expensive. Her insurance doesn't cover half of them."

"It's generous of you to contribute when you have your own family to consider." Marla watched her reaction.

Debbie stifled a sob. "I won't be able to help anymore if I'm arrested." She covered her face with her hands. "Oh, Marla. I've done a terrible thing, and you're the very worst person to tell. You'll go straight to your husband."

"Dalton is good at what he does, Debbie. Whatever you're hiding, he might already know. He's investigating a murder case, not the association's bookkeeping. That *is* what we're discussing, isn't it?"

Debbie nodded.

"Did Cherry find out you were cooking the books so you could support your sister's medical expenses?"

"Do you think I killed her? I didn't . . . I never . . . Cherry was my friend!" Her eyes widened. "Your husband doesn't think I'm the killer, does he? I'd never harm anyone, I swear!"

No, you'd just steal from our homeowner funds so we have to pay extra assessments. That hurts our wallets. Marla sympathized with her motives but not with her actions.

"Is Gene the only person who's onto you? Or did Cherry know? She was the treasurer, after all." Marla scanned the office. From the disorderly piles of papers scattered around, she surmised Debbie could barely handle her volunteer position. Cherry struck her as the more organized type. Had the treasurer caught on to Debbie's deceit?

"Cherry didn't suspect a thing until Ron Cloakman got wise," Debbie stated in a defiant tone. "He thought *she* was skimming the cream off the top. It's only money that I should be paid for this job. Jimmy wouldn't let me tap into our household account to help Hannah. What other recourse did I have?"

"Your sister has no family of her own?"

"She's divorced with two kids. If anything happens to her, those poor children will be left without a mother. Their father has remarried, and they've already said they don't want to live with him. Hannah has depleted her savings. Costly medications are her only other option, but she can't afford it."

"I'm so sorry." What choice did Debbie have, indeed? Still,

there had to be an alternative to stealing. "Hey, I might know something that can help. Have you heard of crowdsourcing?"

Debbie took a tissue from a box on her desk and dabbed at her eyes. "No, what's that?"

"It's where you ask strangers online to fund your project. I believe there are programs for healthcare needs. If you want, I can check into it for you."

"Would you? Oh, I'd be so grateful." Debbie's eyes moistened. "No one else understands, and Jimmy will hate me when he realizes what I've done. He's meticulously honest."

At a loss for words as to how to respond, Marla changed the subject. "Tell me about Gene. Have you seen any correspondence between him and Erik Mansfield?"

Debbie's nose scrunched like a rabbit's when it sniffed a carrot. "We sent letters out to various contractors soliciting bids, but that was during Alan's reign as president. I presented the responses at our last Board meeting."

"And what happened? Did you guys vote?"

"It's up to the membership to vote, but Gene pointed out how Erik's proposal was superior to the others, even if the cost was higher. Erik's company would throw in more extras and use better materials."

"So Gene pushed his bid as the top choice?"

"His arguments made sense, even though I knew he had a personal interest in it."

"How long has Gene been on the Board? Do you think he's been getting kickbacks from other jobs we've panned out?"

"I couldn't say. He's been a director for the entire three years this community has been open. He keeps getting beat for president, though."

"Why? How long is the incumbent allowed to stay in his role?"

"Alan's term was coming up for renewal, but there's no question he would have won again with his charisma." Debbie tossed her crumpled tissue into the trash.

"People liked him so much more than Gene?" Marla found that hard to believe.

"Alan may have been pigheaded, prejudiced and prideful, but he was a stickler for the rules. People appreciated his leadership."

I see how he followed the rules with his own interests. "Did he examine the budget, or did he leave that entirely up to Cherry to present to the membership?"

"Alan looked it over. He wasn't a fool. He'd taken on the window problem and aimed to make Beamis Woodhouse replace the faulty parts."

"According to Beamis, it's not his fault. Ethan Lindberg, the manufacturer who supplied the vinyl extrusions, is to blame. His product melts in the heat, causing the windows to leak."

"So you're saying this fellow Ethan supplied the vinyl frames? He sold defective parts to Beamis, whose company used them to make our windows. Then the builder bought these windows from Beamis and installed them?"

"You got it." Marla gave a mental prayer of thanks that her house hadn't been involved.

Debbie's mouth cracked into a grin. "So we could sue all three of them!"

"If you want to go that route. I thought Gene hoped to avoid the court system and costly lawyers and just get other bids for replacements."

"Of course he does, so he can get a kickback. That's just wrong. We have a good case. Thanks, Marla. I'll present this information to Tom Raskins. He's standing in for vice president."

"Do you think he'll be fair?"

"He's a good man." With a pained expression, Debbie twisted her hands together. "I'll have to turn in my resignation. I'm sorry for what I did, Marla. Please don't think too badly of me."

"I understand, Debbie." In truth, Marla didn't. The woman had faced desperate times and embezzled from her neighbors. Turning to theft usually made things worse in the long run.

Marla wondered whether she should tell Debbie about Ethan's connection to Alan Krabber. Had Alan realized his son was responsible for the defective product that sabotaged their development?

She could just imagine Alan's volatile reaction upon hearing he had an offspring from the woman who turned her back on him. A Jewish woman. She'd bet that was what had soured Alan on her religion. His vitriol had been born from hurt and a sense of betrayal. Then what was this ministry he'd supported and that had paid him a regular income?

She believed Debbie who'd said she didn't kill anyone. So who did that leave? Ethan? He would have bumped off his dad right after they'd first met, not now. And he would have had no reason to murder Cherry Hunter. The answers had to be closer to home.

"Who else knew about your, uh, indiscretion?" she asked Debbie. "Ron Cloakman found out money was missing, but he thought Cherry was to blame."

"She was furious at him for accusing her and told Gene. He realized it was me. I'd set up the lockbox arrangement, you see."

"So you two were watching each other's backs, so to speak. He'd keep quiet about you if you supported the bid from Erik Mansfield."

Debbie bowed her head. "That's right."

"People saw Ron talking to Cherry at the garage sale, so I'm guessing that was the first time he spoke to her about the HOA's problematic finances."

"If I were you, Marla, I'd tell your husband to take another look at Ron's company. I don't know that they're doing so well. Those Native Americans have asked for a permanent injunction against further building in this neighborhood. That ruling would kill his master project."

Maybe Ron *had* been warning Cherry against exposing the burial site that day. When Alan told the developer about his discovery, he may have mentioned Cherry was the one who'd verified his find. Ron might have lied about the true purpose of his conversation with the association treasurer, although Marla had no doubt he'd also accused her of embezzlement.

Another neighbor entered the office, and Marla took her leave. Troubled thoughts plagued her as she went to work. Had Dalton verified Ron's alibi for the night Alan died?

Then again, what role did Herb Poltice play? Was he such a fanatic that he'd attempted to exact revenge on the pair who'd defiled his ancestral burial site?

She waved a greeting to Luis at the front desk and to the other stylists as she strode to her station. Had Herb been the one snooping in Alan's yard the day Spooks fell down the hole? He could have been attempting to uncover more bones for himself. But that didn't make sense. Herb wanted to preserve the site, not cause further desecration. And it was illogical for him to kill the two people who could serve as witnesses in favor of an injunction. The issue was bigger than him alone.

And what about her own near-miss incidents? Who was to blame in that regard? The intruder she'd surprised had been inside Alan's house, not in his yard.

One fact was certain—Alan and Cherry were connected through the discovery in his backyard. That had to be the linchpin.

In her opinion, only one person stood to gain the most from

silencing them. The finger of guilt pointed irrefutably to Ron Cloakman.

Chapter Eighteen

"How's Dara doing?" Nicole said as Marla plopped her purse on the salon counter and plugged in her appliances. "Will she be okay?"

"She's fine. I called the hospital and they're releasing her this morning."

"I hope she doesn't sue. Those cupcakes were meant for you." Nicole gave her an appraising glance.

"Yes, and she wasn't supposed to eat them!" Marla gestured to the interior. "If she sues us, I'll counter with accusations of theft. I'll bet Dara can account for our missing inventory."

"You don't have any proof, since you're the only one who caught her in the act. Unfortunately, the cameras hadn't been activated yet."

"Maybe, but I'd have plenty of character references in my favor. Let's hope it doesn't come to that."

"What was in the food? Could it have killed her?"

"No, it wasn't a lethal dose. The drug was an antihistamine commonly found in many medicines. What's scary is that Alan Krabber ingested something similar before he died."

"The drug or the cupcakes?"

"Maybe both."

"Was Dalton able to trace who sent them?"

"Not so far, although his lab tech might have lifted some prints off the box. It didn't have a label, so we're assuming the pastries didn't come from a shop. You can buy bakery boxes in any kitchen supply store."

"You think this was a warning directed at you?"

"Yes, and it worked. I need to be more careful, but I'm not going to stop my inquiries."

"What does Dalton say?"

"He's clammed up. Usually, that means he's getting close to solving the case. Anyway, let's talk about more cheerful topics. What do you have going on this morning?"

Nicole pointed to her printed schedule. "My first appointment is a thermal heat treatment. I hope I remember how to do one."

"If you want a quick refresher, we have a video in the back."

Nicole would be tied up all morning with that procedure. The special process relaxed and straightened hair. Its effects could last up to four months.

"No thanks, I'll be okay." The sleek stylist glanced at her watch. She wore skinny pants and a blousy top. Several bracelets clinked on her other arm. "It's almost time. I need some more coffee before I get started."

"Me, too. I'll walk you back." Once they were ensconced in the break room, Marla addressed an issue of concern. "Did you make plans for Luis's going-away party?"

Nicole grinned, a flash of white teeth in her warm mocha face. "Arnie is bringing platters over on Friday. I can't believe this is Luis's last week."

"I'm grateful he's coming in on Saturday since I have to leave early. We're having eighteen people over for Passover."

Nicole's eyes bugged. "How will you get everything done in time? Have you started cooking?"

"Not yet, but I'll manage."

"You always do." Nicole filled her mug with coffee, cream and sugar. "What do you have first?"

"A cut and blow on a new customer. At least, I don't

recognize his name."

Marla approached the day with her usual cheer, putting aside the hundred things on her mental list until later. Working at her chair functioned as a form of meditation. When combing, cutting, or curling, she could forget about everything else. All that mattered was the art her fingers could create. And it never got boring. No matter how many times she blow-dried people's hair, she designed the results for each client's unique texture and volume.

She'd just put down her coffee cup on her station counter when Luis signaled to her. Marla went up front to greet the client and walk him back to the shampoo station. Her jaw dropped when she regarded the familiar face.

"Robyn! Luis told me someone named Robert was coming."

"He must have heard me wrong." Robyn Piper regarded her thoughtfully through her black framed glasses. "I thought I'd check out your place. I need my hair restyled anyway."

"Come on back." Marla accompanied her, stopping a minute to run her fingers through Robyn's straight brown hair. "What did you have in mind?"

"Cut it shorter, but not too much. I've had bad hairstylists who hack your hair off."

"Show me where you want it," Marla suggested.

"Somewhere around here." Robyn demonstrated a range from chin to shoulder length.

"Do you still want it one length or layered? Did you bring pictures of what you like?" Lots of times, people expected Marla to be a mind reader. Or they wanted a style worn by a celebrity but one that wouldn't work on their type of hair.

"I'm afraid not. And can you do anything about the color? It's so mousy. My hair looks like mud. Plus, it has no shine."

Marla led Robyn to her chair where she discussed the possibilities for a makeover. Robyn agreed somewhat tremulously to a layered cut and color. While Robyn put on a smock, Marla consulted Luis about her schedule. She'd need more time with this appointment than anticipated.

Maybe Robyn had come to check out the salon regarding Marla's job offer. Ads hadn't brought in any more candidates for the receptionist position. Marla had spoken to a couple of women referred by other stylists. One of them didn't want to work Saturdays, and the other person hung up the phone after Marla said group health insurance was available, but the woman would have to pay for her own portion. What she needed was an energetic person who enjoyed meeting new people and who had decent computer skills.

Robyn probably looked at this job as a comedown from her higher-paying corporate position. Marla didn't want to pressure her for a decision but would hire her on the spot.

"I love it!" Robyn exclaimed after Marla finished restyling her hair. She gazed at herself in the mirror and grinned like a cat who just drank a bowl of cream. "I swear, you've made me look ten years younger."

"You look great. Here, take this ticket up front. I've given you a discount as a first-timer and a Royal Oaks resident."

"Sure." Standing, Robyn fumbled in her handbag and withdrew a twenty-dollar bill. "Here, I appreciate you altering your schedule for me."

"Thanks." When she'd first opened, Marla hadn't accepted tips as the owner. But she changed that policy not long afterward, feeling customers wanted to show their gratitude and felt awkward when she turned them down. She stuck the money in her drawer and pointed to her daily printout. "Actually, Luis makes up our schedules. Saturday is his last day."

Robyn swallowed and averted her gaze. "Um, does your offer still stand?"

"Honey, if you want a job, you've got one."

"Really? Because I've decided I need a break from corporate America. It would be fun to work here. It's lively, and I'd get to meet new people. I'd like to give it a try."

Marla's spirits soared. "When can you start?"

Robyn smiled. "When do you need me? I've been enjoying my time off, but I'm starting to get restless. I don't like being idle."

"We're closed Sundays and Mondays. Can you begin on Tuesday?"

Robyn clapped. "I'm so excited. I have errands to run today, but could I come in tomorrow to see what Luis does?" Her eyes gleamed behind her glasses.

"Absolutely. This is fabulous. Nicole, meet our new receptionist!" Marla made the rounds, introducing Robyn to her staff. They extended friendly greetings.

"Welcome aboard," Luis said. "I'll be happy to show you the ropes. You'll like this job. It's a cheerful place to work. Marla, your first client on Thursday is scheduled for one o'clock like you requested."

"Okay, great. I have things to get done in the morning."

First thing on her list for Thursday was the appointment for the fence estimate. Dalton dropped Brie off at the school bus stop while Marla took the dogs out. It would be wonderful when she could just let the animals out in the backyard.

Around the corner, she spied Angela working on her plants. Stray wisps of hair curled around the older woman's face under a wide-brimmed hat. She used a hoe in her garden, clearing a patch of land. The tool had seen better days, judging from the rust stains on its surface.

Spooks strained on his leash and barked. Lucky joined in at the sight of another hound across the street. Marla nodded to the other pet owner.

"Hey, Marla." Angela stopped her exertions and waved.

"Hi, how's it going?" Marla winced when Lucky halted to pee on Angela's lawn. She tugged on Spooks's taut line. The poodle kept barking even after the strange dog moved away.

"I'm trying to put my herbs in before it gets too hot. Say, how's your husband's investigation coming along? I don't feel particularly safe knowing there's a killer roaming the neighborhood. I'm surprised no one's been arrested yet."

I'm with you, pal. "Sorry, Dalton won't share the details."

"That's too bad. Do you know at least if they're close to catching the guy?"

"I have no idea." Uncomfortable with the topic, she changed the subject. "What are you baking? Something smells good."

The scent of warm bread emanated from Angela's house. Marla loved the cooking aromas when she walked around the block. You could always tell when someone was roasting a chicken or having a barbecue. Hadn't Angela said she'd worked in a bakery?

"Easter is next weekend. I'm making some sweet breads and donating them to the local nursing home. I do it every year. They're very appreciative."

"How kind of you." A lick of surprise hit Marla at Angela's generosity.

"Bread symbolizes life and is an important part of Easter rituals. It's amazing how much our two faiths have in common." Angela put down her tool and trudged across the grass toward Marla. "Judaism is the basis for Christianity. I have no doubts in that regard. And the Lord was born of your disposition. However, He sacrificed himself so we could live free of sin. If you accept his teachings, you'll join us when He returns to claim his followers. That day is coming sooner than you think."

"Thanks, but this is my cue to move on." Marla tightened her grip on the dog leashes. Spooks continued to snarl in an uncharacteristic manner. What had gotten him so riled? The poodle must sense her discomfort.

"I can give you a loaf to take home," Angela offered with a friendly smile. "I've already made a couple of batches. My braided egg bread is the best."

"Oh, really? That sounds like challah. I'm sure it's divine, but you might as well save it for the people in the nursing home." She strode forward, not caring if she was being rude.

No wonder the woman lived alone. Who would listen to her ramblings on a daily basis? Marla sucked in a breath of fresh, warm air and increased her pace. She'd better get home before the fence guy appeared.

A truck had pulled up to the curb in front of her house by the time she returned. She put the dogs inside the house. Ignoring their barking, she hastened around her yard to the rear, where Dalton was talking to a scrawny fellow with a craggy face.

"Marla, this is Ralph Emerson. My wife, Marla."

She shaded her face with a hand. "Nice to meet you."

"We were just discussing the merits of different types of fences," Ralph said. "Why don't I take the measurements, and then I can come inside and show you the options."

"Good plan." Dalton took Marla by the elbow and steered her toward the front.

"I just ran into Angela Goodhart," Marla said, watching where she stepped. The ground was moist from the sprinklers. "She's as nutty as Alan about religion."

"What did she say?"

Marla told him. "I still wonder about that letter I got addressed to Alfred Godwin but with her address."

"I thought she'd said the name was erroneous but the mail was meant for her. How could she tell? What was on the return address?"

"I don't remember, but I may have written it down somewhere, just in case. Why, do you suspect Angela?"

"We suspect everyone. She stays home a lot. Doing what?"

"Angela is a graphic designer. Haven't you interviewed her?"

He nodded, his expression sober. "We've interviewed everyone associated with either Krabber or Cherry Hunter."

"And? Any conclusions yet?" She opened the front door and entered the air-conditioned interior. The cooler air evaporated the perspiration on her skin. Already, the rising sun was heating the air. It could reach into the eighties today.

"We still have a few puzzle pieces to put together. A word of caution—trust no one. You should remain on guard, especially after those cupcakes."

"Did your tech get any clear prints off the cake box?"

"Maybe." Dalton's expression shuttered, and Marla knew that was all she'd get.

She didn't have much time to do anything else before the fence person, Ralph, rang the doorbell. The dining room table had been cleared off in preparation for Passover, so Marla sat him there. She and Dalton took seats opposite each other. Ralph spread out various brochures.

"Let's start with the purpose of your fence," he said. "What's your prime concern: privacy, pets, or security?"

She and Dalton glanced at each other. "We want to let the dogs out in the yard," she replied, swinging one of the pamphlets over to her side.

"Security and privacy go hand in hand," Dalton stated, folding his arms across his chest. "I don't want to see into my neighbor's yard and vice versa." He tapped on one of the brochures. "This type appeals to me, preferably in white."

Marla stared at him. "I favor a chain link fence. It won't make me feel cooped in. I like to see the shrubbery."

Ralph aligned his booklets. "Vinyl is a popular option. It's less expensive, doesn't rot or warp like wood fences, and it doesn't require painting. On the other hand, wood is very attractive. We use cedar or redwood, and you can choose from a wide variety of styles. You'd have to consider the amount and size of the knots as well as the surface finish."

Marla examined the pictures. Even the wood fences varied from designs where you could see between the posts like an old-fashioned picket fence to a more solid look that afforded better privacy. The type of wood would have to be resistant to termites and moisture.

"Don't overlook your metal fences. They're known for durability," Ralph said, his tone earnest. "Steel, wrought iron, and aluminum give you more choices."

Dalton shook his head. "I like wood. We'll have to think about where to put the gates."

"Between the chain link fence and a solid wood, which is cheaper?" Marla asked.

"The chain link, of course. And it'll last forever."

"Why don't you write us up two estimates? Give us one for the type of wood fencing my husband likes and another for a chain link. You can choose the decorative tops," she told Dalton. They'd dispute the merits of each type later. Or maybe she'd get her mother's opinion.

Before Dalton left, Marla said, "I'm going to set the tables now for the Seder. That'll be one less thing I'll have to do on Saturday. I can't start cooking until tomorrow."

"What time will you be home tonight?" Dalton asked, putting one foot forward as though he were eager to scoot out the door.

"My last customer comes in at seven. I'm hoping to be out by eight. It's your turn to make dinner," she reminded him.

"I thought we'd have ravioli. That's an easy fix."

Marla grimaced. "I don't eat flour products on Passover, and that includes pasta. We'd have to freeze any leftovers. Plus we just had spaghetti the other day. Why not throw some salmon on the grill and make a salad?"

"Okay, you got it."

"You'll have to tell me what to make for Easter besides the turkey. Do you have any special holiday foods? A delicious aroma was coming from Angela's house. She was baking some type of traditional sweet bread."

"Oh?" He squinted at her. "Did she offer you a taste?"

"As a matter of fact, she did. I politely declined. She bakes the breads and donates them to the nursing home."

"Good for her. After the cupcake incident, I suggest you refrain from sampling anyone else's food except for family members."

"I've learned that lesson, thank you."

She proceeded to lay out the place settings on the white tablecloths covering the extended tables. *Don't forget the Haggadahs,* she reminded herself. She had retrieved the box of prayer books last night. She also needed small dishes to set around for horseradish, salt water, and the hard-boiled eggs that were part of the ritual. What else? Oh, yes. Plates for the matzo.

She was in the midst of placing wine glasses out when her cell phone trilled. The caller I.D. showed Ronald Cloakman.

They exchanged pleasantries while she wondered at the purpose of his call.

"Can we meet?" Ron said in his baritone voice. "I need to talk to you about your husband's case."

"Why don't you speak to him directly?"

"I'd rather keep this discussion between us. I know you're busy, so I'll come your way. I'd hoped to catch you before you went to work."

"Where do you want to meet?"

They agreed on a time and place. After hanging up, Marla rushed into the bathroom to put on her eye makeup and hoop earrings. She chose a stylish skirt and top ensemble to wear that looked feminine and yet professional. By the time she was dressed, had made a few phone calls, refilled the dogs' water dishes and checked her email, the time had arrived for her to dash out the door. She made it to the diner where they'd agreed to meet right before Ron showed up.

They settled into a booth without any nearby patrons so as to ensure their privacy. The real estate magnate looked debonair in a long-sleeved gray dress shirt tucked into a pair of pressed trousers. His tie had streaks of silver like his hair.

They made small talk while the waitress poured them each a cup of coffee and delivered their meals. Marla ordered a buttered English muffin, while Ron went all out with an omelet and hash browns. Marla waited until they'd taken their first few bites before getting to the point.

"What did you want to see me about, Mr. Cloakman?"

He cleared his throat. "Call me Ron. Your husband and his ice queen partner came to see me again. They seem to think I'm the murderer."

"Why do you say that?"

"Unfortunately, I have no one to vouch for my whereabouts on the night of Alan's death. As you know, Alan had told me about the bones. He'd used Cherry to authenticate their historical value. The detectives think I had a viable motive to silence them both."

"It's a valid point. How much potential income will you lose if building in this community is permanently suspended?"

"A considerable amount. Alan wanted money in exchange for his discretion. I didn't have to murder him to gain his cooperation."

"So he was blackmailing you?" *We figured as much,* she wanted to say aloud.

Ron narrowed his eyes into tiny slits. "I brought you here to tell you I'm innocent."

"You'll have to admit, Ron, the case against you doesn't look good. People saw you talking to Cherry at the garage sale. Were you berating her for informing the Indian tribe about the burial ground? Did you warn her to keep her mouth shut?"

His wide shoulders hunched. "I already told you why I spoke to her. The association's financial reports were inaccurate. I'd come to the conclusion that she must be at fault. As treasurer, it was her duty to manage the HOA's finances."

"No doubt she denied your accusations."

"That's right. She reminded me that Debbie Morris had been in charge of setting up the lockbox. When I said the income reported didn't match the number of households, Cherry said that's because some homes were in foreclosure, and the association was having trouble collecting those dues. At least, that's what Debbie had told her."

"So why didn't you suspect the secretary instead of Cherry?"

"I knew Cherry's background. Let me explain." He sat back while the waitress refilled their coffee cups. "I'm a history buff, and I had looked into some references Miss Hunter had cited in a recent journal. You knew she taught at the university? Well, the sources she quoted didn't exist. She had made them up! Can you imagine?"

Marla stared at him. "What? You mean she falsified her data?"

"That's what I thought, but I gave her the benefit of the doubt and asked her about it at the garage sale. The look on her face confirmed my suspicions."

"Oh, my." Marla hadn't seen that coming. Did Dalton know?

Ron's lips thinned. "I said I would inform her department chairman unless she kept quiet about the bones. She needed her job with two kids in college. She'd already told the tribal shaman about Krabber's discovery, so it was too late for that. But if it came to a court case, I advised her to bite her tongue.

I'd reveal her secret if she testified in the tribe's favor."

So did you get rid of her and Alan as potential witnesses for an injunction? "Maybe she wouldn't have spoken up any further," Marla suggested. "Cherry ratted on Alan to the tribe because he'd come on to her and then cast her away. It was her way of getting back at him. I don't think she'd have taken it beyond tossing the dirt in Herb's lap."

She swallowed convulsively as another thought crossed her mind. "Good God, Cherry was the one who authenticated the bones. Do you think she falsified that report, too?"

Chapter Nineteen

Marla leaned forward, her gaze fixed on Ron across the table. "Cherry wanted to claim credit for the find because it would boost her status at work. Could she have invented the possibility of a burial site for that purpose?"

"Nah, the bones were real enough." Ron shoveled a piece of omelet into his mouth and chewed in silence. "Now that the authorities have been called in, they'll excavate for more evidence. The historical value of any artifacts will be objectively determined."

Marla tilted her head. "That's assuming they find anything else. What if Cherry planted the bones, knowing Alan planned to dig a hole in his backyard?"

"Despite her failings, I can't see Cherry cooking up such an elaborate scheme. And why? To get back at Krabber, who'd spurned her?"

"Correct. She might have anticipated the headache it would cause him in his role as president. Look at what's happened. Construction in the community has come to a halt. As a result, the potential for dues from new residents will decrease, meaning our monthly payments might rise to cover expenses. Cherry's involvement could lead to more widespread damage than she imagined."

"That's for sure." Ron scarfed down a forkful of potatoes. "Still, the lady might have had issues in the past, but I don't believe she invented this discovery."

No, but maybe she'd doctored part of her report. "Did you tell my husband what you've just told me?"

"No. I didn't want to soil Cherry's memory. For the sake of her sons, you understand. I'm sharing this with you now because I figured you'd understand."

Marla bought his sincerity. As for Ron's role as a suspect, he didn't have to kill Cherry to shut her up. All he had to do was threaten to expose her false publishing resources, in which case the professor would lose her teaching position.

She drank a long sip of coffee. A memory sparked that prompted her next question.

"Do you think Cherry hit on Alan for money to keep his news quiet? I saw her coming out of a jewelry store several weeks ago. She was admiring a tennis bracelet on her arm and implied she'd gotten a bonus at work."

"It's more likely Krabber paid her for the job of authenticating the bones."

"Oh yes, that makes sense." Marla considered other possibilities. Had Dalton checked into Cherry's ex-spouse? She wondered if their parting had been on amiable terms. How many years ago had they divorced? Did the guy have any contact with Alan Krabber that could link the two cases?

The developer's cell phone rang. He squinted at the screen before answering.

"What is it?" he snapped. Pressing the phone to his ear, he listened a moment. "I'll think about it, okay? And stop with the demonstrations, or I'll have you cited for disrupting business."

He clicked off and then stared at Marla. "That was Herb Poltice. He had the nerve to set up a protest outside my office the other day. Herb should be happy with the halt to further construction at Royal Oaks."

"So what did he want?"

His jaw tightened. "Never mind. Miss, can we get the check?"

Ron called to the waitress. He got out his wallet and counted out a few bills. "Thanks for coming today. I'd appreciate it if you'd get the detectives off my back. They're looking at the wrong fellow."

"Can I leave the tip?" Marla gathered her handbag.

He waved in a dismissive gesture. "It's my treat. Listen, if your husband wants to question somebody, tell him to target Angela Goodhart. That woman is strange. I've attended quite a few Board meetings for the community, and she's always there, even though she isn't an elected official. She and Alan were tight, if you know what I mean."

"I'm not sure that I do." When he didn't elaborate, Marla slung her purse strap over her shoulder. "Do I have your approval to tell Dalton everything you've told me?"

"Yes, that's why I asked you here. Just see to it that word about Cherry's misdeeds in the professional arena don't come to light. I wouldn't want to shred the woman's reputation when she can't defend herself."

Marla was touched that he cared. "Thanks for confiding in me, Ron. I hope this issue with Herb's tribe gets resolved soon."

The waitress returned with the bill. Ron left the appropriate amount plus a generous tip on the table, and they both rose.

Outside, Marla considered stopping by the police station to report on her conversation but decided not to bother Dalton. She'd tell him at dinner. Instead, she texted him that she'd heard from Ron Cloakman.

She didn't believe he was the killer. He'd mentioned Angela, but she discounted that idea. What motive would Angela have? Besides, Dalton must have already gone down that road.

He phoned when she was in the middle of a highlights. Marla noted Dalton's name on her caller I.D., but didn't answer. After setting the timer for her client's coloring agent to set, she went outside for a breath of fresh air and to return his call.

"I have news," Dalton said abruptly on the other end. "Philip Byrd was assaulted last night in front of his house."

Marla's heart lurched. "Is he all right?"

"He's got a concussion, but he'll live. He was in the hospital overnight for observation. I spoke to him earlier. He couldn't tell who hit him. It was too dark. He'd just pulled into his driveway and gotten out of his car."

"He's lucky to be alive." Marla thought of Cherry Hunter, who had been attacked but hadn't been so fortunate.

"Killing him doesn't seem to have been the goal. His house keys were stolen."

"His keys? Did someone rob his house?"

"It doesn't appear so. I met him there when he came home from the hospital, and we walked through the place together. He said everything was accounted for as far as he could tell. But he'd also kept Alan Krabber's keys on that same ring."

"Oh, dear." She gazed at the parking lot where the sun gleamed off the cars. "Was Alan's house the target? If anyone had lurked in his yard last night, the dogs would have barked."

"Not necessarily, if it was someone familiar to them. This person must have followed Byrd home from Krabber's house one day. How else would he know where Byrd lived? It makes me believe even more strongly that the culprit lives in our neighborhood."

"But what would he want next door?" Her conversation with Ron Cloakman fresh in her mind, Marla scrunched her forehead. It put the developer farther out of range as a suspect.

"You tell me. What's this about you hearing from Cloakman earlier?"

Marla repeated the gist of their conversation.

"You met him alone? Was that wise?"

She heard the censure in his tone. "We picked a public place."

"Why talk to you and not me?"

"Come on, Dalton, we both know I'm much less intimidating. Ron felt you suspected him of murder and that you'd stopped looking elsewhere. Maybe it was Herb Poltice who assaulted Philip and stole his keys. What if he'd found out Cherry had falsified her research sources and feared she'd done the same thing with the bones? He'd want evidence himself of the discovery. It could have been him digging holes in Alan's backyard the day Spooks fell down the pit."

"So why would he need to get into Krabber's house? Listen, I'm going to meet Byrd over there when he's ready. He's got a locksmith at his place now changing the locks, but then he wants to do the same for his uncle's place. Want to join us?"

"Really? You'd allow me to come?"

"Kat is busy, and I don't see the harm. Besides, Byrd might be more relaxed with you around."

Her face fell. "I still have to blow dry this one client, and then I have others right afterward. I'm booked solid until dinnertime."

"Byrd isn't available yet anyway. I want to question our neighbors again in the meantime."

"What for? He's the one who was attacked."

"His neighborhood has already been canvassed. If the purpose of the assault was to gain entry to Krabber's house, it seems logical to look there. Did you see any strangers outside this morning?"

"I left fairly early to run errands. Why, do you believe someone broke into Alan's place in broad daylight? You said Philip was hit last night."

"I'm just thinking of all the angles. I'll ask around to see if anyone noticed anything out of the ordinary. After I check in with Byrd on his time frame, I'll get back to you."

"Don't forget to talk to Angela. This will give you an excuse to see her." Marla hung up and resumed her duties.

Work kept her occupied, and she didn't have a chance to even glance at her cell phone until two hours had passed.

Byrd has a headache and is resting, so he'll meet us at the house between six-thirty and seven, Dalton texted. *He'll ring our doorbell before he goes inside. The locksmith is coming, too. That's the only time he has available after regular hours.*

Marla wrote back that she might be late but she'd meet him there. She worked fast to finish her last customer. Robyn had come in that day as promised, staying for a few hours in the morning to follow Luis around and then stopping by again to see how he wrapped up the day. A swell of sorrow hit her at the thought of Saturday being his last day. He'd been a stalwart supporter through all her trials. She'd miss his reassuring presence.

Robyn had a confident air about her, though, and carried herself well. She dressed with style and would easily make a good addition to the team. Robyn didn't seem the type to take any guff from anyone. Hopefully, she could bring the salon up to speed in regards to social networking, plus she might think of some new marketing initiatives.

By the time Marla escorted her last client to the front desk, Robyn had left. Marla reviewed with Luis what they had yet to cover with her. She'd promised to pop in on Saturday with any final questions.

Satisfied that everything was in order, Marla prepared to depart.

"Can you close up?" she asked Nicole, who had a late appointment.

"Sure as peanut butter goes with jelly." Nicole laughed at Marla's confused expression. "You go on home to your husband, girlfriend. I'll shut this place down."

"Thanks." Marla unplugged her tools, cleaned off her counter, and gathered her purse. "See you in the morning."

Her phone rang on the way out. Thinking it must be Dalton asking where she was, Marla didn't glance at the caller I.D.

"Marla, where are you?" her mother said.

"Why, what's up? I'm on my way home. Is anything wrong?"

Marla crossed the parking lot. Clouds wafted overhead in an azure sky. It was a glorious spring day, the last month before humidity strapped them in for the summer.

"I promised to get the horseradish for Passover, and I forgot. Can you buy some? If they're out of red, the white will do."

"I'll get it tomorrow. Is that all?" She didn't mean to be sharp, but she had to go.

"Um, well, I hate to drop this on you, but Roger called and said he could come after all."

"No way." Her voice expressed her dismay. "We're stretched tight as it is. Tell him it's too late."

"I can't do that, bubula. We can always squeeze in one more."

"Why do you always forgive the jerk? He's taking advantage of you."

"His son is poisoning him against me. The man is confused. We'll work it out."

Marla beeped her car key remote. "Sure, Ma. Whatever."

Roger's fickle behavior put a pall on her mood, so she approached Royal Oaks fifteen minutes later with a glum heart. Two cars were parked in Alan's driveway, she noted before pulling into her garage. One of them she recognized as the nephew's vehicle.

As Marla entered her kitchen, Brianna glanced up from where she was doing her homework at the dinette table.

"Hey, Marla. Dad is next door. He said you should go over when you got home. The rice is already cooked. He just has to throw the salmon on the grill."

"I could bake it. That might be quicker." Marla dropped her purse on the counter and then stooped to pet the dogs dancing around her ankles. "I have my cell phone in my pocket if you need me."

"I'll expect a full report when you return."

Brie's imperious reply made Marla smile. She hastened across the lawn to Alan's house, where a locksmith was changing the front door lock. Brushing past him, she announced her presence in a loud voice.

"We're in the bedroom," Dalton yelled from down the hall to her left.

Her footsteps tapped on the ceramic tile as she headed that way. Doors opened to three bedrooms off a short corridor. A glimpse showed her the room facing front was set up as a home office. The corner room served as a den filled with bookcases and a worn couch, plus another computer desk. She was surprised Alan didn't have any guest facilities, but maybe that sofa held a pull-out sleeper.

As she rounded the corner, she noted a walk-in closet on her right and the master suite dead ahead. What was upstairs in the loft then?

Philip had a bandage on his temple, shadows under his eyes, and a wan complexion. The lanky man at thirty-six was one year younger than Marla. His fatigue lines made him look older.

"I'm glad you're all right," she told him, standing just outside the master bedroom threshold. "Has any other news come to light on the attack?"

"Just that we know what they took," Dalton said, his face grim as he approached her. "Krabber's emergency supplies are missing."

"What? That's weird." Marla glanced at the stripped-down queen bed, the wood armoire, and the book lying on a nightstand. A sense of emptiness pervaded the place.

"It would make a good haul for the flea market. We're approaching hurricane season."

"What about other valuables, like jewelry or cash?"

Philip spoke in a hushed tone as though he didn't dare disturb the spirits. "I'd already taken Uncle Alan's wristwatch and his gold rings home for safekeeping. He didn't have any other jewelry worth taking."

"Portable electronics? Thieves like tablet computers and laptops."

"He had a laptop but I haven't seen it. It's possible he stashed it somewhere out of sight."

"Anyone who watches the obituaries would know this house was vacant," Dalton remarked. "A clever crook could have discovered Philip's relationship to the deceased and looked him up. Hence the assault and theft of the key."

"I don't buy that. Why not just smash in a window? As you said earlier, it's more likely the thief was someone from here who followed Philip home."

"We've been talking about Ethan Lindberg," Dalton said.

"You think Alan's son is behind this episode?"

"It's possible. Philip says he's never met the guy, or at least he doesn't recall meeting anyone of his description."

"But why would Ethan bash you on the head?" she asked Philip. "Because he felt the inheritance belonged to him?" That sounded more Machiavellian than Marla would give Ethan credit for, but then hadn't he orchestrated a scheme to sell inferior products to building suppliers?

"Why don't you get your fingerprint specialists in here?" she said, planting her hands on her hips. "There might be evidence of the intruder."

"Philip doesn't want to file a report. He just cleaned up from our last sweep through."

She gave the nephew a sympathetic glance. "I'm sorry you're having so much grief."

His shoe scuffed the floor. "I just wish my uncle's killer would be found. It's hard coming in here and reliving those horrifying images each time. I can't wait to sell the place."

Marla opened her mouth to offer to help when she caught Dalton's quelling glare.

"I'd feel the same way in your position," she said instead in a soothing tone. "Say, did you ever get in touch with those workmen Alan hired to put up his fence? I'd gotten the impression they might know something about him that he wanted kept quiet."

"Unfortunately, we weren't able to trace them," Dalton replied. "Philip found an estimate but it was handwritten without an address or phone number."

"Too bad. So where do we go from here?"

"*We* don't go anywhere." Dalton grasped her elbow and guided her toward the main entrance. "If Philip decides to report a theft, that's his decision. My job is to stop a murderer from hurting anyone else."

"Amen," Philip added. He accompanied them to the front door, where the locksmith was putting the finishing touches on his work. "Thanks for coming over, both of you. It's helpful to know you're nearby if I need anything."

Marla shook his hand. "Stay safe, will you? Watch your back until this thing is over."

Philip shot Dalton an inquiring glance. "I hope this incident won't distract you from your investigation, Detective."

"We're getting closer to a solution. But Marla is right. Be careful while this person is still on the loose."

"Are you nearly ready to arrest someone?" Marla asked on their way across the lawn. Dry grass crunched underfoot. She should check the frequency of their sprinkler schedule.

"Kat is waiting on one more piece of information that we hope will solidify things."

"You're not going to share it with me, are you?"

He chuckled at her resigned tone. "Just keep your head down and stay out of trouble until we wrap this case. Listen to me for a change, you hear?"

"Of course, darling. Don't I always?"

Unable to figure out who might be guilty from the number of suspects, Marla decided to leave those worries to her husband while she focused on the upcoming holiday instead.

Friday dawned bright and sunny. She reviewed her mental list of chores while she leashed the dogs for their morning walk. Dalton had left to drop Brianna off at the school bus stop and then head into work. She didn't have to be at the salon until ten and hoped to make the farfel stuffing for tomorrow first. A boxed mix made it easy but she added sautéed onions and mushrooms. Tonight she could assemble the Passover plate, so that would be ready.

Outside, she walked toward the next street over while considering what else she could prepare before the day ended. She wouldn't have much time tomorrow after work. Absorbed in her thoughts, she didn't look up until Spooks barked and yanked on the leash.

"Marla, just the person I wanted to see!" Wearing gardening gloves and busy weeding the beds around her crown of thorn plants, Angela stretched to her full height. A hat protected her face from the rising sun. The smattering of makeup she wore barely concealed a cluster of sunspots on her tanned complexion.

Marla forced a smile. "Hi, Angela. Getting your outdoor work done early?"

"Yes, it's supposed to get up to eighty-five later. I was hoping you'd come by."

"Oh, why is that?" The less she saw of the woman, the better. What was wrong with Spooks? He strained on the leash, snarling at Angela while Lucky sniffed the grass.

"I use a wig when I want my hair to look longer. I'd like to wear it to church on Easter, but it needs to be freshened up. Can you come inside for a minute and take a look?"

The blonde took off her hat and ruffled her unkempt layers of hair. It was already a decent length. Why not just add extensions?

"Bring the wig into my salon, and we'll discuss the options. I'm in a hurry—"

"Maybe you don't work with wigs? I can take it elsewhere, you know, but I thought you could see it on me while you're here. Then you can take it along with you to fix. Come on, I won't keep you long. And bring the dogs."

"Well, I don't know." Marla glanced up and down the street. No one else was around.

As they spoke, Angela had sidled closer. Before Marla could move away, the woman snatched the dog leashes from her hand.

"Follow me. I won't take up much of your time," Angela said in a firm tone, striding toward the front door.

Spooks yipped, resisting the tow. Lucky, on the other hand, must have liked what she smelled because she pranced along eagerly. The aroma of freshly baked goods emanated from the house.

Marla hurried after them. "The dogs aren't used to your place and might soil the carpet. Give me back their leashes, Angela."

"Don't worry, I have tile floors. Besides, it's cooler inside." Angela pushed open the front door and tossed her hat on an accent table in the foyer.

The nerve of the woman! If Angela wanted her services so badly, she could come into the salon like everyone else. Marla didn't do house calls, although she had contemplated it at one time.

"Close the door so the mosquitoes don't get inside," Angela

said after Marla trailed her into the hallway. "The wig is in the kitchen. Can I give your pets a treat? They're good little fellows." Angela led the dogs forward, evading Marla's thrust for them.

Marla swung the door shut and rushed after her. She didn't want Angela giving the animals anything to eat.

Inside the kitchen, Angela opened an inner door and shoved the animals inside the adjacent area.

"Go on, your treat is in the laundry room. Enjoy!" She slammed the door closed.

Spooks barked madly, thudding against the door from the other side. Lucky was silent, so Marla surmised she was consuming whatever treat Angela had provided.

Wait a minute. That implied she'd planned this maneuver ahead of time.

Marla's gaze zeroed in on the range where a tray of cupcakes sat cooling on a rack. Connections zipped together in her mind like Lego pieces.

"You!" she said, rounding on Angela.

But it was too late. Her eyes glinting with malice, Angela pointed a gun at Marla.

"I see you've figured it out. Take those car keys hanging on the hook over by the garage door. We're going for a drive."

Chapter Twenty

Marla drove as Angela directed. With a gun pointed at her head, she didn't have much choice. Not yet, anyway.

"Your husband wanted me to come into the station for more questioning. I need to give him something else to think about," Angela said in a cold tone. "He'll be worried when he learns you never came into work. Your dogs will be a casualty, too. I wouldn't want them leading the cops to my house."

"Why are you doing this?" Marla's fingers gripped the wheel. She hoped Angela hadn't poisoned the dogs, but that was a real possibility. Her heart beat a frantic rhythm in her chest. How could she get away?

Her mind calculated the options even as she focused on the road. Angela had kept enough distance from her at the house so Marla hadn't been able to make a move. If she'd attempted to snatch a knife from the counter, Angela would have shot her. It might have made a mess, but the zealous light in Angela's eyes told Marla she wouldn't hesitate.

"Someone might have seen me go inside with you," Marla said. "How do you know a neighbor wasn't watching?"

"The people across the street had gone to work. I didn't see anyone else."

Angela kept her attention focused solely on Marla, who wished she knew more about weaponry. That gun looked small enough to tuck inside a purse, and yet she had no doubt it would be deadly when fired at close range.

"Your daughter takes the school bus during the week," Angela continued with a sneer. "Your husband drives to work. You take the dogs for a walk. It's the same routine every day." She clucked her tongue. "As the wife of a police detective, you should know better."

Marla's knuckles went white on the steering wheel. Stalled at a red light, she pressed her foot on the brake pedal. Angela lowered the gun and pointed it at her belly until traffic moved ahead. When Angela indicated she should head west, Marla got an inkling of her plan.

Her gut clenched, and ice water sluiced through her veins. Angela intended to take a side road off Alligator Alley, shoot her dead and dump her body in the Everglades.

Familiar exits whizzed by as she sped down the highway. Dalton had warned her and Brianna never to get in a stranger's car. If they did, their lives could be over. The only way out would be to crash the vehicle and pray the air bags cushioned the blow.

She began looking for light poles, emergency call boxes, or mile markers where she could veer to the right. She'd have to hit the car on Angela's side hard enough to disable her. If she went too slow and they were both just stunned, Angela could still shoot. And yet, what would be her own chances of survival if she hit a pole at sixty miles per hour?

Her face popped out in a cold sweat, and her hands grew slippery on the wheel.

"I should have figured it out a long time ago," she said, her voice raspy. "You're the one who sent me the cupcakes at my salon, aren't you? I should have remembered you were in charge of the baked goods at our rummage sale."

"I'd hoped you would eat them at work and fall asleep on the drive home. It would have served as a warning to you."

"Another stylist sampled them and had to be taken to the

hospital. You must have dosed them pretty high. Is that how you disabled Alan Krabber before tying the noose around his neck and pushing him off his second-story balcony?"

Angela chuckled, an evil sound. "Alan had learned about my bingo addiction. He accused me of cheating him out of his share of our money. I said we should talk about it and brought over some of my cupcakes. He had a sweet tooth and loved them."

"When was this?" Marla risked a glance in her direction.

"That Sunday after the annual HOA meeting. He'd told me about the fence going in the next day, and I thought it was a sign of approval from above. I knew your husband wouldn't be happy that Alan hadn't done a survey."

"So you set your plan in motion?"

"That's right. I told Alan he could eat the blue frosted cupcakes on Sunday. They had a secret treat inside. He loved surprises, and I'd put chocolate kisses in the middle. But he couldn't eat the cupcakes with red frosting until after dinner on Monday." She winked. "They had cherry pie filling, his favorite."

A chill raced up Marla's spine. The woman talked about Alan as though she were fond of him. "Why did it matter when he ate them?"

"I'd laced the red ones with sedatives. Once he got drowsy, I'd only have a short window in which to do my work. I called him around seven on Monday, and he told me he'd just finished dinner. He'd loved the cupcakes and had eaten three of the red ones. Everyone loves my baking," she boasted.

"And then?" Marla prompted, her gaze darting to the side of the road. Across the canal stretched a river of sawgrass. That wouldn't help her. Where did Angela plan to cut off the highway? There were boat ramps but not many side roads.

Her stomach clenched at the notion of plowing into a pole. Angela's Lexus was a newer model, so she had faith in the airbags. But dare she take the risk? What alternative was there?

Tears pricked her eyes. She didn't want things to end this way, and certainly not from her own stupidity. Had she listened to her instincts, she would never have set foot inside Angela's house.

"How did you get in Alan's house if he was unconscious?" she asked to soothe her nerves while her mind sought alternatives.

Angela seemed in a talkative mood. Or else she knew Marla wouldn't repeat anything she said. The woman's gaze held steady, and so did the weapon in her hand.

"I let myself in the front door with a spare key he'd given me. I'd waited until the neighborhood quieted and it was dark outside. Alan had gone to bed, which made things easier. I took the desk chair, heaved him onto it, and wheeled it to the balcony. It wasn't hard to loop a computer cable into a noose and knot the other end of the line to a post."

"So you put the cable around his neck and shoved him over the railing?"

"Yep. The man was so heavy, I was afraid the post would break, but it held. He didn't wake up once."

"How could you know your method would work? What if his neck was too thick?"

"I'd printed out instructions from the Internet. I stayed until his face turned blue and his chest stopped moving."

Angela had planned everything out in detail, just like she had lured Marla into her house. Marla's breathing, coming in short pants, seemed to squeeze from her chest.

"How did you get his signature on a suicide note?"

"You're slowing down, Marla. Either speed up or shut up."

Marla pressed her lips together and accelerated. From the corner of her eye, she spied Angela's disdainful smile.

"I had Alan sign a bunch of papers for our business. I'd

slipped a few blank pages in there in case I needed them someday. He was so blinded by the money coming in that he didn't see past his nose."

"And what business was that?"

Angela laughed, a harsh sound in the air-conditioned interior. "I can't believe you haven't guessed by now. After all, you delivered that item of mail to me. That was a dead giveaway."

"The envelope addressed to Alfred Godwin? Who is he?"

"Alfred Godwin runs the StayTrue Ministries. You're looking at him."

"What? That's *you*?" Different pieces of the puzzle fell into place.

"All of the signs indicate the end is near. Deliverance is almost upon us. Sinners are so afraid of being left behind that our sales of survival gear have gone through the roof."

"Oh. My. Gosh." Alan hadn't been collecting hurricane supplies. His deliveries and pickups had to do with their ministry business. He and Angela must have been partners who sold those goods to gullible followers. "What was Alan's role? He managed the retail sales?"

Angela snorted. "Alan did all the computer stuff, while I wrote the scripts. We even had podcasts online and a radio talk show. There's still time to save your soul, Marla. Give yourself to the Lord, and your death will take you to a higher plane."

I don't think so. She sensed from Angela's alert posture that they were nearing their exit. She'd have to make her move soon. Her gaze scanned the unending stretch of road ahead. Where was a pole when she needed one? She resisted the urge to test her seatbelt. Angela might guess what she had in mind.

"Alan thought you were using the profits from your business to play bingo?"

"He threatened to expose me as a fraud despite what it would do to the ministry," Angela said, her voice dripping with venom.

"I couldn't let him destroy the church we'd built. It would devastate our followers."

Not to mention ending your lucrative empire. "Why did you kill Cherry Hunter?"

"Alan stupidly wrapped the bones he'd given Cherry to authenticate in one of our mockup ads. I'd scribbled some notes on the sides. Cherry figured out our connection and suspected that I might have been involved in his death. The woman was dumb enough to ask me about it."

"So you attacked her one night and bashed her on the head? With what? The same tool you hit me with outside Alan's garage?"

"My hoe. Handy implement, eh? I couldn't let Cherry give me away to the cops. Then you went snooping next door. I was inside Alan's house, making sure I hadn't left any evidence that would lead back to me."

"Why didn't you finish me off?"

"The gas fumes were supposed to do that. I didn't think you'd wake up in time to save yourself."

Marla cringed at her matter-of-fact tone. "Was that you digging in Alan's backyard to search for more bones? Did you throw Spooks in that pit?"

"No. I could care less about those bones. It wasn't me."

"And Philip Byrd . . . did you intend to kill him?"

"Hell, no. After he changed the locks on Alan's door, I needed to get inside again. I didn't want to smash a window in case he'd installed an alarm system. I had to retrieve our stock. We had orders to fill, and I didn't want to disappoint our customers. I'd planned to get them the day you interrupted me, but I had to leave fast after putting you inside the garage."

"So that's why you took his hurricane supplies. We'd thought he was just afraid of natural disasters."

"Your husband found some clue that led him to me, didn't

he? That's why he wants me to come in, but I'm not planning to oblige. I'll keep driving once I take care of you. Whatever I need is packed in the trunk."

Angela had planned this finale all along, and Marla had played her tune. Would she live to make amends for her actions? She could bear Dalton's anger if only she survived.

Her heart thumped so wildly she thought she'd faint. Bile rose in her throat. Did she have it in her to take the risk that might save her life?

Angela's voice hardened. "After the rest stop, there's a turn off to a fishing camp. I want you to take it. I'll make it a quick kill, I promise. Then you can join Satan with the other nonbelievers."

"You'd better pray to your god first." Marla wrenched the steering wheel to her right.

At sixty miles per hour, the car careened toward the side of the road. A series of light poles stood by the exit just ahead. Marla headed for the nearest one. A final thought of regret and sorrow for her loved ones flashed into her mind.

"No!" Angela screamed, throwing up an arm.

Marla gritted her teeth, bracing for impact. The pole loomed in her vision.

A jarring crash drove her body forward against the seatbelt.

An explosion and pressure to her chest.

And then nothing.

CHAPTER TWENTY-ONE

Marla shifted on her cushioned chair at the Passover table, while her brother Michael led the last of the service before the meal. Battered and bruised, she'd at least suffered no life-threatening injuries in the car crash that had saved her life.

The same couldn't be said for Angela, whose body lay in the morgue until her next of kin could be notified. Funny how no one knew if she even had any relatives. She'd been single, never married, presumably without any siblings. It must have been a lonely life, but maybe she preferred it that way. Or was that why Angela had turned to religion, to fill the emptiness in her soul? She seemed to have truly believed in the gospel she preached.

"We can eat!" Michael exclaimed, closing his Haggadah until later.

His kids fidgeted and giggled next to Arnie's children. Marla glanced around the table at her family and friends, a glow of warmth lighting her from the inside out and penetrating the drug haze that held her upright. Her spine hurt something terrible. The doctor in the emergency room had said the hairline fracture would heal on its own. There wasn't much else she could do about it except rest.

Everyone had pitched in to help prepare dinner. Thank goodness she'd done all the food shopping and had set the table ahead of time. She just wanted to enjoy everyone's company. Her only regret was missing Luis's going-away party. Dalton had driven her to the salon earlier that day so she could say goodbye.

Seated next to her, he shot her a concerned glance. She took his hand and squeezed, sorry for the anxiety she'd caused him. He'd nearly gone ballistic when he received a call from her in the E.R.

Roger got up and waddled into the kitchen to help Anita serve the first course. While Marla could barely tolerate the heavy-set man and didn't care for the way he treated her mother, she was grateful for his assistance. Maybe he was just eager to eat.

Dalton's mom regarded her from across the table with a frown of puzzlement. "So Marla, this woman who wanted to shoot you was posing as a religious minister?"

She nodded, her shoulders stiffening at the pain that slight movement caused to her neck. Physical therapy would help down the road, but first she had to give her body time to heal.

"That's right. The murders had nothing to do with the bones Alan found in his backyard. They had everything to do with the lucrative Rapture scam Alan ran along with Angela." Marla took a gulp of water. She couldn't fulfill the ritual of drinking four glasses of wine during the service and had taken tiny sips instead. Her pain medication already left her feeling woozy.

"You've heard of the Rapture, I presume?" Marla asked her Christian mother-in-law. At Kate's nod, she continued. "Angela wrote all of their material and managed their finances. Alan handled their computer sites and retail sales. He also served as their voice, doing podcasts and radio talk shows as Alfred Godwin, the fictional minister."

Dalton jabbed a finger at Kate, participating in her first Seder along with her husband, John. "My partner and I suspected Angela, but we were waiting for one final piece of information. Kat was tracing a source of income in Krabber's account. We'd determined it came from StayTrue Ministries. Since that was a business account, we needed to know who'd signed the original documents."

"I looked up their website on the Internet," Marla said. "It gets thousands of hits."

"The bank manager told us someone named Alfred Godwin had established the account. I remembered Marla mentioning his name, and things started to come together. Angela was a co-owner on the account. And she'd set up the post office box. She was supposed to stop by for questioning on Friday. We would have nailed her then."

Brianna spoke from her place next to Dalton. "So this all started when Mr. Krabber found out that Angela played bingo? Why would he think she was cheating on his payments?"

"He didn't trust women, not after his fiancée had betrayed him," Dalton replied. "So he threatened to expose Angela as a fraud. I guess he didn't care if he'd be implicated in the scam. He had enough money from all the donations people had sent in and from their sales of survival gear. But monetary gain hadn't motivated him to get involved in the first place. Nor was he a believer like Angela."

"I get it," Marla said. "Being rejected by his fiancée turned him against her kind. He was motivated by bigotry."

"Angela wanted the money though, didn't she, Dad?"

Dalton smiled proudly at his daughter as Anita and Roger placed plates of gefilte fish at each person's setting. "Yep, and they were making millions. Their income provided more money than they could possibly spend before the end of the world. StayTrue Ministries grossed over one point five million dollars last year."

"Yet they both kept modest homes and didn't appear to be high spenders," John said, eyeing the gefilte fish as though it might jump off the plate.

"Don't forget Angela's bingo habit," Marla remarked. "She had a pretty nice car before I totaled it, too. Apparently, Alan saved his money into a generous nest egg."

Dalton lifted his fork. "Rapture profiteers are nothing new, but they're using technology to their advantage now. Besides various apps, you can buy cloud storage for information you want to preserve for left-behind relatives. Books and movies on the subject are hugely popular. There's even insurance for your pets, so they can be placed with atheists after you ascend."

"That's a bit extreme, wouldn't you say?" Kate arched her eyebrows.

Marla was fortunate to have such tolerant in-laws. Thank goodness Roger had controlled his usually boisterous manner. His loud voice had led the singing during the service, though.

"Most Rapture schemes are run by folks who hope there is no ascension," Dalton said with a thoughtful frown. "They're making tons of money. The better ones don't give any dates for this great event and purposefully remain vague. Believers can be very suggestible. Who else would buy this crap?"

"Exactly." Marla scooped up a bit of beet horseradish on her fork with a piece of gefilte fish and put it in her mouth. Chewing and swallowing, she regarded him with a jaded eye. "How could devout followers be suckered into investing money for these items? Supposedly they're going to Heaven. What good are survival kits and freeze-dried foods for them?"

"They're buying these items for family members who won't be so lucky. Or maybe they're sinners, afraid they won't be allowed into a celestial afterlife." Dalton stuffed a forkful of fish into his mouth. He'd learned to appreciate the ritual food.

"At least we know why UPS stopped so often at Alan's house," Marla said, sniffing the mouth-watering aroma of chicken soup. "The deliveries were from his manufacturers and the pickups were the ministry's logo gear going to buyers."

"Would you believe there's a genre of literature called Rapture erotica?" Arnie's wife, Jill, said. At her husband's surprised glance, she added, "No, I don't read it, but I've seen it advertised. Those folks spend their time before disaster hits by having wild sex. I suppose you can justify any type of weirdness by saying the end of the world is near."

"Don't forget the apocalypse believers," Roger called from the kitchen, where he assisted Anita in dishing out bowls of matzo ball soup. "Those freaks don't care about religion. They just rant on about the end of days."

Marla tilted her head. "You're right, there's a larger component to this than I'd first realized. I've been doing more reading on the topic. The Rapture prophecy may be a religious aspect of a greater movement. Have you heard of Preppers? They're survivalists who believe in disaster preparedness to the extreme. Three to four million believers live in the U.S. alone. They're afraid of everything from a natural disaster, to a worldwide flu pandemic, to economic collapse and war in the Middle East."

"I'm not surprised after Katrina and the Asian tsunami and Superstorm Sandy," Dalton said.

"Don't forget the earthquake in Haiti," Jill added. "But there will always be unpredictable events in the world."

"True, so why not look on the bright side instead?" Dalton leaned forward. "I saw a TV show recently about genetic research regarding the flu virus. This virus needs two specific proteins to propagate. In order to produce the second one, messenger RNA goes through a process called splicing."

"What does that mean?" Marla's brow wrinkled. This was getting too technical for her. She supposed learning about science boosted Dalton's crime-solving skills.

"During splicing, two ends of the long molecule join together, while the intervening segment is discarded. One of these splicing sites may offer an opportunity as a switch. If it can be turned off, the two sites won't be able to come together. Thus, the virus can be stopped from spreading."

"It sounds ingenious, but who knows how far away such a solution might be?" Marla spread her hands. "In the meantime, Preppers are training in self-defense and first aid; stockpiling survival gear, weapons, and food supplies; and are even building secret retreats and bunkers. Books, TV shows, podcasts, and blogs offer advice, same as for the Rapture movement. The bad thing is when it inspires fanaticism that hurts others." She leaned back in her chair, having said her piece.

"In Alan Krabber's case," said Dalton, "his attitude was caused by a woman who jilted him. And learning he'd had a son who was raised by another man must have added fuel to the fire."

"What's happening with Ethan and the windows?" Marla asked.

"Based on the information I provided, Gene is threatening a class-action lawsuit unless Ethan works with Beamis to replace the faulty parts. I think Ethan will probably settle. It'll cost him less for replacements than for attorney fees."

"What's going to happen to this community regarding the archaeological study, Dad?" Brianna broke off a piece of matzo and bit into it.

"Ron Cloakman offered to donate a tract of land in one corner for a museum to commemorate the site's heritage. I hear that Herb is advising his tribe to accept the proposal."

"It's a reasonable offer, and one that respects each party." Marla hoped both sides accepted this solution so building could resume. She bent her head, ignoring the pang in her neck. "It's terrible that Cherry had to die because Angela was afraid she might give away her role in the ministry."

"At least Cherry's kids won't find out how their mother fictionalized her research sources at the university. That'll be kept under wraps." Dalton leaned back as Charlene, who'd risen to help, started serving the soup course.

Marla gave a nod of gratitude to her sister-in-law. Used to being on the move, this lack of mobility frustrated her.

"Who threw Spooks down the pit, Marla?" Arnie asked, stroking his dark moustache. He and Jill had contributed the desserts, as promised. "Did that Indian guy do it to find more evidence of an ancestral burial ground?"

"Herb said it wasn't him. We're assuming Cherry dug the holes in Alan's yard, looking for more bones to submit to her lab. She must have panicked when Spooks ran back there."

A pause in conversation ensued while everyone enjoyed Anita's soup contribution. Marla loved her mother's soft matzo balls.

"Your kids are growing up so fast," she told Arnie with an affectionate smile. "Speaking of children, did I tell you guys that Tally wants me to hold a baby shower for her?" She groaned in mock distress. "I don't have the slightest idea of what to do."

"I'll be glad to help," Kate said with a broad grin as tiny crinkles appeared beside her hazel eyes. She exchanged a bemused glance with Marla's mother.

"Count me in," Anita said. "Maybe this will inspire you to think about babies, bubula." She gave a conspiratorial wink at her *mechutonesteh*— relative through marriage—across the table.

"All right, you two." Marla waved her spoon. "Don't get any ideas. I like things just the way they are."

"Hey, Dad," Brianna said, dipping her hard-boiled egg in salt water before eating it like Marla had done. "I noticed the fence and stone pathway are gone next door."

Dalton cast Marla a triumphant smile. "That's right. Byrd took care of it this morning. He's having that hole in the yard filled in as well. I believe he's keeping the old guy's boat, though."

"By the way," Marla said, "did Dalton tell you he's been offered a new position as vice president of security at Royal Oaks?" She beamed at him with pride.

Dalton squared his shoulders. "It's a responsibility I won't take lightly. Never mind the security guard issue and community watch. I'm going to call for other changes as well."

"Like what?" Marla said. Was the political animal in him surfacing again?

"For one thing, we should obtain sealed bids for all major projects, and these bids should be opened in front of the entire Board. That way, one individual can't have the chance to make a deal on the side."

"That sounds reasonable."

"We should periodically check the pricing on goods and services to make sure no one is taking advantage of us. And we can require two signatures on expenses over a certain limit."

"Hopefully, the rest of the Board members will agree with you."

"More importantly, this neighborhood can go back to being a peaceful community."

"Amen to that." Marla paused, approaching a sensitive topic. "How did Detective Minnetti react to your solving the case?"

"You mean, to *your* solving the case? Kat and I are still adjusting to our partnership, but the road will get smoother. She isn't quite accepting of your role yet, though." Dalton smiled at her in the special way he had just for her.

A coil of warmth permeated her body, making her wish she was whole again. But she'd have plenty of time to show him her love and to enjoy her extended family.

"I have some advice for you. I should have mentioned it sooner. It's valid for everyone." Dalton's gaze swept the company and then settled on her.

"What's that?" She stared into his smoky gray eyes, feeling a swell of affection.

"Hereafter, vary your routine. Angela got to you because you followed the same route with the dogs every day at the same time. Be more unpredictable."

She nodded, appreciating his wisdom and his concern. Dragging her gaze from him, Marla glanced at each person around the table. Her heart burst with joy.

Being together with her loved ones was all that mattered. Life was short, and no matter what might come around the corner, people should live each moment to the fullest. Being fearful of the future, like the apocalypse followers, took away from the present. The here and now was what counted.

She lifted her wine glass in a toast. "L'chaim." *To life.*

"And to our next adventure," Dalton said, clinking her glass.

"What adventure? I just want to get back to normal."

"And you will. That's why I planned a few months ahead. I hope you can clear your schedule."

She stared at him. "For what?"

He winked. "Our honeymoon. It's about time we took one, don't you think?"

MARLA'S RECIPES

Chicken Spaghetti Casserole

16 oz. cooked spaghetti, vermicelli, or angel hair pasta
9 oz. package Perdue Original Roasted Chicken Breast Short Cuts
16 oz. package frozen peas and carrots
2 cans Healthy Request cream of chicken soup
1 small jar pimento, drained
1 cup grated cheddar cheese, divided

Combine all ingredients in a greased 9 × 12 baking dish, reserving some grated cheddar to sprinkle on top. Bake at 350 degrees until browned and bubbly, about 20 minutes. Serves 6–8.

Pot Roast

3 to 4 pound flat cut brisket
2 Tbsp. olive oil
1 large yellow onion, sliced
1 can cream of mushroom soup
1/2 cup water
3/4 cup brown sugar
1/4 cup vinegar
1 tsp. Worcestershire sauce
1 tsp. mustard
1/4 cup Marsala wine

In a Dutch oven on top of the stove, brown meat in 2 Tbsp. oil on both sides. Add sliced onions. Blend together other ingredients in a bowl and pour over meat. Cover and simmer for 2 1/2 to 3 hours or until meat is very tender. Add water to moisten pot as needed during the cooking process. Allow to cool for a few minutes, then thinly slice meat across the grain.

Israeli Couscous with Mushrooms

2 cups large grained couscous
Low-sodium chicken broth
8 oz. fresh gourmet mushroom blend, coarsely chopped
2 Tbsp. olive oil
2 garlic cloves, chopped
1 tsp. fresh thyme
2 tsp. Worcestershire sauce

Preheat oven to 400 degrees. Mix together mushrooms, garlic, olive oil and thyme, and spread in aluminum foil–lined baking pan sprayed with cooking spray. Bake for 20 minutes. Meanwhile, cook couscous in chicken broth according to package directions. When done, stir in mushroom mixture and Worcestershire sauce and serve hot.

Salmon Croquettes

1 large can salmon or 2 small cans, drained and flaked
Egg Beaters
Garlic powder
Plain bread crumbs
Cooking oil

Add salmon to large bowl. Pour in enough Egg Beaters to moisten. Add a sprinkle of garlic powder and a toss of plain bread crumbs. Mix thoroughly. Form into patties. Fry in cooking oil in large skillet until browned on both sides.

Brisket with Dried Plums

3 1/2 lb. flat cut beef brisket
2 Tbsp. olive oil
2 medium onions, sliced
1 cup beef broth
1/4 cup Marsala wine
3 Tbsp. balsamic vinegar
3 Tbsp. honey
1/2 tsp. ground ginger
1/2 tsp. ground cloves
1/2 tsp. cinnamon
1 cup pitted dried plums (prunes)
2 lb. sweet potatoes, peeled
1 cup dried apricots

Preheat oven to 350 degrees. Trim fat off brisket. Heat oil in heavy Dutch oven and add meat, browning on both sides. Remove brisket. Add onions and sauté until wilted, about 5 minutes. Meanwhile, mix beef broth, Marsala wine, vinegar, honey, ginger, cloves, and cinnamon in a bowl.

Put brisket on top of onions in pot. Pour broth mixture over meat. Cover and bake for 2 hours. Then add sweet potatoes, cut into chunks. Scatter on dried fruit. Cover and bake for 1 more hour or until meat is tender.

Transfer meat to cutting board, and spoon out fruit with slotted spoon. Cut meat thinly across the grain. Serve with fruit and pan juices.

For more recipes, please visit Nancy's website: http://nancyjcohen.com.

ABOUT THE AUTHOR

Nancy J. Cohen is an award-winning author who writes romance and mysteries. Her humorous Bad Hair Day series features hairdresser Marla Vail, who solves crimes with wit and style under the sultry Florida sun. Several of these titles have made the Independent Mystery Booksellers Association best-seller list. Nancy's imaginative romances have also proven popular with fans. Her books in this genre have won the HOLT Medallion and Best Romantic SciFi/Fantasy at The Romance Reviews. Active in the writing community and a featured speaker at libraries and conferences, Nancy is listed in *Contemporary Authors, Poets & Writers,* and *Who's Who in U.S. Writers, Editors, & Poets.* When she's not busy writing, Nancy enjoys reading, fine dining, cruising, and outlet shopping. She likes hearing from readers. Please contact her at nancy@nancyjcohen.com or http://nancyjcohen.com.